I0817832

DESERT SWARM

DESERT SWARM

Book 3

of the

Tarizon Saga

by

William Manchee

Top Publications, Ltd.
Dallas, Texas

Dedication

The Tarizon Saga is dedicated to my grandchildren, Joshua, Alex, Isabella, Andrew and Travis.

Desert Swarm

Tarizon Saga, Book 3

Top Publications, Ltd.
Dallas, Texas

ISBN 978-1-935722-68-7

1
The Accident

Jack Carpenter got into his F-250, started the engine, and eased out of the gravel parking lot adjacent to the job site of Inyo Concrete Construction Company. It was the first Friday in March 1959 and his company was in the process of pouring a new warehouse slab for a local food distributor. He was tired and not anxious about the long drive home to Shoshone, California. It was damn near a five hour drive and if he stopped for dinner he'd be lucky to be home by midnight. Ordinarily he'd have gotten a motel for the night and then left at the crack of dawn when he was fresh and well rested, but he'd promised his son, Jake, that he'd take him hiking along the Armagosa River on Saturday and maybe do a little fishing.

Divorce had not set well with Jack. He loved his wife, Angela, and was totally shocked and dismayed by her sudden desire to be free of him. He thought she'd been happy but he'd been wrong. She said she was tired of being alone all the time and he could understand that, but a man had to make a living. He'd thought she understood that. Angela was a school administrator and they'd met when he was pouring the foundation for a school in Bishop. It had been love at first sight, at least for him. When he saw those big brown eyes for the first time and felt the warmth of her smile he simply melted. He knew immediately she was the woman he wanted to be with for the rest of his life.

Unfortunately, Angela wasn't as taken with Jack and it took a long courtship to convince her to marry him. Perhaps that was the mistake he'd made. She liked him but didn't love him the way he loved her. He was so happy when she finally said yes, he couldn't think of anything else but getting a ring around her finger and having her wake up next to him each morning. He'd spent a lot of time with her the first few years but his business grew and prospered, demanding more and more of his time.

Jake had been a surprise. He came about a year and a half after they'd been married. Jack was ecstatic with the news that he was to be a father, but Angela wasn't so thrilled. She wanted children but not immediately. She said she had some living to do before she got saddled with children. In time, however, she came around and seemed to be happy about the prospect of being a mother. At least that's what Jack wanted to believe.

When the baby came it was hectic as it always is with a newborn. When Jack was home he took care of Jake at night so Angela could sleep. But when Jack was gone for a few days and Angela didn't get much rest, she was angry and bitter when he returned home and they were often at each other's throats. Eventually Jack had to hire a nanny as Angela made it clear she couldn't deal with the baby alone.

This worked pretty well for four or five years but it was expensive and there were times it was difficult for Jack to pay the nanny. The construction business was erratic. Sometimes it would be booming, but just as often it would crater leaving him with little work or income. Fortunately, ICC had a good reputation and was the first company called by the locals when there was a foundation needed or a driveway to be poured. But when Jake reached his eighth birthday, Jack refused to pay for a nanny anymore arguing that Jake didn't require that much extra care to justify the expense. Angela complained bitterly about his decision because over the years the nanny had become more of a housekeeper and cook than a nanny. Her attitude toward Jack took a nose dive when he refused to reverse his decision.

In retrospect, Jack realized he'd made a mistake marrying Angela. She was outgoing and social and he was more introverted and laid back. It was a good combination when they were alone together. He was a patient listener and tried hard to make her happy, but when she wanted him to go out to social events or out with her friends, he wasn't happy. A lot of times he was tired and simply wanted to sit down in front of the TV and relax. If he refused to go out, Angela would be angry and not talk to him for days.

It was while they were apart that trouble would brew. Angela couldn't stand sitting home, so she'd get a babysitter sometimes and go out with her girlfriends. Shoshone was a small town and there wasn't a lot going on, so they would sometimes drive to Las Vegas to see the shows and do a little gambling. It was on one of these trips that Angela met Curt Lawson. Lawson was a well-respected deputy sheriff working out of Independence, California. He was in Vegas with some of the other deputies letting off a little steam. They met at a blackjack table and hit it off immediately. Angela was attracted to Lawson's rugged good looks, recklessness, and cocky disposition. Lawson was married too, but that didn't stop him from taking Angela to his room and having his way with her.

The affair lasted over a year before Jack found out about it. It probably would have gone undetected much longer had Curt not put in for a transfer to the Sheriff's Substation in Shoshone. Living now in close proximity, they saw more of each other and people began putting two and two together. Jack was well liked in the community so he was quickly informed of Angela's betrayal.

Jack would have probably forgiven Angela for the indiscretion but Angela was too proud to continue the marriage with infidelity hanging over her head. She filed for divorce immediately and kicked Jack out of the house. She blamed him for what had happened—his long hours away from home and neglect of the family.

Jack was devastated by the divorce and fell into a deep depression after it became final. The only thing that kept him from burying himself in a bottle was his love for Jake and his determination to continue to be a good father. Jack's father, Andrew, had been a good father although Jack hadn't appreciated that fact at the time. It was only after Andrew's untimely death at age fifty-two that Jack realized how lucky he'd been to have such a fine person as a father. Jack wanted Jake to feel the same way about him when he died. One of Jack's deepest regrets was that Jake had never known his grandfather. The thought of that often brought tears to his eyes.

At 8:30 p.m. Jack stopped at Mona's Café for dinner. He was a frequent customer there and knew all the waitresses. Dolly Watson perked up when she saw him walk in the door. She was divorced like Jack and silently hoped to connect with Jack someday, however, Jack had yet to show any interest.

"Hi, Jack," Dolly said as he sat down in a booth. She put down a cup and filled it with coffee.

"Hi, Dolly," Jack replied with a heavy sigh.

Dolly frowned. "Tough week, huh?"

"Yeah. One of our trucks broke down, so I had to babysit the job for three hours until another one could be called in. I was supposed to be on the way home at three not six."

"That sucks. You look tired. Maybe you shouldn't try to make it home tonight."

"Oh, I'll be all right. Two or three cups of coffee and I'll be wide awake."

"You know, I have a place just down the road. I've got a guest room. You're welcome to crash there anytime."

Jack smiled at Dolly. He'd always liked her but never thought of her in a sexual way. Her bright blue eyes, long blonde hair, and pleasant smile were alluring enough, though he'd usually gone for brunettes. He gave her a hard look. *Was she flirting with him? Had she just invited him home*? In the past, he'd been a happily married man and had resisted the natural urges to flirt with women. But, those days were over now. He was free to flirt if he wanted to. He wondered what caused Dolly's divorce and why she didn't have a steady boyfriend now.

"That's really nice of you to offer, but I promised my boy I'd take him hiking in the morning. He'd be devastated if I didn't show up."

"You could call. I'm sure he'd understand."

"Oh, he'd understand, all right. He'd understand he wasn't the most important thing in my life."

Dolly shrugged. "Okay, just a thought. What can I get you?"

Jack smiled broadly. "I'm sorry. It's—"

"No. You're right. Kids are important. What can I get you?"

"One of those big juicy hamburgers and a large fry."

"How about some apple pie for dessert?" Dolly suggested.

"Yeah. That sounds good."

Dolly forced a smile. "Coming right up."

Jack silently screamed. He'd offended Dolly and felt badly. He was angry with himself for not being able to accept that his relationship with Angela was over. He knew he needed to get on with his life and that there was no reason for him to feel guilty whenever he talked to a pretty woman. He took a deep breath and when Dolly returned with his hamburger he looked up at her anxiously.

"Hey. Ah. You know. I'll be coming by this way on Sunday."

"Really?"

"Uh huh. Ah. You got anything going on Sunday afternoon?"

Dolly studied Jack a moment and then cocked her head. "Well. Let me think."

"You like rock climbing? We could head up to the Alabama Hills. It's beautiful up there."

"I don't climb mountains," Dolly advised sternly.

Jack smiled. "This isn't rugged mountain climbing. It's more hiking and sightseeing. We could have a picnic. Or, if you prefer we could go to Lone Pine and catch a movie."

Dolly smiled broadly. "Okay. A picnic and a movie. That sounds like fun. I'm supposed to work Sunday night, but maybe Barbara will trade shifts with me."

Jack grinned. "Okay, then. It's a date."

"Yes, it's a date," Dolly agreed.

Jack felt exhilarated as he drove off from Mona's Café. He hadn't had a date since the divorce and it felt liberating to finally be free of Angela's yoke. And if things went well Dolly would invite him back to her place when the evening was over. The thought of that put a smile on his face. But his euphoria didn't last as the monotony of the road finally overcame his caffeine fix and he began to yawn. The clock on his dash advised that it was 11:08 p.m. He flipped on the radio and turned to some hard rock to help keep him awake. That worked for a while but soon even the harsh noise couldn't keep his eyelids opened. He dozed off but was quickly awakened by the drumming of his tires on the shoulder of the highway. Instinctively, he swerved to the left to avoid going off the road, but his momentum was too much and his truck rolled right off the highway and down the side of the mountain.

Remarkably, the truck righted halfway down and, after plummeting down the mountain for more than half a mile, Jack managed to slide to a stop just before striking a huge red boulder. He got out of the truck dazed, walked away a few yards, then blacked out. When he awoke, hours later, he was lying flat on his face and ached all over. After rolling over and sitting up, he touched his tender nose and discovered dried blood on his mouth and chin. Suddenly remembering he had to get home to pick up Jake, he struggled to his feet and started looking around in the darkness for his truck, but could see nothing. Disoriented, he began walking away from the highway and into the desert. As he walked he worried about his truck and wondered if it would still run when he found it. He dreaded the thought of having to call a wrecker and explain what had happened. He was glad he wasn't bleeding and didn't seem to have been seriously hurt, but still his body ached all over and his ribs were sore from where he'd hit the steering wheel.

Soon he regretted that he'd started walking. He realized he should have known better, but blamed his imprudence on the horrible headache he was experiencing. Now he was hopelessly lost and had no idea which way to go. It was pitch-dark and he had only the stars and a half moon to provide him light. Frustrated, he decided to sit down at the foot of a large boulder and wait until morning when he could see where he was going. He knew he shouldn't sleep after suffering a head trauma so he vowed to stay awake. His mother was a nurse and had given him that advice on many occasions.

She'd left Shoshone when his father had died and now lived and worked in LA. He hadn't seen her for a while and made a mental note to find time to do that soon.

At first light, he was up and heading north where he thought he'd find the main highway. He had no idea how far he had wandered during the night or what direction he'd gone, but he figured it couldn't be too far. A half hour into his trek his stomach growled and, for the first time, he thought of water. He was in the middle of the Mojave Desert without any! He shook his head, thinking what an idiot he'd been. He knew he couldn't have been that far from the highway when he got out of his truck, but now he could be miles from it. It was his practice to always carry plenty of water in his truck but that would do him no good now. Luckily it was spring and though the temperature would easily reach 90°, it wouldn't be the 110° plus that summer would bring. Either way, though, he knew he was screwed if he didn't find water within a few hours.

As he reached the top of a hill he looked off in all directions hoping to see the highway or some sort of civilization. He didn't see a highway but he did see, off in the distance, what appeared to be some kind of structure or the remnants of one. If there had been a house there he figured it was possible that there might be a well or a road he could follow back to civilization. He immediately set off in that direction praying he would find a way out of his predicament.

When he got to the structure he was very disappointed. It looked like someone had built a foundation and began to build the walls but had stopped. It was an unusual material, he thought. It looked like rock but there were no seams or veins of cement holding the rock together. It almost looked like the material had been poured into molds like concrete and then left to set. But he'd never seen that kind of construction before and couldn't imagine that someone would use something so advanced out in the middle of nowhere.

Jack looked around for a well or a road leading up to the structure but saw nothing but undisturbed terrain. He walked around the foundation and was astounded by its rectangular size. He guessed it was about the size of a football field. *Surely nobody in their right mind would build something like that out here. The cost would be astronomical and what would be the purpose?*

The sun was up fully now and he could feel the temperature rising. He knew he had to find water soon or he'd get dehydrated and his energy level and general health would deteriorate rapidly. He took off in a northerly direction again, still believing he'd have to come soon to California Highway 127 which ran right through Death Valley. He could have gone a different way and avoided such a desolate terrain but he loved the desert and enjoyed the scenery.

He walked another hour and was beginning to feel a little lightheaded when he heard the noise of traffic in the distance. A wonderful wave of relief washed over him as he knew the highway must be just ahead. Ten minutes later he stepped over a ridge and saw it below. A smile crept over his sunburned face. He skidded down the embankment and stumbled onto the highway. A motorist swerved to miss him and honked his horn irritably. Another car slowed and rolled down the window.

"You all right, mister?" A middle-aged woman asked.

"No. No, I'm not. I was in an accident. Can I get a lift into town?"

"Sure," the lady replied reaching over to unlock the passenger door. "What happened?"

"Fell asleep and ran off the road."

"Where's your car?"

Jack shrugged. He explained what happened as they took off toward Shoshone. Thirty minutes later the woman dropped Jack off at his doctor's office. He thanked her and then went inside and took a seat. A woman at the front desk recognized him.

"Jack?" What are you doing here? I didn't have you down for an appointment today."

Jack looked up and tried to smile. "I know, Melba. Sorry, but I rolled my truck and I've been wandering in the desert for the last three hours. You think the doctor could take a look at me?"

Melba got up quickly and called the doctor. Then she opened the inside door and rushed over to him. "You don't look so good, honey. Come on back. I'm sure the doctor can squeeze you in."

"Thanks," Jack said as Melba helped him up. "You wouldn't have a glass of water, would you?"

"Yes, of course."

Melba took Jack back to a treatment room and then went to get him a glass of water. When she gave it to him he drained it and handed her the glass back for more.

"Don't drink too much at one time," Dr. Fairchild advised as he stepped into the room.

Jack nodded. "Hi, Doc. Sorry, to bust in on you like this but it was kind of an emergency."

"No problem. So, what happened to you?"

Jack explained the situation while Dr. Fairchild examined him. When he was done he said, "Well, you were lucky to walk away from an accident like that. You could have easily been killed. I'm still worried about your head. I want you to stop in at the hospital in Bishop and have them run a cat scan."

"Okay. I'll be near there on Monday. Can you set it up?"

"Yes. Melba will take care of it for you. In the meantime, you should go home and rest."

"Right. I will," Jack lied. He knew there wouldn't be any resting. He'd have a lot of explaining to do to Angela. And Jake would be disappointed if they couldn't at least go out for a while. He thanked Melba and left.

Angela and Jake were just pulling up outside when Jack walked out of the doctor's office. Jake jumped out of the car and ran over to his dad. "Are you okay?" he asked worriedly.

"Yeah, I'm fine."

"So, thanks a lot for ruining my day," Angela spat. "I was supposed to be in Vegas right now with Lynn and Shirley. They were pissed that I had to bail on them."

"I'm sorry, Angela. The reason I was on the road at midnight was so you could go out with your girlfriends. I obviously didn't want to fall asleep and total my truck. I damn near died."

"Hmm. Too bad you—"

"Mom!" Jake protested.

"Okay. Okay. I didn't mean it. It's just so typical of your father."

"Can we go home? I need to lie down and rest for a bit. I'm not feeling so well."

"Sure, Dad," Jake said giving his mother a scathing look. "Come on. We'll take you home."

Jake helped Jack into the car and they headed to the home that Jack had actually built himself with the help of a few of his contractor buddies. He thought having a house he owned free and clear would provide his family with a measure of security, but the court had awarded the home to Angela and left Jack with nothing but his truck. It didn't seem fair, but Jack hadn't hired a lawyer and was so sick about losing Angela that he hadn't felt like fighting.

"After I get a little rest, maybe your mother will let us borrow her car and we can go look for my truck."

Angela sighed. "You shouldn't be driving in your condition. Melba said you had a concussion."

"I have to find my truck and it would be better if Jake were with me in case I faint or something."

"You're crazy if you think—"

"I'll stay on the highway. Don't worry. There's plenty of traffic. You can come along if you want."

"No. I've got plans."

When they got home, Jack slept for a few hours and then he and Jake loaded up Angela's car with plenty of food and water and took off. It was mid-afternoon and the temperature, according to the sign in front of the bank, was 93°. After about forty minutes they got to the area where Jack figured he'd run off the road.

"Okay, I'll drive by slowly and you look off to the right side of the road and see if you see my truck."

"Got it," Jake said getting on his knees and poking his head and shoulders out of the passenger-side window. After about ten minutes he pointed and screamed, "There it is. Over there."

Jack pulled the car to a stop and they both got out. The embankment was steep but not too difficult to climb down. It only took them about five minutes to get to the truck. When they got there, Jack examined it carefully. The roof was caved-in pretty badly from the truck rolling and it would definitely need a new paint job, but Jack figured it would be salvageable. At least he hoped it was as he only had liability coverage and if it was a total wreck he'd have to buy a new truck.

"Let's see if she'll start," Jack suggested.

"You got the keys?" Jake asked.

"No. But they should be in the ignition."

"Can I try to start it?" Jake asked.

Jack smiled. "Sure, just leave it in park and put your foot on the brake."

"I will," Jake promised and tried to open the cab door. It wouldn't budge.

Jack grabbed the door handle and yanked hard but it wouldn't move for him either.

"Shit!" Jack exclaimed. "Try the other side."

Jake ran around the truck and opened the passenger door without any trouble. He climbed in and crawled over to the driver's seat. The key was in the ignition, so he put his foot on the brake and tried to crank it. Nothing happened.

"Let me look under the hood," Jack said moving to the front of the truck. "Pull the hood latch."

Jake had helped his father work on the truck before, so he knew his way around the cab. He pulled the hood lever and it popped up. Jack slipped his fingers underneath the hood and lifted it up. After a moment, he stuck his head out and said, "The battery cables came loose. Now try it."

Jake focused on the brake and the ignition again and tried to crank the engine one more time. This time the engine began to turn, but it didn't start. Jack waved his hand to wait a moment and then made sure all the sparkplug wires were tight. When he signaled he was ready, Jake cranked the engine and it finally turned over and came to life.

"Yes!" Jack exclaimed. "Thank God!"

Jake turned off the engine and then got out of the truck. "Can you drive it out of here?" he asked.

Jack looked up at the road in the distance. "I'll need a wrecker to pull it up the embankment. Let's just lock it up for now and then you and I can go get some dinner. I'm starving. I'll get a wrecker out here tomorrow morning to pull it back on the road."

Jake agreed and they hiked back to Angela's car and headed back to Shoshone. The next morning Jack went to a local wrecking yard and body shop where he knew someone with a tow truck. Joe Small had been a childhood friend and they'd hung out a lot as teenagers. He didn't usually work on Sundays but since Jack was an old friend he made an exception. When they got back to the yard with the truck, Jack asked him for a favor.

"Listen, can I borrow your Jeep until you're finished with the truck? I've got a date this afternoon and I'd hate to have to cancel."

"You've got a date?" Joe asked seeming amused.

"Yes, my first one since the divorce. I'd hate to miss it, plus I want to do a little exploring. I found a rather strange foundation out in the desert and I'd like to check it out a little closer."

"A foundation? Why would you care about a foundation?"

"I don't know. It just wasn't right. I've never seen this type of building material before. I'd like to try to identify it. It might be something I could use in the future."

"Okay, you can drive it next week and when you come home on the weekend your truck should be as good as new."

"Thanks, Joe. You're a lifesaver."

On the way to Mona's Café to pick up Dolly, Jack breathed a sigh of relief. He'd have been heartbroken had he been forced to cancel on Dolly. He liked her and, despite aching all over, couldn't wait to go out on their first date.

2
Love in Death Valley

Dolly answered the door immediately after Jack knocked. She was dressed in light blue shorts and a pink halter top that left little to the imagination. Jack gave her lean body a onceover and then smiled. “You look great!”

“Do I? I wasn’t sure what to wear.”

Jack looked down at her tan flats. “I’d switch to sneakers. They’ll give you better traction if we do any climbing.”

Dolly nodded. “Okay. I’ll go change them. Come in,” she said, stepping aside to give him room to enter.

“I almost didn’t make it,” Jack confessed in a loud voice so Dolly could hear him in her bedroom.

“Oh, really? What happened?”

“I fell asleep on the way home last night and rolled my truck.”

“Oh, my God!” Dolly exclaimed as she walked back into the living room with a new pair of Converse sneakers on. “I noticed your nose was a little swollen. Are you alright? We can do this another time.”

“No. I’m fine, but I would like to alter our plans a bit, if you don’t mind.”

“Oh. Of course. If you’re not feeling well, we don’t have to go out.”

“No. That’s not it. While I was wandering around in the desert yesterday, I came across some interesting ruins that I’d like to show you. I’ve never seen anything like it.”

Dolly frowned. “Ruins?”

Jack laughed. "Yes, ruins. But, the area is quite beautiful and we can still have our picnic."

Dolly shrugged. "Sure. I didn't know you were into archeology."

"I'm not usually, but being in the construction business different types of architectural designs and unique building materials interest me."

"Well, let's go. You've got me curious now."

"I hope you don't mind taking a Jeep. Our sightseeing will be off-road."

Dolly swallowed hard. "Oh. Well, it's a good thing I didn't have my nails done."

Jack laughed. "I promise you our next date will be more conventional."

Dolly smiled tentatively and followed Jack outside where they got into the Jeep and took off back toward Shoshone. When they got to the spot where Jack ran off the road, he told her to hang on as they started down the steep embankment. When they got to the spot where the F-150 had rolled to a stop Jack stopped to survey the scene.

"Okay. This is where the truck ended up. I'm going to look around and see if I see my footprints. I have no idea which way I went."

Dolly nodded and smiled warily as Jack began examining the ground. After a minute, he found some tracks and ran back to the Jeep.

"Okay, I think I wandered off in that direction. Let's drive that way awhile and see what we find."

After twenty minutes Jack stopped the Jeep and looked around for anything that looked familiar.

"It was dark so everything looks different," he commented.

"If you suffered a concussion you might be experiencing some memory loss as well. I hope we can find our way back to the road."

Jack looked over at her. "Oh, I remember now. There was a large boulder I slept under." He looked around and scanned the horizon until his eyes fixed on a rock formation that looked familiar. "There it is, I bet."

They drove over to it and Jack jumped out to look around. "Ah hah!" he said, pointing to a spot where the grass had been padded down. "That's where I sat up against the boulder."

"Weren't you worried about snakes and scorpions?" Dolly asked.

Jack laughed. "No. I've spent a lot of time backpacking and found that most animals will leave you alone if you don't bother them. My main concern was water. I should have never wandered off without any."

"Well, you didn't exactly know what you were doing."

"No. Okay, I went north from here. I had the rising sun to work with so I'm pretty sure if we go north now we'll run into the ruins."

"Good. I'm getting hungry. Maybe we can have our picnic there. Is there any shade?"

Jack thought about that a moment.

"I don't remember any trees but I'm sure the walls of the ruins will provide some shade."

"Good. Let's go."

They traveled another ten minutes before they came to the ridge overlooking the ruins. Jack stopped the Jeep and pointed to the structure in the distance.

"There it is."

Dolly looked at it with obvious disappointment in her eyes.

Jack laughed. "Okay, I know it doesn't look like much from a distance, but wait until you see it up close. It's really quite unique."

When they finally got to the ruins Jack did a double-take. "It looks different today," he noted.

"Different? How do you mean?"

"I don't know. Bigger, I think. The walls are a little higher too. But that can't be possible."

"What kind of rock is that?"

"I don't know. That's what piqued my interest. It's solid rock or some kind of crystal. It almost looks like it was poured into a mold."

Dolly ran her hands over the surface of one of the walls. "It's very smooth and hard."

"Yes. That's one thing I wanted to do, check its strength and brittleness."

He went back to the Jeep and pulled out a tool chest. After setting it down near the wall where Dolly was standing, he pulled out a hammer and chisel. "Let's see how strong it is," he said and struck the chisel hard with the hammer. The surface didn't give. "Wow. Not even a mark."

"If it's so strong, why did the building fall down?"

Jack opened his mouth but nothing came out. "You're right. This isn't a ruin. There's no rubble. It looks more like an abandoned construction site."

"But why would someone build something so big out here?" Dolly asked.

"I don't know. Maybe they were going to build a big airplane hangar and were planning to build the runways later."

"Right, but you said there was no road out to this place."

"That's true. At least I didn't see any evidence of one."

"Well. I'm going to set up our picnic. I'm famished."

"Good idea. While you do that I'm going to take some photos and gather a few samples of this material if I can chip any of it off."

"Sounds good," Dolly replied and walked back to the Jeep to get the picnic basket.

While she was setting everything out, Jack took dozens of photos from every angle and then set out to chip a piece of the crystal off one of the walls to take home to study under a microscope. It took a while to get his sample. A hammer and a chisel didn't work so he had to resort to a sledge hammer. Finally, he tucked a six-by-eight-inch piece of the crystal under the seat of the Jeep and walked over to where Dolly had a blanket spread in the shade of the six feet wall.

"So, that's one tough wall," Dolly noted as she wiped a bead of sweat off Jack's face.

He nodded. "You got that right. I wonder what in the hell they were building out here."

"And who started to build it without men and equipment?"

"Unless they brought them in with helicopters. Maybe this was going to be some kind of government building. A missile silo, perhaps."

"That could be. They usually build those away from populated areas."

"I bet that's it," Jack said excitedly. "That's got to be it."

Thinking they'd solved the mystery they ate heartily, talked, laughed, and finished off a bottle of wine. As the sun began to set and Jack was about to suggest they go home, Dolly took his hand in hers and kissed it.

"You know, I was going to invite you in when we got to my place, but it's much more romantic out here."

Jack looked at her longingly and then nodded. "That's a good point. Perhaps–"

Dolly leaned in and kissed him again, this time on the lips. He closed his eyes enjoying the sweetness of her lips and the pleasant scent of her body. Then he put his hand behind her head and pulled her into him hard. She responded by pushing him down on the blanket and straddling him as she pulled off her halter top. He gasped at the sight of her naked breasts. She took his hands and pulled them up to her and while he caressed them, she began unbuttoning his shirt. When his shirt was clear she came down on him and they kissed hard, their tongues exploring and caressing the interiors of each other's mouth. Suddenly, Jack rolled Dolly off him and pulled off her shorts with one quick jerk. She wasn't wearing panties. He took a moment to take in the beauty of her naked body. He could feel his heart pounding in his chest. Impatient, Dolly sat up and began unbuckling his pants. She wasn't making much progress, so he rolled on his back, pulled them off and kicked them away. Then he was on her and felt himself slip inside. She moaned in delight as she took him in gratefully and they began to make love under the hot desert sun.

3
The Expert

George Palmer, a tall blond who looked like a basketball player but actually had no talent for the game, was just finishing up his first year as a teaching assistant in the Geology Department at Deep Springs College in Lone Pine, California. He had taken this position because the deserts of the world fascinated him and Deep Springs was located in the Mojave Desert, near the infamous Death Valley, two of the most fascinating places on the planet in his mind. He didn't particularly like teaching, but his job gave him lots of time to roam around and study the desert terrain and the wonders it contained. So, he gladly put in his time lecturing, counseling and grading exams in order to be able to enjoy his passion.

Another perk of the job was the women who attended his classes and hung on his every word. It seemed like there was always a couple of them hanging around asking questions or just wanting to talk. He was a decent looking guy but not a hunk by any stretch of the imagination, so he figured it was his intellect that attracted them rather than his looks or personality. On a few occasions, a student ended up in his bed and he'd have to take it easy on them at exam time to avoid his indiscretion being reported to the dean.

It was Sunday night, during one of his indiscretions with a student named Cindy Lee, that he received a phone call from Jack Carpenter. He'd met Jack when the school was having a new wing built for the science department. Jack had spent a good deal of time there supervising the pouring of the slab for the building.

The two met in the cafeteria one afternoon and had an interesting discussion about the science of mixing concrete and ways to make it stronger.

"Hey, Jack. How are you?"

"Fine. Sorry to call you on a Sunday, but I figured it would be hard to get you during the week with your teaching schedule and everything."

"That's true. No problem. It's been awhile."

"Yeah. When are you guys going to start that new gymnasium project you were talking about the last time I was there?" Jack asked.

"Oh, that's on hold for a while. Contributions have been a little light these days, you know, with the economy the way it is."

"Tell me about it. I've got three trucks idle."

Cindy sighed deeply and gave George a look.

George put two fingers to his lips and blew Cindy a kiss. "So, what can I do for you, Jack?"

"I came across something a little weird north of Shoshone in the Funeral Mountain Range off of Highway 127. It's in Death Valley and I remembered you mentioning that you were an expert on the geology out there."

"Yes. I am. What do you mean by weird?"

"It appears to be an abandoned construction site which is weird enough for Death Valley, but what's really interesting is the material they were using to build the hangar, missile silo or whatever it was they were building."

"There hasn't been any construction in Death Valley to my knowledge in a long time," George said. "It's a protected area. You couldn't build anything without the permission of the Park Service."

"If it was a missile silo maybe you could."

"I don't know. I doubt it. The environmental lobby would go nuts if they found out about it."

"Right. Maybe that's why they stopped building whatever it was supposed to be. Anyway, I'd like you to take a look at it. I'd like to find out more about the material they were using. It's amazingly strong and durable. I couldn't even scratch it with a hammer and a chisel."

"Is it a metal?"

"No. It's a rock or crystal of some sort."

"Huh. That does seem strange. When can you show it to me?"

"How about on Saturday? I'm tied up with a couple of jobs right now."

"Fine, where should I meet you?"

"Meet me at nine o'clock at Mona's Café. You know where that is?"

"Sure, I've eaten there before. I'll see you then."

George hung up slowly. Jack's telephone call had intrigued him. He wondered why someone would be building a hangar out in the middle of the desert.

"Come back to bed," Cindy moaned. "I'm not through with you yet."

"Sorry for the interruption, love. You want to go on a field trip next Saturday?"

"Sure," Cindy replied. "Do I get extra credit?"

George laughed. "Right. Like you need it."

During the night George couldn't stop thinking about Jack's call. The next morning before class he put in a call to his contact at the National Park Service, Randy Perkins.

"Morning, Randy. How's it going?"

"Not so great, actually. These budget cuts are a bitch. I don't know how I'm supposed to cut back six percent when we don't have enough money now to maintain all the services needed in the Park."

"Hmm. I've got the same problem here in the Geology Department. Contributions are down so we have to cut back too."

"I hope this economy turns around pretty soon. I'm tired of this crap."

"I know. Listen. You know Jack Carpenter. He's a concrete contractor out of Shoshone."

"Right. I think I've met him. He's been out here a few times on one project or another."

"Well, he says he's stumbled on a construction site in your park—out near Bat Mountain."

"What? That's impossible. There aren't any construction projects going on out there that I know anything about."

"He says it appears to have been abandoned, but that it was a large project, an airplane hangar or maybe a missile silo, perhaps."

"What the hell? He must be mistaken. There hasn't been anything like that in the Park in the ten years since I've been here---certainly not a missile silo."

"Yeah, he said it was pretty weird."

"No. It's not just weird, it's impossible. The park boundaries aren't marked very well, so the site may be on private property."

"Right. That's probably it. I'm going out there on Saturday to take a look at it. If it turns out to be on park property I'll let you know."

"Please do. If I've got a missile silo at my back door I'd damn sure like to know about it."

"I'll call you either way," Randy said and hung up.

George didn't think much about Jack Carpenter and his mysterious discovery the rest of the week until Friday when Cindy stopped by his office.

"So, when do we leave for our field trip?" she asked.

"Field trip?"

"Yes, Jack Carpenter, remember?"

"Oh, right. Well, why don't you come by my place tonight so we can get an early start in the morning?"

"You dirty old man," Cindy replied with a wink.

"Well, we'll save time that way."

"Right....Should I bring anything?"

"Ah. Yeah. Lots of water, sun screen, and some snacks. I doubt we'll be there too long, but you never know."

"Okay. I'll drop by tonight and bring my nightie."

George laughed but his mind had already shifted gears to the field trip. Building a large structure like an airplane hangar out of rock was pure insanity, a missile silo, however, was a different story. Could the government have developed a new alloy or concrete mixture that could withstand a nuclear detonation? The prospect of that made him stop by the library on his way home. He had some research to do before the field trip.

The next morning, he and Cindy were at Mona's Café at eight-thirty. They ordered coffee and a light breakfast. At 8:45 Jack, Dolly and Jake walked in and joined them.

"Hi, George. This is my son, Jake. It's my visitation day so I had to bring him along. I hope you don't mind."

"No, not at all," George said. "This is your expedition. You make the rules."

"And this is my girlfriend, Dolly."

"Nice to meet both of you," George said. "This is Cindy, one of my geology students. She's coming along to take notes and assist me."

"Hi, Cindy. It's nice to meet you," Jack said.

They all talked while they ate breakfast and at 9:30 took off for the discovery site. Jack still had his friend's Jeep and George brought a pickup with off-road tires that he used for exploring in the desert. At 10:45

they reached the site and got out to look it over. Jack's mouth dropped as he took in the structure.

"What the hell!" he exclaimed.

George looked over at him and frowned. "What's wrong?"

"The walls. Look at them, Dolly. They've grown!"

"Yeah. They sure have," Dolly agreed. "They're taller than when we were here last week."

"That's impossible," George said dryly. "Rock doesn't grow."

Jack laughed. "Well, I've got the proof right here in my backpack."

Jack rummaged around in his pack and pulled out an envelope of photos he'd had developed. "Take a look at these," Jack said as he handed the pack to George.

George looked through the photos and compared them to what was before him. He shook his head and handed them back to Jack.

"It's not possible. It must be the lighting. It almost looks like the walls are higher."

Jack took a deep breath. "The walls have grown, trust me. Take a look at this material and tell me what you make of it."

"Jack," Dolly exclaimed. "Look at that."

Jack went over to where Dolly was standing. "What about it?" he asked.

"That wall wasn't there last week. Look at your pictures."

Jacked leafed back through the photos and smiled at Dolly. "Good catch. How do you explain this, George?"

Jack showed him the photos which showed only flat ground where they were now looking. George looked at Cindy.

"You better start taking pictures, honey. This is the most bizarre thing I have ever seen."

Cindy went back to the truck and got her camera. "What is being built here?" she asked.

George shrugged. "I don't know, honey. It's gonna be big whatever it is."

"If the walls are taller now than they were last week, where is all the construction equipment?" Cindy asked. "Who's in charge of this place?"

"That's what I'd like to know," George said. "Randy over at the Park Service doesn't know anything about it. I wonder if we're inside the Death Valley boundary."

"I don't think it is," Jack said. "I checked the deed records at the courthouse yesterday and as best I can tell we are on private property owned by Bat Mountain Corporation."

"Never heard of it," George said.

"Neither have I, but it's a Nevada corporation and it's been buying up real estate around this area for several years. By my rough calculation it owns nearly three thousand acres."

"Were you able to get any information on its officers or stockholders?"

"No. Just the name of the law firm that filed the papers."

"Why would anybody want land out here?" Dolly asked. "There's no water and there isn't enough vegetation to sustain any kind of livestock."

"That's a good question," Jack said. "The only reason that I can think of is that they plan to bring in the utilities and build the roads after the building is constructed."

"Hey, Dad," Jake said. "Can I climb that boulder over there?"

Jack looked over at the pile of gigantic red boulders 200 yards ahead. He remembered when he was young he liked to climb too. “Sure, just be careful and stay where I can see you.”

“Alright,” Jake said and ran off.

“That still doesn’t explain how this wall is growing,” George noted.

“Could they be working at night when it’s cool?” Dolly suggested. “Maybe they fly in their equipment at night and take it away in the morning when they leave.”

Jack laughed. “I doubt it, but the only way to find out is to camp here tonight and see what happens.”

“They may not work on the weekends,” Cindy noted.

George nodded. “True, but that doesn’t matter. I need to set up a camp here anyway to figure out what’s going on and I have a feeling it might take a while. If there’s anything happening at night, we’ll figure it out soon enough.”

“Dad! Dad! Come look at this,” Jake screamed from the top of a boulder. “Look, Dad! Look.”

They all began running toward the spot where Jake was pointing. When they got to it they just stared in amazement. Before them was a large circular area completely flat and totally devoid of vegetation.

“What the hell?” George said.

“They must have had a bulldozer out here for a week to level this area,” Jack observed. “How big do you think it is?”

“It looks to be at least fifty yards across. I wonder what it’s for,” Dolly said.

George bent down and pulled up a dark chunk of rock. “This rock looks like it was subjected to a lot of heat.” Then he noticed it. The ground was compressed. “You know, it almost looks like something landed here.”

“What?” Jake said, having come down from the boulder. “You mean like a spaceship?”

George laughed. “No, there aren’t any aliens running around. It was probably something that was built by the military. That’s what I bet this place is—some kind of experimental site used by the military.”

“I doubt that,” Jack said. “The military would put up fences and keep people away.”

“Not if they didn’t want to attract attention. It was just a freak accident that you ran into it.”

“Well, anyway, it doesn’t explain why the structure is still growing?” Jack noted. “I guess we’ll just have to wait and see what happens. In the meantime, I’ll do some more research on Bat Mountain Corporation. And you can get some samples and figure out what this substance is and how it can be growing.”

George nodded. “We need to keep a lid on this. If the press gets a hold of it we’ll have every nut job in the state coming out to see where the aliens landed.”

Dolly smiled. “Well, I’m afraid a lot of people already know about it. It’s been the talk of the café all week.”

“Right. But nobody knows about the landing site. I need time to photograph it and take some samples before everybody and their mother comes out here.”

As they were talking the sound of rotor blades could be heard in the distance. “Shit! There’s a helicopter coming,” George said.

They all looked to the east and saw the green chopper approaching. “Oh, it looks like the National Park Service. It must be Randy.”

The helicopter set down a hundred yards away and two men came rushing over to them.

“Hey, George. Jack,” Randy said. “I got curious and decided to come out and see this for myself. What the hell is it?”

“It looks like something landed here,” George said. “Whatever it was it burnt off the vegetation, compressed the soil, and melted the rock. Some kind of experimental aircraft I'd suspect."

"Huh," George said looking around. "Ah. This is Greg Arnold from the Department of Defense. When you mentioned there might be a missile silo out here I put in a call to him to see if that was remotely possible."

"The structure is over there," George said pointing in the direction they'd come. "We just discovered this landing site a few minutes ago."

"The military doesn't have any record of a missile silo here," Greg said.

"Oh, by the way. This isn't Park Service property. We're a few miles outside of Death Valley."

"Right," George said. "Jack figured out it's owned by a company called Bat Mountain Corporation. They've been buying up a lot of property in this area for several years."

"Is that right?" Greg said. "I'll have to check them out. I can't imagine why someone would want to buy a bunch of desert property."

"Come over here and see the structure. You won't believe it," George said.

They all walked back to the building site and Jack showed them the pictures and pointed out how the walls had grown several inches in the last week.

"That's hard to believe," Randy said shaking his head.

"It looks like its growing like a coral reef or a stalagmite in a cave," George suggested. "But those processes take hundreds, if not thousands, of years."

"I'm going to have to get some scientist out here to study what's going on here," Greg said. "The government's going to want to know."

"I hope not," George said. "I want to study it myself for a while. If your people come in they'll kick everybody out and won't share with the academics."

"Not necessarily. It doesn't appear to be a threat to national security or a health hazard so it will probably take them a few weeks to get out here. In the meantime, you can do your research and get a jump on everyone else."

"You won't put a burr in anybody's saddle?" George asked.

Greg shook his head. "No, if you promise to keep me updated on any new developments."

"Thank you," George said. "I will."

The group continued to discuss the situation until mid-afternoon when Randy and Greg flew off. Then everyone pitched in to set up camp so the site could be monitored 24/7.

Jack had to get Jake back to his mother, so he and Dolly left to do that but promised to return with dinner and some supplies. He cautioned Jake not to discuss what they had found with anyone and he promised he wouldn't. Jack and Dolly planned to stay overnight and spend Sunday at the site but they both were tied up the following week with work. George said not to worry as he would have at least two students at the site at all times the following week.

Not much happened on Sunday with the exception of the continued growth of the walls. Jack calculated they had grown five inches in the 24-hour period from noon Saturday to noon Sunday. That translated to a growth rate of roughly fifteen feet per month. In addition, several more interior walls began to materialize. George also determined that the crystal substance being used to build the walls were made of natural ingredients indigenous to the area with the exception of a chemical bonding agent that he could not identify. He also noted that under a powerful microscope there appeared to be molecular movement of some sort, but he couldn't determine how or why it was happening.

Back at the defense department Greg Arnold's report of the strange discoveries in the Mojave Desert was getting scant attention. The military was focused on a deteriorating situation in Southeast Asia and threats from China and the Soviet Union. Although Greg knew the government needed to get out to Death Valley soon he kept his promise and didn't put a burr under anyone's saddle just yet.

4
Media Storm

On the following Friday George got a telephone call from Tim Whitfield, a reporter from the Inyo Register. He indicated he had heard rumors of some sort of archeological dig going on out in the desert and wanted to know more about it. George took a deep breath and let it out slowly. He hadn't wanted the press involved, but knew it was only a matter of time before they got wind of it. Perhaps if he down-played it, they'd lose interest in it as a story.

"Yes, we've been studying an abandoned construction site. It's near Bat Mountain so we're calling it the Bat Mountain Site."

"Okay. So, what's so interesting about it?" Tim asked.

"Ah. We're interested in the building techniques that were employed. They're rather unique."

"You mean the fact that the walls are growing?"

George sighed. "Who told you that?"

"I have my sources."

"Was it one of my students?"

"I can't say. What about the landing site? Do you think aliens landed there?"

"No. That's ridiculous. It was probably some sort of aircraft. You know the air force is always testing them. It could have been a vertical lift fighter or a helicopter."

"Can I see the site?"

George thought a moment. "Okay, I suppose but only on the condition that you don't disclose the location. I don't want a bunch of people coming out and interfering with my work."

"No problem. You give me an exclusive and I'll keep the location secret."

"Okay. You've got a deal. Meet me at my office here at the college tomorrow at ten and I'll take you out to it. Come alone."

"I'll need my cameraman," Tim protested.

"Alright. You and your cameraman, but that's it."

"Excellent. I'll see you tomorrow."

After he hung up he called Cindy and told her about the new development.

"Who do you think leaked it?" Cindy asked.

"I don't know. I thought maybe you might know."

"Probably one of the freshmen. I was afraid this was going to happen."

"I'll need you to come with me tomorrow. I'm going to make this jerk wear a blindfold. I don't trust him."

Cindy laughed. "You think he'll let you do that?"

"He will if he wants the story."

"You better tell Jack. He won't like picking up the newspaper and finding a story about his discovery."

"Right. I'll call him tonight. He won't be in his motel room until after six."

The next day Tim Whitfield and Andy Anderson, his cameraman, showed up at George's office. After they went over the ground rules one more time, they all piled into George's truck and took off. When they got to Mona's Café they stopped and met Jack and Dolly for lunch. When they were done George made Tim and Andy put on blindfolds which they wore until they got to the camp. When George pulled Tim's blindfold off at the edge of the landing site his mouth dropped.

"Holy shit! This is unbelievable," Tim exclaimed. "Have you figured out yet what kind of experimental craft made this footprint?"

George shook his head. "No, we don't have access to classified information, but the Defense Department is sending a team here in a week or two. I'm sure they'll figure it out."

They took the blindfold off Andy's head and he began taking photos of the site. He also got some shots of Jack, George, Cindy and Dolly. Then they walked over to the construction site. The walls were over six feet tall and dozens of new interior walls were taking shape. George showed them pictures of what the site looked like when they first discovered it.

"Jesus! And you don't have any idea how or why these walls are growing each day?"

"Not a clue," George confessed.

"It's a miracle," Andy said. "You know, one of those things you read about in the Bible."

Everyone turned to Andy. "No." George said, "I'm sure there's a rational explanation for it. We just haven't found it yet."

Andy started walking around the perimeter of the site taking pictures from every angle. "You know, it kind of looks like the beginnings of a cathedral."

Jack frowned. "A cathedral? How do you figure that?"

"Well, it's rectangular with a large interior for the congregation to worship, a place up front for an altar, and rooms front and back for the priests and their staff. I spent some time in Germany when I was in the Army and this looks like the beginnings of a cathedral—a big one."

"Shit! Don't put that in your article," George said to Tim. "We don't want flocks of worshipers coming up here."

"I'll just report the facts, but the photos speak for themselves. If people think it looks like a church, I'm not going to be able to convince them otherwise."

George groaned. "Wonderful."

They let Tim and Andy wander around for about an hour and then took them back to George's office. Tim said the story would probably be in the paper's Sunday edition. After they'd gone George saw he had a message from Greg Arnold. He immediately called him back.

"I just got word. They'll be sending a team in on Monday."

"Monday. I thought I'd have another week at least," George protested.

"After I turned in my report, somebody ordered some aerial photos of the area and that landing site got somebody's attention."

"Hmm. I bet."

"Okay. Thanks for the heads up."

George picked up the phone and called Jack. "This weekend may be our last opportunity to figure out what's going on out there." He explained what was coming down.

"Oh, well. I doubt you and I could ever figure it out. It's best the experts take over."

"I know, but it would have really been a feather in my cap had I been able to do it."

"Well, can't you write a scholarly paper about it or something?"

"Yes, I've already got that done. I'm submitting it to Geology Magazine tomorrow. Hopefully they'll publish it."

"I'm sure they will. Particularly when the newspaper story hits the stands and people start talking about it."

5
Local Buzz

When Dolly got to work at 4:00 p.m. on Sunday for the evening shift, the café was bustling with customers. As soon as the cashier spotted her she pointed in her direction. "There she is."

Dolly frowned. "What's going on?"

"You didn't see the morning paper?"

"No. I don't subscribe. I usually read it during my breaks at work."

"Well, most of these folks are here to see you."

"Me? Why-?"

Dolly was interrupted by a tap on the shoulder. She turned around to see who it was and was surprised to see the Mayor, Jeb Russell and his wife Eloise.

"Mr. Mayor, Eloise."

"Hi, Dolly. Read about you in the paper today."

"You did? I haven't seen the article yet."

"You and Jack found something pretty mysterious, huh?"

"Oh, yeah. We did."

"Do you think aliens landed there?" Eloise asked.

Dolly chuckled. "Nah., I doubt it, but you never know."

"I heard the government was going to take over the site," the Mayor said.

"Yeah, you heard right. The Department of Defense is coming in next week, I think."

"Were you scared camping out there during the night?" Eloise asked.

"No. The place is pretty much deserted now."

"What about them walls that just keep on growin'? the Mayor asked.

"Well, we didn't camp too close to them, so I don't think we were in any danger."

"Where exactly is the site?"

Dolly hesitated. She knew Jack wanted to keep the exact location secret and the newspaper reporter had been blindfolded.

"I'm not sure. Jack drove me out there and I really didn't pay that much attention as to how he got there."

Dolly excused herself and went into the kitchen. Mona smiled when she saw her.

"Well, look who the cat brought in."

Dolly laughed. "Are all these people really here to see me?"

"Most of them are, but don't think you're going to get a bonus or anything."

Dolly laughed. "I didn't think I would, but that's a thought."

Mona frowned.

"Just kidding."

Dolly put on her apron and went out into the dining room to start taking orders. At every table, she went through the same question and answer session about the alien landing, the missile silo or the cathedral that God was raising in the desert. At her break, she found the newspaper and read the article.

Miracles in the Desert

Is it possible that aliens landed right here in Inyo County? Did the government build a missile silo without informing the local population? Or, is God raising a cathedral in the desert to herald the Second Coming of Christ? These are some of the questions that citizens will be asking in the wake of an extraordinary discovery by Jack Carpenter, a longtime resident of Shoshone, a little over two weeks ago. After falling asleep at the wheel, his truck went off of Highway 127 and rolled six or eight times down a steep embankment to the valley floor below. Miraculously, Jack walked away from the wreck, confused and disoriented from a concussion he had suffered, but otherwise okay.

Normally a victim of this type of accident would sit tight and wait for help to come, but for some strange reason Jack was drawn away from his vehicle and found himself wandering in the desert without an ounce of water. Whether this was due to his confused state of mind or the guiding hand of God, I'm sure will be the subject of much future debate. But the fact is Jack stumbled upon something quite extraordinary, a phenomenon that might have never been discovered to the end of days had fate or God not intervened.

Out in the desert, many miles from any habitation, Jack found a building under construction. A building that he would soon discover was alive! Although that seems impossible, Jack documented his discovery with photographs that conclusively prove that this structure, whether it is to be a missile silo, a cathedral or an airplane hangar, is building itself at the rate of 5" per day. If you do the math that's over fifteen feet per month! So, no matter what it turns out to be, within a few months it should be finished, unless it just keeps rising to the heavens.

Unfortunately, this reporter was not allowed to have the exact location of this site and had to agree to be blindfolded to get the story. But after seeing the structure and an adjacent circular landing site right out of a science fiction novel, there is no doubt it will be quite visible to anyone flying overhead. But you better hurry as I have been informed the Department of Defense is about to take over the site and may soon be restricting the airspace around it.

For the past few weeks Jack has only allowed a select few to visit the site including his girlfriend, Dolly Watson, who you can find waiting tables at Mona's Café in Independence most afternoons, his son Jake, and Professor George Palmer, who teaches at Deep Springs College in Lone Pine. There's been a few of the Professor's students allowed out there too, to help him do his research and Randy Perkins of the Park Service. Soon the site will be crawling with federal agents trying to figure out if aliens have landed and if this living church is a threat to our national security or a gift from Almighty God.

Tim Whitfield
Photos by Andy Anderson

Dolly set the newspaper down and swallowed hard. She was starting to realize her life was about to drastically change and she didn't know if that was good or bad. It was exciting for sure, but she didn't know if she wanted celebrity status. She'd always been a small-town girl and liked it that way. She was also worried about Jack and how all this would affect their relationship. Privacy was important for two people while they were trying to figure out if they were in love and she feared they wouldn't be seeing much of that in the weeks to come. Then again, if they survived the ordeal their relationship might even grow stronger. Dolly got up and went back into the fray.

6
Stardom

On Monday morning when he got to school Jake thought he'd been mistaken for a teenage movie star. Everyone was stopping him to ask about the story, whether aliens had really landed and if his dad was actually from another planet. Girls, who wouldn't ordinarily have given him the time of day, suddenly were his best friend, following him around and hanging on every word. Jake liked the attention but didn't have many answers for the barrage of questions. At lunch, he was called to principal Paul Barnes' office.

"Well, Jake. You've become quite the celebrity."

Jake shrugged. "I guess. I really didn't do anything."

"You're too modest, Jake. I'm sure you were a big help to your father out there in the desert."

"Well, yeah. I helped him set up camp and gather wood for a fire—that kind of stuff."

"So, tell me about the landing site. Did it really look like a spaceship had landed there?"

Jake nodded. "Actually, it did. It must have been a big ship, too. The circle was fifty yards across."

"Wow. That big?"

"Yeah, and the ground was all black where the thrusters must have burned away the brush. I've got a piece of melted rock if you want to see it."

"Sure. Do you have it with you?"

"Yes," Jake said digging into his backpack. He pulled out a black flattened rock and handed it to him.

The principal took it and studied it carefully. "This is extraordinary. It does look like it was subjected to some significant heat."

"What about this living wall? Is it really growing?"

"Absolutely. I've been out there three or four times and each time the walls are taller than they were the time before. The first time the wall was up to my belt and now it's up to my nose."

"Holy cow!" Barnes exclaimed. "Where exactly is this wall?"

"I don't know exactly. The truck went off the road about seven miles north of town. From there it's about four or five miles."

"Which direction?"

"Ah, east I think."

"Well, thanks a lot for stopping by, Jake. You think your dad might be willing to come visit and talk to the other students?"

Jake felt proud that his father was being asked to visit the school. He smiled at the principal and nodded. "Sure, I'll ask him if you want."

"Do that. I think the kids, and maybe even their parents, would love to hear more about what's going on out there."

Jake left and went back to the cafeteria. He was immediately surrounded by students who wanted to know what the principal wanted. As he was talking his stomach started to tighten. He realized he'd screwed up. He'd told the Principal where the site was located. *Crap! Dad's going to kill me.*

7
The Church of the Living Desert

After Jake had left his office, Principal Barnes called his pastor, Reverend John Little, of the Church of the Living Desert. Reverend Little had read the story in the Inyo Register and was fascinated by it. He had to know where God was raising up this great cathedral in the desert but the location wasn't revealed in the article. So, he wondered how he was going to find out where it was. As he was thinking, the answer came to him. There was only one high school in Shoshone, so Jake Carpenter would be a student there. Luckily for him the Principal, Paul Barnes, was a member of the church.

"Okay, I got the location for you," Barnes advised.

"Thank you, Paul. I am going to organize a pilgrimage out there this afternoon. This is too good an opportunity to pass up."

"Yes. I think God has finally answered our prayers."

Two years earlier the church had lost its affiliation because it could not afford the financial commitment demanded by the mother church. As a result, two thirds of the members had left, leaving the little church in dire financial straits. But Reverend Little was not a quitter and stubbornly refused to close the doors. His father had been a preacher in a suburb of Dallas and had a huge congregation. John hadn't followed in his father's footsteps because his father had groomed his big brother to take over the church when he retired. He didn't like his brother much and wasn't about to live in his shadow, so he set out on his own. To make ends meet he'd sold insurance for a while, then became a broker-dealer selling deferred annuities, but eventually turned back to his roots when he saw an advertisement for a pastor for the Church of the Living Desert.

"Can I borrow a couple of school buses to take people out there?" Little asked.

"Sure, but they can't be taken off the road. I'd get hell from the school board if one of the buses got damaged."

"We won't take them off the main highway. We'll get some Jeeps and pickups out there to shuttle people to and from the site. Some people may have to walk, but that's okay. Jesus wandered around the desert for forty days and forty nights, so eight or nine miles is nothing."

"Be sure you have plenty of food and water. We don't want anyone dying on this pilgrimage."

"Amen to that," Reverend Little said. "I want to be the first one out there so we can stake out the prime real estate. I have a feeling it's gonna get crowded when folks figure out where it's located."

"You're probably right," Barnes agreed.

After the three school buses had finished their routes that afternoon they lined up in front of the church. An excited crowd of about a hundred-fifty faithful had gathered and began climbing onto the buses. A dozen or so other vehicles including pickups, Jeeps, and motorcycles joined the motorcade when it took off thirty minutes later.

The atmosphere on the buses was electric. The passengers sang hymns of hope and salvation in anticipation of the promised miracle in the desert. Reverend Little was elated with what was happening. He knew this was the beginning of great things for his ministry if he could just stay in the forefront and not get elbowed out by the Catholic Diocese or the Baptists. To insure being in the spotlight he had invited not only the reporter for the Inyo Register but also reporters from the Sacramento Bee and the Los Angeles Times. He'd also alerted an old friend, George Putnam, at Channel 11 News in LA. The reporters had met him at the church and were on the buses. The Channel 11 news crew was scheduled to meet the pilgrims at the accident site on Highway 127. He prayed they'd be there when they arrived.

8
Mob Scene

George Palmer and a dozen or so students and faculty from Deep Springs College were at their camp taking advantage of possibly the last day they'd have exclusive access to the Bat Mountain Site. Jack, Dolly and Jake had also come to take one last look as well. Nobody knew what would happen exactly once the feds took over the site, but they feared they'd be kept away. As they were all gathered around discussing their theories and observations, they heard cars in the distance.

"Who the hell is that?" Jack asked.

"I don't know." George replied. "I wasn't expecting the feds until tomorrow. Maybe they sent an advance team out to secure the site."

After a few minutes two sheriff's cars rolled up on the ridge overlooking the site and stopped. Eight deputies got out of the vehicles and peered down at them. Two of the deputies approached the camp. Jack recognized one of them, Curt Lawson, his ex-wife's boyfriend.

"Afternoon Jack," Curt said seeming amused.

"Hi, Curt. What's going on?"

"We got a heads up that a mob of people is about to descend upon this place, so I thought we'd better come out and make sure they behave themselves."

George stepped forward. "Thank you, Deputy Lawson," George said. "I really appreciate you coming out here. We didn't think anybody knew where our camp was located."

"Well, your secret is out, I'm afraid. There are a dozen vehicles and a couple of school buses already parked out on Highway 127."

Jake's mouth dropped open when he heard that school buses had come. "Oh, crap!" he exclaimed looking over at his father. His father looked back at him expectantly. "I'm sorry, Dad. I told our principal where the site was located. He asked me and I just blurted it out before I realized it. I'm sorry."

Jack sighed. "It's okay. It was just a matter of time."

"So, how do you want to handle this?" Deputy Lawson asked.

"I've got some rope. Can you keep everybody on the ridge? It's a good spot to watch what's going on. Perhaps we can let small groups down to get closer looks from time to time, but if we can keep the bulk of the crowd away that would be helpful."

"Okay. That should work."

Twenty minutes later the area was cordoned off and deputies were stationed at even intervals to make sure the perimeter wasn't breached. When the first wave of vehicles arrived, they were warned to stay back behind the ropes. Soon the ridge was populated by hundreds of pilgrims straining to get a better look at the living cathedral that they'd heard so much about. After a while Jack and George climbed to the top of the ridge and brought down Reverend Little, Principal Barnes, the reporters, the Channel 11 News crew and eight others for a tour of the site. The walls had grown yet another foot since the photos were published in the newspaper, so nobody questioned the claim that the walls were alive.

"It is a miracle!" Reverend Little exclaimed. "I feared the newspaper article had been exaggerated but, if anything, it understated the magnitude of this phenomenon."

"Yes," Principal Barnes agreed running his hands across the surface of one of the walls. "This is extraordinary. It looks like gray ice but it's hot and hard as steel. I've never seen anything like it."

"It's a gift from God and we are the lucky recipients of his generosity."

"Well, I'm afraid the government might have something to say about that," George interjected.

"Of course, they'll have to study it for a while but eventually they'll have to give it back to the people and I intend to become its custodian once that's done."

"But how? The property belongs to Bat Mountain Corporation. I'm afraid they'll decide who becomes custodian."

"True enough. That's why I must find out more about this Bat Mountain Corporation. You have any ideas on that front?"

"Ah, not really. Maybe Deputy Lawson knows a private detective who could look into it for us," Principal Barnes said.

Reverend Little nodded and looked around for Deputy Lawson. When he spotted him, he approached and said, "Deputy Lawson."

"Hi, Reverend," Lawson replied.

"Thank you for responding so quickly. I don't know if I could have kept my people from wandering all over the site."

"Yeah, it's a good thing you called. You know, if your people plan to stay out here for any length of time, you better get some port-o-potties and some tents where people can get out of the sun. A medic wouldn't hurt either. Being out in this sun for any length of time can cause dehydration, heat stroke, and numerous other ailments."

"Yes, excellent idea. I'll have that taken care of immediately. In the meantime, I had a question for you."

"Okay."

"Ah. Have you ever heard of this Bat Mountain Corporation?"

"The company that owns this property?"

"Yes."

"No. Never heard of them until I read the article in the Register."

"So, if you were trying to contact them, how would you go about doing it?"

"I will be trying to contact them. They need to know what's going on out here."

"You don't think they are behind this?"

Deputy Lawson laughed. "I doubt it. If they knew what was going on, I'm sure they would have put up fences and hired security to keep people away."

"Well, if you are able to contact someone, would you give me their contact information? I'd like to offer our services in helping preserve the integrity of the site."

"Sure. I'll let you know as soon as I make contact."

"Thank you, Curt. I appreciate it."

Reverend Little walked away and rejoined Principal Barnes. "Okay, that went well. Lawson's going to try to contact Bat Mountain Corporation and once he has their contact info, he'll pass it on to us."

"Good."

Reverend Little looked up at his congregation gathered on the hill above them. Dark clouds were gathering to the west and the wind was beginning to gust. "Well, I guess it's time for a sermon."

Barnes nodded. "Yes, I'm sure everyone is quite curious as to what's happening."

"Indeed. Come on," Reverend Little said as he made his way up the hill.

While the tour had been going on, some of the members of the church had constructed a make-shift pulpit on top of a large boulder that sat on the hill. With the help of a ladder Reverend Little climbed to the top to address the throng.

"Welcome! Children of God," he began, "Before you behold a miracle. From out of bedrock your Lord is building a church. I know it's hard to believe. You're told every day that miracles don't happen. But now you know differently.

"But why now? And why here? These are the unanswered questions. Although the scriptures can be interpreted in different ways, I have a few suggestions I'd like you to consider. In Revelation 1:7 it is written '*Behold, he cometh with clouds; and every eye shall see him, and they also which pierced him: and all kindred of the earth shall wail because of him.'*

"Of course, this is but one of the many proclamations of a Second Coming of Christ. '*For as the lightning cometh out of the east, and shineth even unto the west; so shall also the coming of the Son of Man be.' Matthew* 24:27.

"We know one day Christ will return to us and when that happens, don't you think there will be a sign--something unmistakable, a miracle, like a church rising from the Earth and reaching to the heavens?

"So, what I believe is that this cathedral is being raised to provide a fitting place for the Second Coming. In Revelation 3:20 it says: *'Behold, I stand at the door, and knock: if any man hears my voice and opens the door, I will come in to him, and will sup with him, and he with me.'*

"Well, I don't know, but it's a possibility that Christ is knocking on the door, that this sanctuary is being raised to herald the Second Coming of Christ. It could be that God wants to focus the attention of the world on this great wonder, so His people can clear their minds of worldly thoughts, and concentrate on the return of our Savior, Jesus Christ.

"In Zechariah 12:10, he says '*they shall look upon me whom they have pierced' and at Matthew 26:64 it is written:* 'Those who condemned Him will also see Him come.' God wants everyone to witness the Second Coming so there is no doubt that the prophecy has been fulfilled.

"So, it is our responsibility to shout out to the world. Christ is coming! Let me hear you say it, Christ is coming."

The crowd yelled out in unison. "Christ is coming!"

"Louder," Reverend Little beckoned.

The crowd yelled out again much louder. "Christ is coming!"

"Yes, he is, so let us tell the world. Christ is coming again!"

Suddenly there was a crack of thunder and a bolt of lightning hit a shortwave antenna attached to a tent.

"Glory, hallelujah!" someone yelled.

Many in the crowd laughed.

Reverend Little smiled as he looked out at the crowd and into the TV cameras that were recording the historic moment. "Now, I know a lot of you have to work and have other responsibilities, but it is important that as many of you as possible stay and keep vigil for none of us can afford to miss the Second Coming of Christ the King. So, talk to your bosses, your family, and your friends and work it out so you can bear witness to the rise of God's mighty temple as it soars to the heavens.

"Thank you and God bless you all."

That night on TV sets all across the nation, Reverend Little's sermon was replayed to millions of listeners, many hearing for the first time the story of the cathedral that was being built without the intervention of architects, the labor of men, the use of equipment, or the need for any materials besides what God had deposited beneath the earth at the beginning of the world. By noon the following day the crowd of a hundred and fifty had swollen to five thousand and Deputy Sheriff Curt Lawson was grateful when he heard the sound of helicopters in the distance and saw a convoy of trucks coming over the hill from Highway 127. It was the expected team of experts from the Department of Defense.

Six helicopters landed behind them and Army troops poured out of each and systematically began securing the area. Then a dozen trucks, buses and vans rolled up and began setting up operations. When the first truck stopped George Palmer and Jack Carpenter went over and greeted the newcomers. Greg Arnold stepped off the bus first along with a military officer. Greg and George shook hands.

"Good morning," George said. "We're glad to see you. The crowds were starting to get a little unruly."

"Yes, so I heard," Greg said. "George, Jack, this is Colonel Benjamin Martin. He'll be in charge of our investigation."

They all shook hands. "Well, I hope you have more luck than we did," George said. "I can't say we did much to solve this mystery."

Colonel Martin nodded. "Well, we'll get to the bottom of it. We all know buildings don't build themselves. There has to be a rational explanation for this phenomenon."

"That's what I thought," Jack said, "but I'm beginning to believe Reverend Little may be right."

"You mean that God is building a cathedral for Christ's Second Coming?" George questioned.

"Yeah. God is the only one I know of who could do something like this."

"Nonsense," Colonel Martin spat. "Just give us time. We've got some of the greatest scientific minds on the planet here. They'll figure this thing out."

"Well, do you need us to do anything?" George asked.

"No, we'll take it from here. I'm sure you all must be very tired. Just clear out your people and we'll contact you if we need anything."

George reluctantly gathered his students together and told them it was time to break camp and go home. An hour later as Jack and Dolly were leaving Jack took one last set of photos. The structure *was* looking more like a cathedral each day, with walls now over eight feet tall. He wondered if the government would ever figure out the mystery, and if they did, whether they would share it with the public. Somehow, he doubted they would.

9
Panic at the Pentagon

Colonel Benjamin Martin, an imposing, no-nonsense man standing six-foot-four, was raised a Catholic but he hadn't been to church since his wife had died of breast cancer six years earlier. He didn't understand how God could let someone suffer the way Carol had those last few months. All his life he'd been told that God had a plan and that we had to accept that whatever happened in life had a purpose, whether we understood it or not. People had to have faith, he was told, trust in God and obey His law without question. If they did this, they'd eventually end up in heaven and enjoy everlasting life. But Ben didn't buy it. He thought that most of what religious leaders spouted off today was just rhetoric, designed to keep people in line and the church's coffers full. It wasn't that he didn't believe in God, he just didn't believe the theologian knew anymore about God than he did.

Since he had never actually witnessed a miracle or believed anybody who claimed to have witnessed one, he was pretty sure there was an explanation for the Bat Mountain phenomenon. His theory was that it was caused by a shift in the Earth's crust or pressure from deep down in the center of the earth—a thermal shaft, an uplift, or perhaps the beginnings of a volcano. The problem with these theories was that they usually took hundreds, if not thousands, of years to accomplish or they occurred after a violent earthquake or volcanic eruption. But there'd been only minor earthquakes in recent years and no volcanic activity in Inyo County for thousands of years. So, when Senator Howard Rawlings, a close confidante of the President, came by the following week to see how the investigation was coming, he didn't have anything new to tell him.

"Senator. It's so nice to see you," Colonel Martin said.

"Yes, likewise. How have you been?"

"I've been better," he replied soberly.

"So, how is our cathedral doing?"

Colonel Martin frowned. "Well, it's not really a cathedral. It's just rock pushing up out of the ground. It may loosely resemble a cathedral but it won't ever have a functional interior or a roof unless someone builds one with traditional building techniques."

"So, how tall is it now?"

"Over twelve feet."

"Wow. Do you think it will ever stop growing?"

"I don't know. There's no way to tell for sure."

As they were talking Randy Perkins from the Park Service joined them.

"Randy," Senator Rawlings said with a nod.

"Hi, Senator. Sorry I'm late, but traffic in the park has been unreal and we were not anticipating this sudden surge in tourists, so we're understaffed. It seems like I've been dealing with one brush fire after another."

"That's alright. I was just trying to coax the Colonel into a bet on when the cathedral will stop growing. He's noncommittal. What do you think?"

Perkins shrugged. "Hell, I don't know. It's a crap shoot since there's never been anything like this ever reported to my knowledge."

"Well, a hundred dollars says it will exceed five hundred twenty-five feet," Senator Rawlings said. "I think the tallest cathedral in the world is about 524 feet so, I'm betting whoever is behind this will be going for the record."

Colonel Martin frowned. "If it's a geological event it could easily top 500 feet, but my money is on a chemical reaction of some sort, so I don't think it will get that tall," Colonel Martin replied. "I'm betting it won't grow more than a hundred feet."

"Okay, I'll take the middle ground," Randy said. "Two hundred fifty feet, the person who comes closest wins, and just so this doesn't drag on for several decades, once it stops growing for a ninety-day period the height is established for the purpose of our bet."

"Now, fun and games aside," Senator Rawlings said with a grim look on his face, "have your people figured this thing out yet?"

"No, not conclusively," Colonel Martin confessed. "Like I said, one theory that our people are throwing around is that someone injected a combination of chemicals into the ground, or they came together by some natural process, and what we are seeing is a chemical reaction."

"That sounds like a viable possibility." the Senator agreed.

"Yeah, but the problem is nobody can come up with a formula that would produce this type of a reaction. Besides, our top geologists have analyzed the gray crystalline substance that's being produced and no one has ever seen it before."

"So, you're back to square one then?" Randy asked.

"Pretty much, nothing that's happened here makes any sense and the brass at the Pentagon are getting pretty nervous. The President is wanting answers but they haven't been able to provide any."

"So, it's looking like a real miracle, then?" Senator Rawlings suggested.

"No. I don't believe in miracles."

"Well, if it's not a natural phenomenon and not an act of God, what is it? I've heard a rumor about an alien landing there."

"I don't believe in aliens either," the Colonel said. "But, it does look like that circular footprint near the cathedral was the result of some sort of aircraft landing. So, either somebody here on Earth has an advanced aircraft that we've never seen before, or someone created the footprint to make it look like aliens landed."

The three men just looked at each other in silence for a moment. Then Senator Rawlings said, "Well, the President isn't going to allow you to suggest aliens have landed, so how are you going to explain what's happening to the American people?"

"That depends on how big this thing gets. Once it stops growing hopefully the public will lose interest in it. But if it grows five hundred feet tall we've got serious problems."

"So, we wait, then," Senator Rawlings concluded.

"For now," Colonel Martin concurred. "We're looking into this Bat Mountain Corporation. They could be behind this—some sort of publicity stunt, perhaps. But so far the FBI hasn't been able to track down any of the board of directors or stockholders."

After a while Senator Rawlings and Randy left, leaving Colonel Martin depressed and defeated. When he took the assignment, he was sure that he'd solve the mystery, given enough time and the proper resources, but none of his experts had been able to figure out what was happening. He couldn't accept the Miracle-of-God or alien theories. They were just cop outs. There had to be an explanation. *What am I missing?*

As he was feeling sorry for himself the phone rang. It was Air Force Lieutenant Mason Andrews who had been researching air traffic over Inyo County during the one-year period prior to the discovery of the landing site.

"Did you find anything?"

"Actually, we did find something that occurred about three months prior to the discovery."

"What was it?"

"The pilots of an American Airlines jet traveling from LAX to Houston, Texas observed a large object entering the atmosphere. At the time, it was thought to be a meteorite. Its trajectory would have put its landing near Death Valley."

"So, was it a meteorite? Do you know for sure?"

"Three fighters were scrambled to investigate but they couldn't find anything on the ground, so it was presumed to have burned up in the atmosphere."

"Very interesting. As it turns out, our landing site is quite soft. Some of our engineers believe something may have churned the ground to about thirty feet."

"What do you mean?" Lt. Andrews asked.

"At first, we thought the site had been compressed due to the weight of whatever landed there, but on a more careful inspection, the ground turned out to be soft like a garden would be after you dug it up prior to planting."

"I see."

"So, one explanation for that would be if the aircraft had burrowed itself into the ground to escape detection."

"That wouldn't be an easy thing to do."

"No, but not impossible. I'm sure we could build a plane with that capability if we thought we needed it."

"Probably," Lt. Andrews agreed.

"So, did the pilots who observed this object descending into the Earth's atmosphere give an estimate of its size?" Colonel Martin asked.

"They said it appeared to have a diameter of about 150 meters."

"That's about right for our footprint."

"So, you think a spaceship entered the atmosphere, landed at your site and buried itself?"

"It's a theory," Colonel Martin confessed. "Not an acceptable one, but something we have to consider."

"We didn't find any satellite photos of that area during that time period, unfortunately. So, the pilots' report is all we have."

"Okay. Send me contact information on the pilots. I may want to interview them."

"Sure."

"Thanks for your help."

"No problem."

Colonel Martin hung up not believing where his investigation was leading him. If he told the brass at the Pentagon that aliens were responsible for what was happening, he'd be reassigned and probably demoted. He had to come up with something else. Aliens were not an option.

10
Deputy Lawson

After the Army took over security for the Bat Mountain Site, Deputy Curt Lawson left and went back to the sheriff's substation. He had promised Reverend Little that he'd check out the Bat Mountain Corporation. He figured whoever picked the name had looked at a topographical map and seen that there was a Bat Mountain not too far from the site and picked that name because of it. Bat Mountain had a GPS location of N 36.33384 and W -116.51588 and stood 4,221 feet above sea level. Presumably Bat Mountain got its name from the many bats, perhaps the legendary Lone Pine Mountain Devils, a large, furry, multi-winged creature with razor-like talons and multiple layers of deadly, venomous fangs, that were often seen by miners and pioneers in the area. He picked up the phone and called Libby Martinez, one of their best investigators, who worked out of the sheriff's office in Bishop.

"Oh, Curt," Libby said. "How's the crowd control going?"

"It's over for now. We've been relieved by the Army."

"Seriously?"

"Yeah. Three helicopters full of them."

"Wow. The Pentagon must be worried."

"Well, I don't blame them. This is some weird shit."

"Hmm. So, does it really look like aliens landed?"

"Kind of, but it could easily have been staged. A couple bulldozers and a flame thrower could have produced the circular landing site."

"Were there any tracks into the area?"

"Nothing heavy. A few Jeep and pickup tracks that Jack Carpenter probably made."

"What about the cathedral? Is it really growing?"

"It's definitely getting bigger, that's for sure."

"Wow. So how can I help?"

"There's a corporation that recently bought up the land around the area—a Bat Mountain Corporation."

"Seriously? Bat Mountain?"

"Yes, there is a peak named Bat Mountain close by actually, so it makes sense."

"Okay. I'll check with the Secretary of State but it might be a foreign corporation or even one offshore, perhaps."

"Find out for me and get me some names of officers or directors that I can contact. The owners of this company must know what's going on."

"Okay. Will do. Give me a few hours."

As Deputy Lawson was going through his telephone messages he found one from Angela. He called her immediately.

"You're back early?" she noted.

"Yes. Saved by the U.S. Army."

"Really? Why?"

"I don't know. I guess your ex-husband's discovery has gotten the Pentagon upset. You don't think Jack had anything to do with this, do you?"

She laughed. "Jack? No. He's way too wrapped up in his work to get mixed up in any kind of conspiracy like this."

"Well, I'd like to talk to Jake, if you don't mind. I've got to cover all the bases."

"Good. Why don't you come over? I'll fix you supper or we can go out after you talk to Jake."

"Yeah. Sounds good, but I'm waiting on a phone call. How about seven? I should be able to get out of here by then."

"Great. See you then."

Curt didn't really think Jack had anything to do with what was going on at the Bat Mountain Site, but he didn't like Jack much since Angela obviously still had feelings for him. Fueled by an inexplicable jealousy, he couldn't pass up the opportunity to disparage him. Even if Jack was innocent, he could cause him a lot of grief simply by conducting an investigation and asking the right questions. A few hours later Libby called him back.

"It's a Nevada corporation formed in March 1958. The only name on the certificate is an attorney, Paul Bradford out of Las Vegas." She gave him the contact information. "I tried to call him but his answering service said he was out of town for the rest of the month."

"Wonderful. There are no names of directors or anything?"

"No. I checked with the comptroller and a no-tax-due franchise tax return was filed and Bradford was the only officer listed on the return."

"Okay. Thanks. Maybe I'll run over to Vegas and check out this answering service. They must have some records on this attorney. Perhaps someone there actually knows him."

"Right. I checked with the Nevada Bar Association already and this is the address they have for him too. He didn't graduate from law school–just took the California bar and passed. Unfortunately, they don't have a photograph."

"Hmm. Okay. Let me know if you dig up anything else."

Curt hung up and started clearing his desk to

leave. Twenty minutes later he was pulling up in front of Angela's house. He was surprised to see Jack's car there. He went up to the front door and knocked. Angela opened the door wide so he could come in.

"Right on time. Jack is going to take Jake for the evening so we can be alone."

"Oh, good. Can I talk to them first? There's a few things I need to get straight."

"Sure, I'm sure that will be fine."

Jack walked into the room with a beer in his hand. He nodded at Curt. "What do you need to get straight?" he asked.

"Oh, some things in that newspaper article."

Jack sat down on the sofa. "Like what?"

"Like, it said after your car went off the road, it rolled several times but managed to right itself before it got to the bottom."

"Right. The truck was rolling and then hit something that changed its trajectory. I was surprised when it finally settled on all four tires. Lucky for me."

"And you weren't hurt at all?"

"He suffered a concussion," Angela interjected.

"True. Nothing serious, though. A few bumps and bruises—a little disorientation."

Angela sighed. "It was a serious concussion the doctor said and you were very disoriented. That's why you ended up wandering around in the desert."

Curt looked at Jack skeptically. "So, have you ever heard of Bat Mountain Corporation?"

Jack nodded. "Not until last week when I discovered they owned the Bat Mountain Site."

"How about the incorporator, Paul Bradford?"

Jack shook his head. "No, but I was going to see if I could track him down."

"Why does that interest you?"

"The same reason it interests you. I want to find out what's going on. I'm a curious person."

"It's part of my job, but it shouldn't concern you."

"It shouldn't concern me? Are you serious? Some bizarre structure made of an unknown substance is growing on my back door and I shouldn't be concerned. Aliens may be landing nearby but I should turn a blind eye to it?"

"Yes. Leave it to the professionals," Curt said strongly.

"Well, I'm sorry. I don't trust the federal government to be honest with the public about this, should they get lucky and figure it out. They'll try to cover it up in the name of national security and you'll go along with whatever they decide to do. So, I'm going to figure this out on my own."

Curt let out a frustrated sigh. "Well, just be careful you don't interfere with my investigation and if you find anything out, I want to hear about it."

"Will you let me know if you find anything out?" Jack asked, amused.

"No. Obviously not."

"Then don't expect any calls from me," Jack spat.

As they were talking Jake walked in. "I'm ready to go."

"Good," Jack said. "Let's get the hell out of here."

Jake looked at Angela expectantly. "Don't ask," she said. "Have a good night, honey."

Jack and Jake left and Angela glared at Curt. "Why are you picking on Jack? He didn't do anything."

"You buy his story he was just wandering in the desert and found the Bat Mountain Site?"

"Yes. Of course, I do. Why wouldn't I?"

"Because it makes no sense. I think Jack knows more about this than he's letting on."

Angela shook her head. “I have known Jack for ten years and he’s got his faults, but one thing is sure, he’s as honest as the day is long.”

Curt shrugged. “Well, for your sake, I hope you’re right.”

11
Stunning News

It was late and Colonel Martin was getting ready to go home when his phone rang. He picked up and found out it was Maria Sutton, a microbiologist working in his lab.

"Yes, Maria. Give me some good news."

"Well, I have news. You'll have to decide if it's good or not."

"Okay. What is it?"

"As you know, I have been studying the crystalline substance found at the Bat Mountain Site."

"Yes, so what did you conclude?"

"It's alive. There is some kind of microorganism within the substance that is making it expand or grow."

A chill darted down Martin's spine. "What kind of microorganism? Where did it come from?" Colonel Martin asked.

"It's very small and our strongest microscopes cannot clearly see it. All we can see are clouds of these organisms. But we do know they are constantly in motion and their activities appear to have purpose."

"What does that mean? Appear to have purpose?"

"They are either following a preset program, instinctively working together, or someone or something is guiding them."

"That's very hard to swallow?" the Colonel said. "You can't expect me to believe that someone is controlling microorganisms?"

"Well, it's only a preliminary analysis, but that's what it looks like to me."

Martin's stomach twisted and he squirmed in his chair. "Thank you, Maria. Let me know if you learn anything else."

Colonel Martin got up and went to the window. He looked out wondering what he was going to tell his superiors. He didn't relish telling them the truth. The phone rang. It was an operator advising him that General Thornton was on the line. Thornton was Colonel Martin's contact at the Pentagon and he'd hoped he wouldn't have to talk to him for a few days.

"General, it's so nice to hear from you," he lied.

"Yes, well the Joint Chiefs are getting anxious for a report. Do you have anything for me?"

Colonel Martin gave him a complete rundown of everything he'd learned to date except the most recent report from Maria. He swallowed hard.

"Oh, and there's one last thing. Our top microbiologist just reported to me, minutes ago, that in her opinion, the crystal substance used in the construction of the Bat Mountain structure is alive with billions of microorganisms and they are responsible for its growth."

"Have you ever seen this microorganism before?" the General asked.

"No sir. It's completely unique."

"So, where did it come from?"

"Well, it didn't come from the site itself. It appears to have been brought in by air and deposited on the site. Apparently, this microorganism propagates quickly."

"Are you saying aliens deposited these microorganisms?" General Thornton asked.

"No, sir. I don't know where they came from but two American Airlines' pilots did report a UFO over southern California that could have landed at the site."

"Wonderful! That's all I need," the general spat. "Keep this new information to yourself, understood?"

"Yes, sir."

"Not a word to anyone. If this leaks out, it could cause general panic around the globe."

"I'll contact the personnel at the lab and remind them that everything they learn is classified."

"Good. Keep me posted if you learn anything else."

"Yes, sir. I will."

12
Spread of the Faith

Reverend Little was not pleased when the U.S. Army came in, moved them off the ridge overlooking the Bat Mountain Site and pushed them back a half mile. His flock couldn't see the growth of the cathedral from their new location and that simply was unacceptable. The next morning, they found a hill that was high enough to provide a clear view of the site so they set up camp there and started selling binoculars along with food and water to help pay for the expenses they were incurring hosting so many people. By the end of the week the crowds had swelled to ten thousand and large campgrounds were opened at Greenwater and the former ghost town known as Evelyn.

Although this view was better than nothing, Reverend Little was not satisfied and repeatedly asked Colonel Martin to allow for escorted tours of the site, but each time he refused. Unable to accept the current situation he reached out to both his congressmen as well as California's two U.S. Senators. The congressman whose district included Inyo County was Joel Stephens from Bishop. After several days Stephens called him back.

"It's not fair to all the pilgrims traveling long distances to see this extraordinary event, to be herded away out of its view," Reverend Little argued. "It's not right."

"Well, the government has a right to set up a perimeter to safeguard the integrity of the site, but they may have gone too far. I'll call Colonel Martin and see if maybe he'll compromise and, at least, allow guided tours during the day."

"I'd appreciate that, Congressman. And I'm sure the pilgrims will as well. Perhaps you'd like to make an appearance at the site and talk to the Colonel one on one, rather than telephone him. It's much harder to say 'no' in person. It would be good publicity too with all the networks there recording what's going on."

There was a moment of silence. Finally, Congressman Stephens said, "You're pretty shrewd, Reverend Little. You'd have made a fine politician."

"Thank you. I'll take that as a 'yes,' then."

"Absolutely, I was planning to come home for the weekend, so let's do this Saturday morning, okay?"

"Perfect. I'll make sure there's a big crowd and all the media is there."

"Okay. See you soon."

Reverend Little hung up feeling encouraged by the Congressman's intervention in his plight. After he'd given instructions to his staff for preparation of Saturday's events, he called Deputy Sheriff Curt Lawson to see if he had dug up any information on Bat Mountain Corporation.

"Yes, it's a Nevada corporation organized by an attorney, Paul Bradford, out of Las Vegas. He's out of town at the moment so that's all the information I have."

"Well, keep me posted if you find out anything else."

Before he hung up he told the deputy about the big crowds expected on Saturday, Congressman Stephens' visit, and asked him if the Sheriff's office could provide some security. Lawson agreed but told him the county's budget didn't provide for officer overtime and he'd have to cover the cost if he wanted them. The Reverend reluctantly agreed making a mental note that he'd have to figure out some new fund-raising ideas to make ends meet.

On Saturday Highway 127 was clogged north and south with pilgrims coming out to the Bat Mountain Site. Reverend Little's people were there in force along with the media. The congressman arrived by helicopter not wanting to get caught in all the traffic. Colonel Martin had reluctantly agreed to a meeting at 1:00 p.m., so there was plenty of time to fire up the crowd before the meeting. Reverend Little took the pulpit to introduce Congressman Stephens.

"Ladies and Gentlemen. As you are painfully aware our elected government has effectively banished us from the Living Desert Cathedral. They have moved us off the ridge overlooking the site so that we are now forced to come here, over a mile away to watch God's Miracle in the Desert.

"So, why are they doing this? Is a cathedral in the desert some kind of threat to National Security?"

The crowd yelled in unison, "No!"

"Have we done anything to interfere with their investigation?"

"No!" the crowd responded.

"Have we been unruly or threatened anyone?"

"No!"

"So, I think the government has forgotten it is the servant of the people, not its master!"

Someone screamed, "That's right!"

Another yelled, "Amen, brother."

"To help us remind our government of their role in this matter, I have asked our representative in Congress, Joel Stephens, to intercede on our behalf and he has graciously agreed to do so. Ladies and Gentlemen, Congressman Joel Stephens!"

Congressman Stephens took the pulpit nodding and smiling to the throng. "Thank you, Reverend, ladies and gentlemen. Yes, I'm afraid sometimes our government does forget its place. They sit up there in Washington with all that power and they forget that their power comes from the people and it can be easily taken away. In a few minutes, I'm going to meet with the U.S. Army and remind them that all of you have the right to monitor what's going on here. I'm sure they will say they are doing this to protect you, but I don't personally see how this Cathedral could pose a danger or threat to anyone.

"So, hopefully they will be reasonable, but if they are not, I'll go to their superiors. If that doesn't work, I'll seek assistance from my colleagues in the Congress to force them to respect the public's right to observe this incredible phenomenon.

"I'm not sure what we are witnessing here—whether it's God's miracle, a fluke of nature, or something else. But whatever it is, you all have a right to see it up close and judge for yourselves, particularly those of you in Inyo County who will be most affected should it turn out to be some sort of threat.

"I'm taking Reverend Little, George Palmer, the first scientist to study this phenomenon, and Deputy Hanson from the Inyo County Sheriff's office in with me to meet with Colonel Martin. Pray that he will be reasonable. God be with you."

The crowd clapped and yelled their approval as the Congressman left the pulpit. Once he was down he led the delegation down the mountain and back over the ridge to the site. The Cathedral how stood over twenty-five feet tall and sparkled radiantly in the midday sun. It was the Congressman's first up close view of the sight so he paused a moment to take it in.

"Wow! That *is* a marvel," he mused.

Colonel Martin and Senator Rawlings met the delegation and invited them in the camp. After a short tour of the site they went into a tent and sat around a large table. Colonel Martin cleared his throat.

"So, I'm glad you decided to visit. I want you to know we are not trying to hide anything here. We're just concerned with the public's safety. That's why we had to expand the perimeter."

"Is there a danger this thing will blow up?" Congressman Stephens asked.

"I don't think so, but we don't know for sure. One of our theories is that this phenomenon is being caused by a chemical reaction, so if that is true the chemicals involved would have to be very powerful and they may be toxic."

"Has there been any detection of toxic gases in the area?" the Congressman asked.

"No," Martin conceded, "but they could be emitted into the atmosphere at any time and I don't want to be responsible for innocent citizens dying."

"Come on," George said. "My students and I were here for two weeks and we never saw anything that would pose a health hazard to the public."

"Well, your ass isn't on the line if something goes wrong," Colonel Martin spat.

"True, but why don't you be honest?" Reverend Little replied. "The government is afraid of the truth. They're afraid that this might be one of God's miracles, in which case the government would have to acknowledge a higher authority."

"Or, the result of an alien visit to Earth and the government is afraid of the public reaction to such a historic event," George added.

"Both of those scenarios are nonsense," Colonel Martin replied. "The government is not worried about either one of them. We are simply trying to be prudent here and understand what is going on before we subject the public to any danger."

"If that is true," George said, "Why don't you let the media set up cameras all around the site so people around the country can watch what's going on in the safety of their own homes?"

There was a moment of silence then Colonel Martin shook his head. "No. I will not have my people living in a fish bowl while they try to figure this thing out. It's not fair to them. They can't do their job properly if they are worried about some armchair scientist second guessing them."

"That's ridiculous!" Reverend Little said. "George's idea is perfectly reasonable and there is no reason to reject it."

"Yes, there is," Deputy Hanson interjected. "All this attention you are bringing to this site is causing the county a lot of money. Our office doesn't have the budget to pay for the deputies needed to control the crowd that's out here now. If you make this pile of rock a national spectacle the crowds will double or triple and we simply won't be able to handle it. Then people *will* get hurt and property will be destroyed."

"I can appreciate the Sheriff's office concerns and I may be able to get Congress to help with the costs," Congressman Stephens said. "But George's idea is reasonable, and it would allow members of Congress to monitor the situation as well."

Senator Rawlings sighed deeply. "You know, Joel. There are national security considerations here. If this is our first alien contact, we cannot afford to be cavalier in the way we respond to it. What if this thing continues to grow until it's ten thousand feet tall? Are we just going to let it? It may be a cancer that has to be cut out before it threatens the entire world."

Congressman Stephens' eyes widened. "Is that what the government believes?"

Rawlings shrugged. "Some of our scientists think that is a possibility, but the fact is nobody knows for sure, so we should err on the side of caution and restrict the site to those involved in the investigation."

"Is that the President's position?" Stephens asked.

Rawlings nodded. "It is. Until we know what this thing is, access to it needs to be restricted."

"Okay. Then I'll have to take this to my colleagues in the House and see if they concur with that position. I personally believe you ought to at least put in a live feed to the cathedral and the landing site and allow weekly tours to the press and selected leaders in the community. The public has the right to watch this event, whatever it turns out to be."

"I'll convey your position to the President," Rawlings assured him.

The delegation left and went back to Reverend Little's headquarters where they held an impromptu news conference.

"Congressman," a reporter yelled. "Did you get any concessions from Colonel Martin?"

"No, I'm sad to say they refused all our requests. They say that until they know exactly what's going on here, it's too dangerous to the public to be involved."

"Congressman," another reporter asked. "Are you satisfied with that response?"

"No, not at all. It was suggested, at the very least, that the press be allowed to put in a live feed to the cathedral and landing site. That way the public could monitor what was happening hour by hour. Also, a weekly briefing for the press was suggested. Unfortunately, both ideas were rejected. I'm afraid things will have to remain as they are for now."

"Reverend Little," another reporter asked. "Are you going to accept the government's position?"

"No. I reject their position and demand they let us back on the ridge immediately. This is a violation of our Constitutional rights. Every citizen has the right to gather and worship freely without government interference. We cannot allow the President to get away with this abridgement to our rights in the name of public safety or national security. Unfortunately, the U.S. Army responds to the President and not to you and me, so we cannot do anything personally to redress this injustice until the next presidential election. In the meantime, however, God answers to no man!"

The press conference went on for some time and when it was over Reverend Little left to go back to his office in Shoshone. He had to do something to get the President to change his mind and be reasonable. He pondered the possibilities.

13
Lone Pine Devils

After the meeting Colonel Martin was angry. He was not used to people challenging his authority and threatening to go over his head. He was carrying out the wishes of the President and the Joint Chiefs for godsakes. *What did Congressman Stephens expect him to do, defy his Commander in Chief?* As he walked around the exterior of the cathedral, he couldn't help but marvel at its beauty. He wondered if God was really responsible for this living miracle or if it was a fluke of nature. He felt helpless for the first time in his life. He'd always been able to handle anything his superiors had thrown at him. He'd always been able to rely on his experience, training, and common sense to solve difficult problems, but nothing about this assignment was common or made sense. He didn't know what to do and he was scared. Scared he'd fail and end his career in disgrace or, worse yet, scared this miracle wasn't from God but from the Devil himself.

It was late when he finally went to his tent and climbed onto his bunk. He tried to sleep but he felt uneasy and tossed and turned for a long time until he finally fell into a shallow slumber. Angry jabs to his face and intense pain to his left eye awoke him. "What the hell!" He screamed, sitting up, arms flaying, trying frantically to brush the creatures off him. Covering his wounded eye and feeling warm blood dripping between his fingers he stood up and quickly scanned the darkness with his functioning eye. The sound of flapping wings sent a wave of terror through him. "Oh, my God!" he screamed as he twirled around to confront his attackers.

A bat landed on his torso and sank its claws through his T-shirt, into his skin and then began biting him ferociously. He grabbed the bat by the wings and tried to pull it off but another bat landed on his head. The second bat went after his good eye while several more landed on his back and head. They were all relentless in their attacks, their fangs ripping into his skin like drill bits. "Oh, my God! Help me! Somebody help me!" he screamed. He stood up, shook himself violently and grabbed another bat by its cold, angry wings. "Leave me alone you bastards!" he wailed but the bats were relentless in their attack finally driving him to his knees. Blood oozed from his eyes and dozens of wounds until he became so weak he collapsed and shrunk into the fetal position.

There were footsteps as soldiers rushed to his tent. The front flaps flew open and dozens of angry bats flew out into the night. The Marine sergeant in command of the night watch turned on a lamp and cringed at the bloody sight before him. "Oh, my God, Colonel! Are you alright?" he asked, but immediately realized it was a stupid question. The Colonel's eyes had been plucked out and his face was a bloody pulp. "Oh, shit! Medic! We need a medic!" He felt for a pulse but found nothing but stillness.

Two other sentries ran in and gagged at the sight. "Oh, shit!"

When the medical team arrived they kicked everyone out, and after satisfying themselves that the Colonel was dead, covered his body with a sheet.

Ten minutes later when the officer in charge, Lt. Herbert Miller, arrived he was apprised of the situation by the medic in charge.

"It looks like he was attacked by bats."

"Bats?"

"Yes, when the sentry who first responded to his screams came into the tent a lot of angry, screeching bats flew out."

"Oh, my God!" the Lieutenant said shaking his head. "I thought the Lone Pine Devil was a myth."

"Apparently not," the medic concluded.

14
The Wrath of God

A little after five in the morning Reverend Little was advised that God had punished the one who had dared meddle with His will. Feeling uplifted he got up and prepared his Sunday sermon to be delivered at the Bat Mountain Site. When he arrived, the pilgrims seemed unsettled as there were rumors something important had happened but no one knew for sure what it was. The crowd hushed as he took the pulpit.

"Good morning my friends and fellow children of God. Do you feel God's power in the air this morning?"

"Yes," someone yelled.

"Well, that's because during the night our Father exacted justice from one who sought to thwart his will. Our Father is a just God but he will not tolerate those who stand with the Devil. Colonel Martin was asked over and over to stand aside and let God's will be done, but he stubbornly refused and tried to deny us God's Miracle in the Desert.

"So, because he thought he knew better than God what was right for His people, God opened the hole in Bat Mountain that descends to the gates of Hell and unleashed the Lone Pine Mountain Demons on the transgressor. Since he could not see what was before him his eyes were plucked out and since he would not obey the will of God his heart was eaten by the bats of hell!"

The crowd was silent, most being shocked at what they were hearing. Several men in suits standing at the back of the crowd began slowly making their way to the pulpit.

"The Lord God Almighty has given us a miracle, a cathedral of unfathomable grace and beauty to herald the Second Coming of Christ. He will not allow any mere mortal to interfere with His purpose. For a man is but a flea before an elephant and has no chance of altering the will of God."

The men in suits arrived at the front of the crowd and one began to ascend the pulpit.

"It is unfortunate that Colonel Martin had eyes but did not see. Had he not stood against the will of God he wouldn't be knocking today on the gates of Hell!"

The man walked out onto the pulpit and pulled his badge out of his pocket. "Reverend John Little? I'm Special Agent William Pierce of the Federal Bureau of Investigation. Please come with me, sir. We have some questions we'd like to ask you in connection with the murder of Colonel Benjamin Martin."

"Sure, I'll come with you," Reverend Little replied firmly. "I have nothing to hide. This wasn't my doing but the will of God. But I will give to Caesar what is due Caesar, as our Lord Jesus Christ commanded."

The three agents escorted Reverend Little to a waiting car and he was taken away still preaching to the pilgrims as the door closed behind him. An hour later he was taken into the FBI field office in Las Vegas and put in an interview room. Agents William Pierce and Melanie Sanders interviewed him.

"Reverend Little," Agent Pierce said. "What do you know about the death of Colonel Benjamin Martin?"

Reverend Little shrugged. "Nothing but rumor."

"Rumor?"

"Your sermon seemed pretty detailed. How did you know he was killed by bats?"

"My assistant, Tom Keller, told me. He said he'd heard it from one of the soldiers working the perimeter of the site."

"Where were you this morning between midnight and 3:00 a.m.?"

"In bed asleep. My housekeeper can vouch for that."

"You were pretty upset with Colonel Martin's refusal to allow your pilgrims back up on the ridge to watch the cathedral grow, weren't you?"

"You know I was."

"Did you decide to punish him for his refusal?"

"I am but a mortal. It is not up to me to punish others, only God can do that."

"You said you were an instrument of God. Did God tell you to punish Colonel Martin?"

"No. The Lord doesn't speak to me, unfortunately. He hasn't spoken to anyone directly since He spoke to Jesus and the prophets. We know his will by his signs."

"Like the Living Desert Cathedral?"

"Yes, a most magnificent sign."

"Do you know who killed Colonel Martin?"

"The Mountain Devils who were unleashed by God upon him."

"Do you know who helped God unleash the Mountain Devils?"

"God doesn't need man to punish His enemies. He has to but think it and it is done."

Agent Pierce sighed and then looked at Agent Sanders. "Okay, we're going to take a break. Just relax. If you need anything, just yell. Someone will be monitoring you while we are gone."

The two agents left the interview room and went into a conference room where an army officer, Lt. Herbert Miller and another special agent, Tommy Rodriguez were waiting.

"So, what do you think?" Agent Pierce asked.

"I think he's lying," Lt. Miller replied. "He knows exactly who killed the colonel because he ordered the murder."

"Well, you're probably right, but we have no proof of that, do we?"

Lt. Miller nodded dejectedly. "No, nobody seems to have seen anything and there wasn't any evidence left in the tent."

"Somebody must have brought those bats in there," Agent Rodriguez said. "They certainly didn't fly in there themselves. The flaps were closed when the body was discovered. They must have made some noise when they were let out in the tent. I don't understand why nobody heard them."

"And I don't think the bats would have attacked the colonel. They just would have tried to escape."

"Unless they felt threatened. Maybe he yelled or moved quickly and spooked them."

"Has anybody talked to Tom Keller and the housekeeper?" Lt. Miller asked.

"Yes, they corroborate his story."

"So, we have nothing?" Agent Rodriguez spat.

"That's about the size of it," Agent Sanders advised. "We have no choice but to cut him loose."

Agent Rodriguez shook his head in disgust. "Do it, then. But we can't let this go. We can't let him get away with murder."

15
The Oval Office

Senator Rawlings was awakened by the persistent ring of his telephone. His wife was a sound sleeper and just turned over as he rolled out of bed and picked up the phone.

"What is it?" he moaned irritably.

"It's the Bat Mountain Site," Jimmy Malone said. "The situation has taken a turn for the worse. The President wants you in his office now."

"Is it so serious it can't wait until morning?"

"That's right. He's got meetings all morning and he wants to see you before breakfast."

"What's happened, for godsakes?"

"Colonel Martin is dead."

"What? You can't be serious."

"Just get in here, now. We've got some tough decisions to make."

"Alright. I'll be there in forty-five minutes."

Jimmy Malone was an agent of the Central Intelligence Agency and assigned as a liaison to the President on several ultra-top-secret projects. So top secret that not even the President's Chief of Staff knew anything about them. The Bat Mountain situation was an unexpected spin-off of one of those projects. About an hour after Senator Rawlings had been summoned he strolled into the Oval Office.

"Howard. Thanks for coming in so early," the President said. "There's been an unfortunate development."

"I heard Colonel Martin is dead. What happened?"

Malone sighed. "Well, believe it or not he was killed by bats."

"Bats?"

Jimmy explained all that had happened in as much detail as he could.

"So, it's pretty obvious that Reverend Little is responsible, but you have no proof," Senator Rawlings summarized.

"That's about the size of it," Malone agreed.

"I was afraid after I left, that the Reverend might cause more problems, but I didn't think he would resort to murder."

"It's revived his dying ministry," Malone observed. "I warned you to leave the Bat Mountain Site alone. It posed no threat to us but now we've got a serious problem."

"It does pose a threat," the President interjected. "If the truth comes out there will be general panic and I'll probably be impeached."

Malone shook his head. "Only a handful of people in the CIA know about the aliens. And the Director and I are the only ones who know there is a connection between them and the Bat Mountain Site. So that's only four people who could leak the story and I think we all can be trusted to keep a lid on it."

"What about the military?" the President said. "As I recall, we had to bring a few of them into the project."

"The only ones in the military who knew about the connection are General Thornton and Admiral Bennett, so the secret is safe," Jimmy assured him.

"So, what do we do now?" the President asked.

"My advice is end the investigation. Have your scientists determine that the formation poses no threat to national security or public health and let it be."

"But it's not going to go away," Senator Rawlings argued.

"I know," Malone said. "Let Reverend Little have his cathedral. In a few years it will just be an unusual rock formation in the desert."

"But it contains an alien life form," Senator Rawlings protested.

"Yes. But it's not a threat," Malone said. "It has no agenda other than to live in peace and be left alone."

"You don't know that."

"I've been assured that is the case."

"If scientists study it long enough, they will discover it's not just a rock formation."

"There won't be any need to study it closely once our scientists have finished their investigation. We'll make our findings available to the public. That should satisfy them."

"They won't be satisfied. They'll keep digging until they find the truth."

"Enough," the President commanded. "I think Jimmy is right. Just let it alone. If letting Reverend Little and his pilgrims' use of the cathedral sparks a rebirth of fundamental Christianity, how bad can that be?"

Senator Rawlings shook his head. "It's your call, Mr. President. I just don't trust the aliens. Playing host to another life-form wasn't part of our agreement. It's just too risky."

"Well, unfortunately we're not in a position to do much about it."

"Yes, sir."

"So, make this mess go away," the President ordered. "Give the public limited access to it but don't let any samples be taken away for close study. That's normal protocol anyway, so it shouldn't raise any eyebrows."

"What about Colonel Martin? We're not going to let his murderer get off scot free, are we?"

"No. If the FBI can get enough evidence to charge him, let them do it, but in the meantime, there is a presumption of innocence."

"Yes, Mr. President," Rawlings acknowledged reluctantly.

Rawlings and Malone got up, shook the President's hand and then left the oval office. Rawlings couldn't believe they were going to just walk away from the Bat Mountain Site. He wondered how it would all play out in the end. Was it possible the whole incident would eventually die down and the threat go away? He didn't think there was a chance in Hell that would happen. The truth was like the air in a tire. It could be confined there for a long time but eventually the tire would wear out and spring a leak or you'd run over a nail and it would escape in an instant.

16
About Face

Reverend Little was surprised when he was released by the FBI. He'd assumed he'd be held at least twenty-four hours. He liked media attention but since he was being released so soon he wouldn't get much. In fact, only two reporters were outside when he was released. That didn't dissuade him from making a statement, however.

"Are you a suspect in the murder of Colonel Martin?" the first reporter asked.

Reverend Little smiled broadly. "I don't know. You'll have to ask the FBI."

"If not, why are you here today?" the second reporter asked.

"I think it's because of what I said this morning in my sermon—that God punishes those who dare stand in his way. Apparently, the FBI didn't think I showed proper respect for the decedent."

"Do you really think God summoned the bats to kill Colonel Martin?" the first reporter asked stifling a smile.

"Yes. That's what it looked like to me. Don't you agree?"

The reporter shrugged. Reverend Little turned, got into his limousine, and drove off wondering what would happen now that Colonel Martin was out of the picture. He was afraid the government would shut down the Bat Mountain Site entirely while a criminal investigation was conducted. When he got back to the Site late in the afternoon he was shocked to see that the Army had left, his pilgrims had been allowed back on the ridge overlooking the cathedral, and the Sheriff's office was back in control. When he saw Deputy Lawson he went over to him immediately to find out what was going on.

"What happened to the Army?" he asked.

"They left about an hour ago. Their commanding officer told me the government's investigation of the Bat Mountain Phenomenon was finished and it had been determined that it did not pose a threat to national security or public health. Apparently, they intend to buy the property and transfer it to the National Park Service for the benefit of the general public."

"My word. Such an about face. Well, like I always say, it's foolish to resist the will of the Lord."

"Right. So, just tell your people to stay behind the perimeter barriers and everything will be fine. But if anybody breaches the perimeter, they'll be arrested. No exceptions."

"No problem. I'll get the word out. Thank you, Curt."

17
Bat Mountain Corporation

Jack Carpenter was starting to lose interest in the Bat Mountain Site when the FBI called. It had been exciting at first but now it had become a distraction he didn't need. His business normally kept him busy six days a week and he was getting behind on some of his jobs because of it. It was a relief when the government took over the site and he could get back to business as usual.

The news that Colonel Martin had been killed by bats, however, blew his mind. He'd heard of the Lone Pine Devil and knew ranchers often blamed the unexplained loss of livestock to it, but he'd never heard of a bat attacking a human in his lifetime. He'd gone exploring in caves before and ran across bats but they'd always kept their distance. He couldn't imagine someone capturing bats and using them as weapons, but admitted to himself it might be possible.

He agreed to meet Agents William Pierce and Melanie Sanders at Deep Springs College where they were also interviewing George Palmer. When he got there, he went over his discovery of the Bat Mountain Site. George had already filled them in on the research he'd done there before the feds took over the site. Both of them were able to provide the agents rock solid alibis so the mood was relaxed.

"So, had you had any problem with bats?" Agent Sanders asked.

"No," George replied. "I never saw one the entire time I was there."

"Me, either," Jack agreed. "I've done some hiking on Bat Mountain over the last 25 years and there are plenty of bats in the caves up there, but I've never heard of them attacking humans."

"What about before that?"

"Well, I thought you might ask about that so I looked it up in an old history book I have. Back in 1878 it was said that 37 Spanish settlers disappeared in this area and their rotted corpses were found by a team of copper miners. Weeks later Father Justes Martinez showed up at a mission near San Diego and claimed the party had been attacked by winged demons sweeping down from the trees in the deep of night."

Agent Sanders frowned. "So, you're buying Reverend Little's sermon?" she asked.

"No. I'm just saying the myth about the Lone Pine Demon is that it is the protector of the environment and natural wonders of the desert. It attacks those who seek to disturb the natural balance of nature in this area. So, the bats attacking Colonel Martin, kind of makes sense, if they perceived he was disturbing Mother Nature. If you believe in the myth, that is."

"Do you believe in it?" Agent Sanders asked.

"No. Not really. Like I said, I haven't heard of anyone being attacked by a bat since I've lived here."

"So, do either of you know anyone in Reverend Little's congregation who might be capable of murder?"

"No," Jack said. "I don't know of anyone in the group that well, but they all strike me as passive types. The only aggressive one in the bunch is the high school principal, Paul Barnes. He pretty much handles logistics for Reverend Little."

"So, Paul Barnes is the chief administrator for the church?"

"Unofficially. The Reverend would tell you *he* handles administration but in reality, he delegates it to Barnes."

"So, if someone was hired to make it look like bats had killed Colonel Martin, you think Barnes would have arranged it?"

"Right. The Reverend couldn't have done it," Jack said.

"So, how easy would it be to catch a bat?" Agent Sanders asked.

"I don't know. I've never tried it, but I was thinking about that today after I heard about the attack."

"Really, did you come up with something?"

"Well, you couldn't sneak up on them. They'd just fly off, but if you could figure out how they go in and out of the cave you could put up netting over the entrance. Then if you turned on a light or created a loud noise, they'd fly into the net and you'd have them."

"Hmm. Interesting idea," Agent Sanders noted.

"I wouldn't want to be the one removing them from the net, though," Jack said. "They'd be pretty pissed off."

Sanders laughed. "No. Me either."

"A better idea," George interjected, "would be to fill the cave with a gas that would knock them out for a while. Then you could gather them up and transport them to the murder site and be gone when they woke up."

Agent Sanders looked at Agent Pierce and nodded. "Right. I bet that was how it was done."

George shrugged. "I wouldn't know what kind of gas to use. Did you catch any of the bats?"

"No, but there was some bat guano," Agent Sanders said thoughtfully. "We might be able to test it for traces of chemical residue."

"Right. And if you found some you might be able to trace it to the killer," Jack said excitedly.

Agent Sanders laughed. “Have you had any law enforcement experience?” she asked. “You seem to have a nose for investigation.”

“Yes, I was an MP during the Korean War. One of my assignments was criminal investigation. I thought about going into law enforcement after I got out, but I would have had to move to the city. There wasn’t much opportunity around here.”

“Well, you’ve been a big help, both of you,” Agent Sanders said as she got up. “If we have any more questions, we’ll call you.”

Jack and George nodded and showed the two agents out. Cindy and Dolly had been waiting in the lounge so they joined them there. They had agreed to go out to dinner after the interviews, so they drove into Lone Pine to their favorite restaurant, the Mt. Whitney. It served great food and had excellent service. The hostess directed them to a booth.

“So, now that the Feds have left the Bat Mountain Site are you going back?” Jack asked.

“No. I asked Randy about it and he said they were opening the area to the press and tourists but that no more scientific study would be allowed.”

Jack frowned. “So, they’ve figured out what’s going on?”

“So they say. The official word is that it is simply a geological uplift. They claim that the rock formation has been buried there for thousands of years and is surfacing now due to a recent earthquake.”

“Does that make sense?” Jack asked.

“Not really. Uplifts take hundreds if not thousands of years. An earthquake could accelerate the process but it would have to be a big one and I don’t know of any around here lately that could have caused this type of geological event. ”

"So, do they think the scientific community is stupid?"

"I guess."

"You're not going to let them get away with this charade, are you?" Dolly asked.

George laughed. "Absolutely not."

"Good. How are you going to prove they are full of shit?"

George shrugged. "I've already collected a lot of data from the site that I'm still analyzing. In the meantime, I have students visiting the site daily to take pictures and keep an eye out for any changes that might be occurring."

"Don't you think it's odd that the owners of the Bat Mountain Corporation haven't surfaced?" Cindy interjected. "If I turned on the TV and discovered the government had set up camp on my land I'd be a little upset."

"That *is* a bit odd," George agreed.

"What do you make of it?" Jack asked.

"Well, whoever owns the property has something to hide, obviously. So, they've gone into hiding and aren't talking."

"Well, I guess Dolly and I need to go to Vegas and snoop around. Maybe we can find the attorney who set up the corporation or someone who knows him."

"Good," Dolly said. "I wouldn't mind doing a little gambling and seeing a few shows."

"Why don't we all go?" Cindy suggested.

Jack smiled. "Okay, then. After work on Friday we'll head on over there."

18
Las Vegas Holiday

On Friday afternoon, they all met at Mona's Café and then loaded into Dolly's big Cadillac El Dorado that she got as part of her divorce settlement with her ex-husband several years earlier. It was a pleasant drive through Death Valley and on to Las Vegas. When they arrived a little after six they checked into the Sands Hotel and bought tickets to see comedian, Red Skelton. Before the show they ate dinner and did some gambling. On Saturday they slept in, had brunch and then began their search for attorney Paul Bradford. They started at the office address he listed on the articles of incorporation for Bat Mountain Corporation. It was on the third floor of a downtown office building. They parked on the street, took the elevator upstairs and found the suite number. The address was Excel Office Suites.

"An office suite. Great," Jack moaned. "They're not going to give us any information."

"Don't be so pessimistic," Dolly said. "You've just got to be upbeat. Let me handle this."

Dolly walked in and went up to the receptionist. "Hi, can I help you?" the receptionist asked.

"Yes. We're here to see Paul Bradford. Is he in?"

"No. Did you have an appointment?"

"Well, no. But I've been trying to get one. What's with him, he won't return my phone calls."

The receptionist shrugged. "Well, I can take a message."

A young woman came out from the office suites, gave Dolly a hard look and then walked out the front door.

"So, how often does he pick up his messages?"

"I don't know. I just take them and leave them in his box. I have no idea when he picks them up."

"Does he get a lot of calls?"

"I'm sorry. I'm not allowed to give out that kind of information."

Dolly let out a frustrated sigh. "Well, you're no help," she said and stomped out.

They all followed her out and loitered in the hall a moment.

"I told you," Jack laughed.

Dolly's eyes narrowed. "Did you see that woman who left here?"

"Yeah," Jack replied.

"Go after her. She looked like she might know something. We'll stay out here in the hall for a little while and maybe someone else will come out who we can question." Jack nodded and hustled off. When he got to the street he saw the woman walking down the sidewalk. He hurried to catch up with her.

"Ma'am," he said when he reached her.

She looked over at him and then stopped abruptly. "Yes, what do you want?"

"Sorry for interrupting your day, but I noticed you just came out of Excel Office Suites."

"That's right."

"Do you office there?"

"Yes, I do. What do you want?"

"Well, my friends and I are looking for an attorney, Paul Bradford. We were told he had an office there too. Do you know him?"

"Not really. I met him a couple of times. He's hardly ever in his office. I don't know why he bothers to have one, he never uses it."

"Do you know where he lives?"

"No. I've never even had a conversation with the man."

"Hmm. That's too bad. He owns some property we'd like to buy and we're willing to pay top dollar."

"You know, I did see him go into a strip club once. We left the office about the same time and I saw him ahead of me in a Red Ford Mustang convertible. He's not a bad looking guy, black hair and blue eyes and a cute mustache. I was going the same way so I watched him, curiosity mainly, until he turned into the Fantasy Strip Club parking lot. That dissuaded any further interest in the man."

"Well, that's a lead."

She smiled. "And a fun one to follow, right?"

He nodded. "Yeah. Someone's got to do it."

Jack thanked her and headed back to the office suite. Dolly and Cindy were talking to a short stocky man when Jack got there.

"Well, thanks for your help," Dolly said as the man strolled off.

"So, did you learn anything?" Jack asked.

"Yes, Mr. Bradford is a straw man for anyone who wants anonymity. Apparently, he's the incorporator and registered agent for hundreds of corporations. He charges $2,500.00 to set up a corporation and a thousand dollars a year maintenance fee. He doesn't have to disclose any information since it is protected by the attorney-client privilege. He says the easiest way to get in touch with him is to make an appointment to arrange to set up a corporation."

"How does your friend know this?" Jack asked.

"He had a corporation set up," Dolly replied.

Jack nodded. "Interesting. I got a lead too."

"Oh really? What kind of lead?"

"Apparently Mr. Bradford likes to hang out at the Fantasy Strip Club on the outskirts of town."

"We should go check that out," George said eagerly.

"I don't want to go to a strip club," Cindy complained.

"You're right," Dolly agreed. "Let's go shopping while they gawk at the naked girls."

Jack laughed. "You girls are very accommodating."

Dolly laughed. "You won't say that after you get the bill. Give me your credit card."

Jack gave Dolly a hard look then cracked a smile and pulled out a card. "Okay, but I wouldn't charge more than a couple hundred bucks on this, my credit limit isn't that high."

"Ah, you're no fun," Dolly said taking the card.

George pulled out his wallet and handed Cindy a hundred-dollar bill. "Here, you can pay for lunch."

Cindy smiled broadly. "Oh! Where can we go that's expensive?"

Jack grinned. "Sorry, this is Las Vegas. Food is the one thing that is always cheap."

"Good. Whatever we have left over we can spend on the slots."

"Fine. I hope you win the jackpot," George said.

They split up with the ladies taking a cab back to the hotel while the men took the car to the Fantasy Strip Club. Even though it was only midday the place was packed with eight girls working the poles and twice that many mingling with the customers. As soon as they found a table, two strippers were on them like bees on spring flowers, dancing around them seductively, putting their nipples up against their faces and letting out sexy grunts and moans. When they had collected their tips and moved on, a barmaid came over and they ordered drinks.

"So, did you really get a lead or was that a ploy to get away from the girls?" George asked.

Jack laughed. "No, it was a legitimate lead."

"So, did you get a description?"

"Yeah, good looking, black hair, blue eyes and a mustache."

"So, what are the odds he'll be here now?"

"Pretty good," Jack said, "since I saw his car in the parking lot."

"You did?"

"Yeah, the red Ford Mustang convertible. It was hard to miss."

George pointed over to a corner of the room. "Is that him?"

Jack nodded. "Yeah. I bet it is. Let's go see if we can get him to talk business."

They took their drinks and walked over to where Bradford was sitting with a stripper on his lap. He looked up at them and frowned.

"The elusive Paul Bradford in the flesh," Jack said.

Bradford narrowed his eyes. "Do I know you?"

"No," Jack admitted, "since you won't return any of my phone calls. But I'd like to get to know you. One of your companies owns some real estate I want to buy."

"What company?"

"Bat Mountain Corporation."

Bradford sighed. "That land's not for sale."

"How do you know? I haven't told you how much I'm willing to pay."

"It doesn't matter. It's not for sale."

"Have you been watching the news? Did you know that a cathedral is growing on the property and the government has seized control of it?"

"That's none of my business. I'm not paid to watch my client's assets."

"Well, I'd like to talk to your client about it," Jack said. "Do you have contact information?"

"No. My clients pay me to make sure they don't get contacted. So, forget about it. You're not getting squat from me."

"Has the FBI talked to you yet about the murder on your client's property?"

Bradford frowned. "What murder?"

George told him about the murder of Colonel Martin and the FBI investigation in progress.

"No. I haven't talked to anyone nor do I have any intention of getting involved."

"Well, you are involved whether you like it or not since you're the registered agent. So, why did your client buy up a bunch of worthless desert property?"

"I don't know. I didn't ask them, nor do I care. Now if you don't mind. I didn't come here to talk business."

Figuring they'd gotten all the information they were likely to get they went back to their table and admired the naked ladies dancing around the poles for a while. When they saw Bradford get up to leave the club they followed him out to his car, keeping a safe distance behind, so he wouldn't see them. When he drove out of the parking lot they were hot on his trail. He drove to a gas station and had his oil changed, then he drove to a McDonald's and bought himself a hamburger.

"This is a waste of time," George complained, "and it's almost time to meet the girls."

"He's killing time. I think he's got an appointment somewhere. We should wait a little longer." He looked at his watch. "It's 3:30 p.m. I bet he's got a 4:00 p.m. appointment with someone connected to Bat Mountain Corporation."

George frowned. "You think he'd be that stupid—to call them the moment we make contact with him?"

"If he's rattled he's probably not thinking too clearly. Finding out about the murder had to shake him up."

Just then Bradford came out of the restaurant, got in his car, and took off back towards town. They followed him and when he parked in a garage next to an office building they parked on the street and went inside. As they went through the front door they saw him taking the elevator and watched the indicator light showing that it stopped on the third floor. They took the stairs and when they emerged out of the stairwell they saw him going into an office. When they approached the door, he had gone in they saw that it was the United States Department of Land Management.

"What the hell?" George said.

"Hmm. That's interesting. Bat Mountain Corporation bought the property from the Department of Land Management."

"Seriously? What do you make of that?"

"I don't know. Maybe the government knew all along what was going to happen on the Bat Mountain Site but wanted to take the property off the government's books so the federal overseers wouldn't be snooping into it."

"But why take the site over if you're trying to distance yourself from it?"

"That was your fault," George said. "Had you not accidentally found it nobody would have noticed the uplift—at least not until it was finished. Had you not noticed that it was growing it would have just been seen as an unusual rock formation."

"That's right. So, they had to take it back over to try to conceal what was going on."

"I wonder what in the hell *is* going on," George said. "I'd sure like to know what they are hiding."

"We'll get to the bottom on it. Don't worry. The cat's out of the bag now, it's just a matter of time."

"Maybe, but we may not have an opportunity like this again."

"What do you mean?"

"The man we want to talk to is in that office right now. Let's go talk to him."

"What? Just barge in there?"

"Yeah, it's a little late to make an appointment," Jack said and started for the door.

George reluctantly followed him inside. Apparently since it was a Saturday there wasn't anybody manning the front desk. They heard voices down the hall to their left so Jack moved in that direction. When he'd recognized Bradford's voice he opened the door and walked in on the two men.

"Well, there's the man I want to talk to. Thank you, Paul, for leading us to him."

Both men stood up. Jack noticed a name plate on the desk identifying the occupant of the office as Riley Wilson. "Who are you?" Wilson demanded.

"My name is Jack Carpenter and I'm interested in buying your property in Inyo County. I've been trying to get a hold of you for weeks, but Paul here doesn't return phone calls."

"The property is not for sale! That's why nobody has returned your calls."

Jack shrugged. "But you haven't heard how much I'm offering?"

"I don't care what you are offering. It's not for sale. So, get out of my office."

"What does Bat Mountain Corporation have to do with the Bureau of Land Management, anyway? I thought it sold the property to Bat Mountain Corporation?"

"It did. It's a matter of public record."

"Then why is Paul here telling you about Colonel Martin's murder?"

"You're trespassing!" Wilson spat. "If you don't leave right now I'm going to call the police."

"Okay. Relax. We're leaving. Just one last question. Why did the government go to all of the trouble to sell the Bat Mountain Site to Bat Mountain Corporation and then turn around and take control of it again?"

"That's classified information," Wilson said picking up the telephone. "Now get out of my office or I'm calling the police."

"Okay, we're out of here. Relax. Thank you," Jack said as they both made a hasty exit.

"You've got balls," George said. "I wouldn't have done that in a million years."

"Well, it worked. Now we know the government is definitely involved and whatever is going on there is *classified."*

Feeling pretty good about what they'd discovered that morning, Jack and George found the girls and resumed their partying. Dolly and Cindy were also in a good mood since they'd done well on the slots and made enough to cover their shopping spree. After dinner and a show, they stopped for a drink at the hotel lounge and then headed to their respective rooms to finish off the night properly. While Jack and Dolly were changing into something more comfortable they talked about the day's accomplishments.

"We should open up our own detective agency," Dolly suggested as she pulled her dress over her head. She was wearing matching red panties, bra and black stockings. Jack's eye's widened at the sexy look.

He laughed. "Yeah, we do make a pretty good team. You should have seen Wilson's face when we barged in on him and Bradford. It was priceless."

"I bet. It was fun asking people questions," she said as she removed her left stocking very carefully trying not to run it. Jack watched her seemingly mesmerized. When she noticed, she smiled broadly. "You want to take off the other one?"

He nodded and knelt down in front of her. After carefully removing the snaps he slowly pulled the stocking down her leg and then planted a kiss on her inner thigh. She put her hands on his head and gently moaned. He kissed the other thigh then ran his hands gently down both legs.

"Oh, man. You've got killer legs," he observed.

She laughed. "Whatever you're doing to them, don't stop."

He smiled at her and continued to kiss and caress them evoking more sounds of pleasure and satisfaction. Then he slipped his hands behind her and unsnapped her bra. It fell away exposing what he thought were perfect breasts, not too large or too small, and naturally beautiful. He gave them an appreciative look and then took one of them in his mouth. Dolly put her arms around him and squeezed him tightly as she moaned in delight. Then Jack picked Dolly up, carried her to the bedroom and laid her naked body on the bed. As he watched her longingly he took off his clothes.

"Come on! Hurry. I want you," she beckoned.

Amused, he deliberately took his time taking off one piece of clothing at a time. Annoyed, she sat up, grabbed his arm and pulled him down on her.

They kissed long and hard and then he was inside her. She stiffened to meet him and then gasped in delight. "Oh, yes! That's more like it. I've been yearning to feel you inside me all day."

"You should have said something. I would have gladly obliged."

"I know," she whispered. "Oh! Keep it coming. Oh my! Yes!."

Jack kept the rhythm going, feeling relieved that Dolly seemed to be enjoying herself. Sex to him was fun and came easy but pleasing a lady was often a real challenge. He desperately wanted their sex to be good, because he liked Dolly and wanted their relationship to last. He didn't plunge into her too hard because he didn't want to climax before she did. That would be a disaster. The steady rhythm he could handle. It felt good and he could stay right there on the edge indefinitely.

"Oh, you're good Jack. Oh! A little harder. I'm almost there. Oh! Ah! Thank you!" Dolly said, her body going limp. Jack leaned down and gave her a long kiss.

"Okay, it's your turn," she advised.

"My turn?"

"Yeah, I know you were holding back to make sure I came. You're a gentleman, Jack. Now it's your turn to let loose."

He felt her clamp down on him hard and felt a surge of pleasure. "Whoa! What was that?"

"That was me telling you to get going?"

He got going, plunging hard and deep inside her. It wasn't long until he went over the edge and let out a sigh. He lay there a moment enjoying the electricity flowing between them, then reluctantly rolled off her and sighed. "Wow! That's the best sex I've had in years."

"You're not so bad yourself, stud."

He looked over at her and smiled. "I aim to please."

"And you did," she said wrapping a leg over him and putting her head on his shoulder. She snuggled up and put her arm around his waist---in for the long haul. He pulled the sheets over them and took a deep satisfying breath. Suddenly he felt tired.

"It's been a long day. I think I'm going to sleep."

"Sleep," she teased. "What if I want another go-'round?"

"In the morning," he said closing his eyes. "Wake me up."

Jack fell asleep almost immediately and Dolly shortly thereafter. Like the sex, it was the best sleep either had enjoyed in years. When they woke up in the morning Jack made good on his promise to go another round and Dolly and Jack knew then that their relationship was going to last a long, long time.

19
Cocoon

Over the next few weeks Park Ranger Randy Perkins supervised the construction of improvements in and around the Bat Mountain Uplift, as it was now officially titled, to accommodate tourists and the press who wanted to visit the site.

Reverend Little's pilgrims set up a semi-permanent camp on the ridge above the site to monitor the growth of the uplift and to conduct daily services. The park service provided rangers for the site itself and the Sheriff's office provided a deputy on duty on the ridge to keep order among the pilgrims.

Everything seemed to be going well until Molly Munson, the curator at the Death Valley Museum, asked Randy to bring her some samples of the strange crystalline stone from the site for an exhibit she was putting together for the museum. Randy wasn't crazy about the task as he knew the stone was nearly indestructible, but he had gone out on a few dates with Molly and wanted to continue the relationship, so he reluctantly agreed.

Expecting a difficult time of it, he brought a hacksaw and a sledge hammer to accomplish the task. He started with the hacksaw but before he'd made much progress the blade broke and he nearly cut off a finger.

"Ouch! Damn it," he moaned sticking his finger in his mouth to sooth the pain. Annoyed by this development he picked up the sledge hammer and began hitting a portion of the wall angrily until he'd managed to break off a rock about the size of a baseball. He wondered if that would be enough but knew in his heart it wouldn't be, so he continued to work until he had multiple samples of various sizes.

As he was gathering his things to leave he was astonished to see the area of the wall that he'd just destroyed starting to mend itself. Mesmerized by what was happening before his very eyes, he didn't notice the crystal strands that were winding over his shoes and around his ankles. When he decided to run to his car to get a camera to record this astonishing development, he fell hard on his face.

"What the hell!" he moaned as he tasted blood from his broken nose. Immediately upon impact crystalline strands the size of thick fishing line began creeping over his wrists and neck while the ones on his feet spread quickly over his ankles. He tried frantically to get up, but the thin strands cut into his skin like razors causing him to scream in pain. "Help! Someone help me!"

Unfortunately, everyone had gone for the day except Deputy Mark Hanson and the pilgrims camped up on the ridge. Many heard the screams but only looked in that direction, curious but not curious enough to breach the security barriers put up by the Army. The crystal restraints dug deeper and deeper into Randy's skin until veins were slit open and he began to bleed out. A half hour later word of the screams finally made it to Deputy Hanson and he went down to check it out. What he found made him gag.

Randy was stretched out on his stomach in a pool of blood but there was no sign of what had caused him to bleed. He knelt down and felt for a pulse. He thought he felt a faint one so he turned Randy over to do CPR, but his eyes were wide open and there was a look of horror on his face that made the deputy shudder. There was no question in the deputy's mind that he was dead. He reported the grisly death to his dispatcher who in turn called Agents Pierce and Sanders of the FBI since they'd already been working on Colonel Martin's murder. The two agents arrived an hour and a half later and just stared at the incredible sight in disbelief.

"What in the hell happened here?" Agent Pierce asked.

Deputy Lawson, who had arrived at about the same time as the two agents replied, "Some of the pilgrims reported to Deputy Hanson that they'd heard screaming down here, so he ran down here to investigate. He found Randy just as you see him now. Then he called it in."

Agent Sanders shook her head. "This is unreal. I've never seen someone killed like this. It's almost ritualistic."

"No man did this," Reverend Little bellowed from behind them. "This was a demonstration of the wrath of God!"

Everyone looked around at the reverend. Agent Sanders said, "You're saying God killed Randy?"

"Not himself, His protector."

Deputy Lawson turned around and shook his head. "What did Randy ever do to anger God?"

The reverend pointed to the sledge hammer. "Look at that. He was trying to destroy God's work. I warned him that God would punish those who tried to thwart His will."

"Nonsense," Agent Pierce said. "Somebody had it in for Randy just like they did for Colonel Martin. But I must admit the killer is very creative in the manner he kills his victims."

"It's obviously somebody who doesn't want the government controlling this site," Deputy Lawson observed. "And you're the only one that I know that has a problem with it, Reverend."

Reverend Little smiled. "Nice try, Curt, but I've got an alibi. I was at my office in Shoshone when this happened and there are a half a dozen people who can verify that fact."

"Yes, but miraculously you were one of the first persons on the scene."

"Of course, I was. I have friends down here. Someone came and got me the moment the word got out that Randy had been murdered."

"Nevertheless, we're still going to need to interview you again," Agent Pierce advised.

"No problem. I have nothing to hide."

As they were talking the FBI Evidence Response Team rolled up and began securing the crime scene. Agent Pierce suggested they should move away from the body and let the team do its work. Special Agent Paula Roberts, the agent in charge of the ERT walked over to the group and shook her head.

"What in the hell happened here?"

Agent Pierce shrugged. "Your guess is as good as mine. The people on the ridge heard screams so they told Deputy Hanson about it and he came down to investigate. This is what he found."

"So, the perp staked his hands and legs in the ground and then choked him with a wire?" Agent Roberts asked.

"That's what it looks like but the blood pooling indicates the wires were tightened at the same time," Agent Sanders said. "There must have been at least two perps and possibly as many as five. We're looking at footprints but there are so many I don't know if they will do us any good."

Reverend Little shook his head in frustration. "I'm telling you God commanded the walls to defend themselves from Randy's attack and they obeyed His command."

"Right, so what are you saying?" Agent Sanders asked. "This so-called cathedral is a living being and can respond to commands from God."

The reverend nodded vigorously. "That's exactly what I'm saying. Isn't it obvious?"

Agent Sanders looked at Agent Pierce and rolled her eyes. "Like I said, case closed. It was an act of God."

Agent Roberts stifled a laugh and said, "Well, I'm going to get back to work. I'll let you know if we find anything."

As he was leaving Deputy Hanson noticed one of the chunks of broken crystal that Randy Perkins had knocked out of the wall laying on the ground. He leaned over, picked it up, and gave it a long look. He was about to take it over to one of the ERT members to log in as evidence, but saw that they had several other pieces, so he stuck it in his pocket as a souvenir.

20
Deadly Souvenir

Deputy Mark Hanson lived with his wife and two kids in an old stone house in Death Valley Junction off of State Line Road. It was an old house that had been built by miners who settled in the area in the early 1900's. He was a good old boy with little ambition and was content with his job as a sheriff's deputy. His wife Amanda loved him dearly and smiled when he walked in the front door.

"Oh, good. You're home early. Now you can eat a hot supper for a change."

One of the disadvantages of being a Sheriff's deputy were the long hours, frequent overtime, and risk that, at any moment, your life could be in danger. Amanda could handle the danger and the long hours, but the overtime that always seemed to come at an inopportune time, angered her. And for the past month there had been so much overtime that Amanda feared the children would forget what their father looked like.

"Children! Daddy's home," she yelled.

Mark made a beeline for the refrigerator, took out a beer and collapsed on the sofa. He was still reeling from seeing the horror in Randy's eyes when he discovered the body.

"Have a tough day?" Amanda asked.

"A horrible day," he replied. "Randy Perkins was murdered and I found the body."

Amanda stopped what she was doing and came over to the sofa and sat down. "Oh, my God! Who murdered him?" she asked.

"Don't know. There must have been several of them, though. They staked him out and then slit his wrists, ankles and neck all at the same time."

"Oh, that's sick!"

"Tell me about it," Mark agreed.

"Why would they do that? Randy was such a nice guy."

"You should have seen the look on his face."

"Don't tell the children. I don't want them to have dreams."

"Daddy! Daddy!" Melissa, their youngest, screamed as she came running into the living room. She launched herself into her father's lap.

"Hey little butterfly. How are you?" Mark asked.

"Fine. You're home in time for supper," she noted.

"Yes, I am. What are we having?"

"Spaghetti!'

"Oh, I love spaghetti," he replied tickling her belly. She laughed and ran to the table.

"I'm hungry, is it time to eat?"

"Yes," Amanda said rising to go put the food out as Josh and David entered the room.

"Oh, boys, I brought you something."

"What is it?" David asked.

"It's a souvenir of the Bat Mountain Uplift," he advised, taking the rock out of his pocket and tossing it to David.

David caught it and began examining it carefully. "Wow. This is cool looking."

"Will it grow like the walls are growing?"

"No. Not likely. The uplift isn't really growing. It's just coming up from under the ground."

"That's not what Reverend Little says," Amanda disagreed worriedly. "He says God has commanded it to grow and it's doing it."

"Rubbish. The government's already done a study and they say it's just a crystal formation that is slowly coming out of the ground due to a recent earthquake."

"I don't know. Maybe you shouldn't have brought it home."

"Nonsense. The kids can take it to school for show and tell. Nobody else has a specimen."

"Yeah, mom," Josh said. "I want to take it for show and tell. Can I take it first, Daddy?"

"Sure, you're the oldest."

"Dad, let me take it first?" Melissa said. "Ladies first, that's what you always say."

"Not this time my little butterfly," Mark said. "Eldest first when it comes to school."

"Oh, shucks, Daddy. That's not fair."

"Don't argue with your father," Amanda scolded. "Okay, supper's ready. Come and get it."

Everyone got up and made their way to the kitchen table. Amanda nodded at Melissa to say grace.

"Rub-a-dub-dub, thanks for the grub," Melissa said laughing. The boys joined in the laughter.

"No. No. Say it right," Amanda demanded.

Melissa took an exaggerated deep breath. "Oh, alright. Thank you, dear Lord, for what we are about to receive from your bounty, and let us be truly grateful. Amen."

"Thank you. That's much better," Amanda said and started dishing out spaghetti.

While they ate, the rock sample Mark had brought home lay on the floor in the living room where Josh had left it when he was called for supper. While the Hansons were eating, Melissa looked over at the rock and was surprised to see it had shrunk. She didn't say anything, but just stared at it as it flattened out and changed color.

"Daddy, the rock looks different," Melissa said.

Mark, who had just put half a meatball into his mouth frowned. "Huh?" he said, his voice muffled from the meatball. He twisted his head to look into the living room. The rock did look different, he thought, but he couldn't put his finger on what had changed.

"What happened to it?" he asked.

"Daddy, I saw it change colors and then there was a puff of gray smoke."

"That's impossible," Mark said irritably.

"You find that rock and take it outside," Amanda said worriedly. "I won't be able to sleep tonight if I don't know where it is. . . . I could kill you for bringing that thing home."

"It's just a rock," Mark replied. "It can't hurt you."

"You said there was another murder. That means there's been two murders ever since the uplift was discovered. How do you know the rock isn't cursed?"

"It's not cursed. Don't be silly."

They all reluctantly went back to the table and finished their dinner. Afterwards they all examined the rock, wondering why it looked different. That night Mark put the rock in a lunch bag and set it on top of the refrigerator, so it wouldn't get lost. When they went to bed Amanda couldn't sleep. Visions of her children strung up with thick wire haunted her. When she finally nodded off her visions turned to horrible nightmares. The next morning when the sun finally came up she jumped out of bed and checked the children. They all seemed fine so she breathed a sigh of relief and went into the kitchen to fix breakfast. After she turned on the gas stove and put on some milk to warm for hot chocolate she decided to go get the newspaper. As she moved past the front door she did a double take. The usually dark brown door was white. She went over to it and was horrified to see it was covered by a hard clear substance. She tried to twist the door handle but couldn't get her hand around it as it was covered as well.

"Mark! Mark! Look at this!" she screamed. "Oh, my God. What's happening?"

Mark came running in from the bedroom and swallowed hard when he saw the sealed doorway. "Quick! Get the kids. We'll try the back door."

Melissa ran into the bedrooms, woke the children and brought them into the family room where Mark was trying to break through the crystal seal over the patio door with a golf club.

"What about the bedroom windows?" she asked frantically.

Mark nodded and ran into the master bedroom.

In the kitchen, the milk began to boil.

In the master bedroom, there were two windows and they were both sealed so Mark went into the bathroom. The bathroom window was small but it appeared normal so Mark went over to it and tried to open it but without success. Up close he noticed the crystal was starting to work its way inward from the wall but hadn't covered the entire window yet, so he took a swing with the golf club and smashed the window to pieces.

In the kitchen, the milk boiled over extinguishing the flame on the old stove. Natural gas began flowing into the air.

"Come quick, there's enough room for the kids to get out," Mark yelled.

Everyone scrambled to the small bathroom. Melissa went out first, then the two boys but the window wasn't big enough for Mark or Amanda.

"Go get help!" Amanda screamed to them.

"Tell them to call the Sheriff's office!" Mark added. "And tell them to hurry!"

As they looked out the window it started to fog over. “Mark? What’s happening? I’m so scared,” Amanda said, her hands trembling.

Mark took her in his arms and held her tightly. “I don’t know, but it will be alright, honey. They’ll break us out of here in a few minutes.”

Ten minutes went by as natural gas filled the kitchen and began spreading throughout the house.

“It’s that rock. It’s possessed by the devil. The evil that’s within it is going to seal up the house and then suffocate us. It’s going to kill us like it did Randy.”

“No. There’s lots of air in the house. It would take hours to suffocate us,” Mark said crinkling up his nose. “What’s that smell?”

Amanda sniffed the air. “I don’t know. Gas? Oh, shit!”

“What?”

“I left milk on the stove.”

Mark ran into the kitchen and saw the burner on the gas stove was wide open. He ran over and shut it off.

“Shit! This can’t be happening.” He looked around frantically wanting to open doors and windows but knew they were all sealed. Then his heart sank when he heard the thermostat come on. “Oh, fuck!” he said as the house exploded into a fiery inferno.

21
Dilemma

Senator Rawlings couldn't believe the news that Randy Perkins was dead. He'd just talked to him hours earlier and had been assured that everything was going just fine. And the way he was killed just boggled his mind. The thought of having to describe it to the President made him nauseous. He'd been honored when the President had come to him about the aliens. The President wanted to consult with the Congress on this matter but felt traditional channels were not appropriate under the circumstances. So he had selected him as a well-respected member of the Senate to be one of the few who would be told about the alien contact. He wished now the President had found somebody else. He called Jimmy Malone to see if he was available for a meeting with the President.

"Did you hear about Randy?" Rawlings asked.

"Yes. I couldn't believe it."

"I thought this was a benign life-form who just wanted to live at peace out in the desert?"

"That's what I was told. But apparently, they thought they were being attacked. Why in God's name was Randy going at one of the walls with a sledge hammer?"

"I'm not sure, but I think I heard someone say he was gathering materials for an exhibit at the Death Valley Museum."

"We told him to leave the damn structure alone. What was he thinking?"

"He wasn't thinking, obviously."

"Shit!"

"We should tell the President before he hears about it on the news."

"Okay, I'll set up a meeting and get back to you with a time and place."

"Thanks."

Rawlings hung up the telephone and then started thinking about an appropriate response to the murder. There would be an FBI investigation, of course, but that wouldn't lead anywhere since they'd be looking for a human being rather than an alien life-form. They'd have to tell the FBI to back off in the interest of national security. They'd object but what could they do if the President gave them a direct order. The telephone rang and he picked up.

"The presidential limousine will pick you up in twenty minutes. We can ride with the President on his way to Arlington National Cemetery for a funeral for an old friend."

"Okay, I'll be out front."

Rawlings hung up and called his office to tell them he'd be in late. Then he freshened up, put on a coat and tie and went downstairs. The limousine was just pulling up. He felt exhilarated being driven around in the presidential limousine with people looking up and pointing at him. People respected power but they rarely appreciated the cost in terms of responsibility. The fate of the nation and maybe even the world lay in the hands of three mere mortals, yet nobody would ever know it unless they made the wrong decisions and the world spun out of control. His stomach tightened with the thought of it. The limousine stopped, Jimmy Malone got in and it sped off.

"So, you got any bright ideas on how to handle this?" Rawlings asked.

"A few, but I'm not claiming they're brilliant. There aren't a whole lot of options."

"What if we tell the aliens to get their damn people off our planet and take their benign life-form with them?"

Malone laughed. "Good plan, except we signed a treaty and they have large space ships with unknown firepower. We can't afford to piss them off."

Rawlings sighed. "It could be a bluff. We haven't seen any demonstrations of their weaponry."

"I thought you agreed we needed their technology."

"I know."

"If we hadn't taken it, the Soviet Union would have and then they would be the most powerful nation on Earth."

"Okay, I get it," Rawlings conceded, "but that doesn't solve our problem right now. Why can't the aliens deal with this life-form themselves?"

"They say all we have to do is back off, leave the area and everything will be fine."

"Right, but that's not so easy with a free press and every religious fanatic in the country going ballistic over this cathedral rising in the desert."

The limousine arrived at the White House and the President got in. "Gentlemen."

"Mr. President," Rawlings said. "Nice to see you."

"Yes, I bet."

Rawlings sighed.

"So, what are we going to do about this latest fiasco?" the President asked as the limo pulled away.

"Well, with two murder investigations underway I think this whole thing is in danger of blowing up in our faces. We have to get the FBI to back off in the interest of national security."

"Right, but if we do that how do we explain it to your colleagues in the Senate?"

"They won't like it, but I can assure them it's a necessary move. Will you have a problem with the Attorney General?"

"No. I can handle him."

"Mr. President," Malone interjected. "How will you handle the press?"

"What would you suggest?"

"Well, with the very bizarre way each was killed I think you could suggest a crazed religious fanatic was responsible."

"Someone trying to make it look like the uplift was an act of God like Reverend Little claims," the President mused.

"Yes, exactly."

The President nodded. "Okay, but you better come up with a good explanation of how both murders took place."

"Right. That's not going to be easy, but we'll come up with something."

"What about the explosion at Death Valley Junction? The press is claiming it's related to the Bat Mountain Uplift."

"What explosion?" Rawlings asked. "I hadn't heard about that."

"It just happened a few hours ago. Three children claim their father, a deputy sheriff, brought a rock sample home from the Bat Mountain Site as a souvenir but it changed shape and color right in front of their eyes. When they woke up this morning all the doors and windows in the house were sealed with the same type of crystalline substance the rock was made of. The kids managed to escape through a bathroom window that hadn't been fully sealed yet but the parents were left inside. The kids ran to neighbors for help, but just as the fire trucks and sheriff's cars rolled up the house exploded."

"Oh, my God!" Rawlings exclaimed shaking his head in disbelief.

Malone shrugged. "Well, it fits in with our crazed religious fanatic scenario."

The President laughed. "Yeah, it does if you can make the press believe any human being could pull all of this off."

"It will have to be a conspiracy," Rawlings suggested. "One man couldn't do all this."

"Yes," Malone agreed. "We won't name names but everyone will think it's Reverend Little and he won't object because it will just give him more publicity."

"That's true," the President agreed. "I've never seen a man who loves publicity, bad or good, the way he does. He's addicted to it."

"There's another problem," Malone interjected.

"What's that?" the President asked, frowning.

"The guy who stumbled onto the Bat Mountain Site, Jack Carpenter, and the professor, George Palmer, who did the initial research there, they've been snooping around looking for the owners of Bat Mountain Corporation."

"Where did you come up with that name?" the President complained. "It sounds like something out of a comic book."

"I did," Malone confessed. "There's a mountain near the site called Bat Mountain so I thought it made sense."

The President shook his head. "Okay, so what's the problem?"

"They managed to find our straw man and followed him to the Bureau of Land Management."

"Oh, you've got to be kidding?" the President moaned. "What else can go wrong?"

"I don't know, but I'm afraid they may have figured out this is a CIA operation."

"Well, that can't happen. I don't care what you have to do, but this can't lead back to the CIA."

Malone swallowed hard. "Yes, sir. I'll figure something out."

"Make this go away, gentlemen. We've got too much at stake here," the President said as the limousine pulled into Arlington National Cemetery. Malone and Rawlings got out at the gate and watched the limousine continue on its way up to the grave site.

"What are we going to do about the explosion?" Rawlings asked.

Malone thought about it. "I'll make the call to the FBI Director and tell them the military is taking over the three investigations. I'll tell him he can verify it with the President. You'll have to get with General Thornton and brief him on the President's wishes."

"Okay, I'll get on it."

"I'll take care of Carpenter and Palmer. I'll send them a clear message to back off."

"What if they don't?" Rawlings asked hesitantly.

"Then, we'll have to shut them up permanently," Malone said coldly.

Rawlings just stared at him for a moment and then nodded. Another limousine pulled up and he got in. On the ride back to his office, he noticed his hands were shaking. "Shit," he moaned. "If I live through this it will be a miracle."

"What was that?" the driver said.

He looked up. "Oh, nothing. Just hurry up, I have things to do."

"Yes, sir," the driver said and stepped on it.

22
The Warning

Jack rolled out of bed, took a look at the room service menu, and then picked up the phone and ordered them a generous breakfast.

"Okay, love. It's time to get up. We've got a long drive home and I want to get back early enough to go see Jake. With all that's been going on he's gonna be pretty freaked out."

Dolly rolled over and sighed. "Can't we stay here a few more days? This has been heavenly."

Jack smiled. "We can take up where we left off at my apartment tonight, or your place if you prefer."

"Yeah. But you'll be distracted with work and I'll have to go in to the café in the morning."

He went over to her and pulled her up and out of bed. They embraced. "Don't worry. In a few weeks, I think I'll have a break between jobs and we can take a long weekend somewhere—maybe go to the Hotel Del Coronado in San Diego. I've heard it's great."

"Hmm. That sounds good," Dolly said. "You promise?"

"I do," he said and gave her a long kiss.

She sighed, then went into the bathroom to take a shower. Jack turned on the TV. The morning news was just coming on. The news anchor had a solemn look on her face.

"This is Jill Collins with the morning news. We have breaking news out of Death Valley Junction this morning where there's been an explosion at the home of Deputy Sheriff Mark Hanson. Jonathan Baldwin is in Death Valley Junction with a report, Jonathan."

The camera switched to a news reporter in slacks and a sport shirt. "Yes, Jill. Just minutes ago, there was an explosion at the home of Deputy Sheriff Mark Hanson and it is presumed that he and his wife, Amanda, are dead. Miraculously, their three children survived the explosion by escaping from a bathroom window. Firemen on the scene say the explosion was caused by natural gas escaping from a kitchen stove but what's strange about the explosion is that somehow the house was sealed up preventing the deputy and his wife from escaping. The bathroom window the children escaped from was apparently too small for their parents to make it out. What we don't know is who sealed up the house, how they managed it, and why?"

"Jonathan," Jill said. "I don't understand what you mean by the house being sealed up."

"Well, Jill. The doors and windows were covered with a clear substance that was very tough and impossible to penetrate, much like the rock substance at the Bat Mountain Site from where Deputy Hanson came after Randy Perkins' murder yesterday. The children claim Hanson brought a rock from the site to the house as a souvenir and that the rock was changing colors and acting strangely last night."

"Wow! That is truly bizarre."

"I'm sure we'll have more details later in the day as the authorities try to sort it all out."

"Thank you, Jonathan."

Dolly came out of the bathroom with a towel wrapped around her. "What's truly bizarre?" Dolly asked.

"Deputy Hanson is dead. His house blew up."

"Oh, my God! How did that happen?"

Jack filled her in on the story. "This whole affair is spinning out of control," he said. "There's something the government is not telling us about the Bat Mountain phenomenon."

"What's that?"

"That it's a living being with a mind of its own."

Dolly frowned. "But how could that be?"

"I don't know but whatever it is, it must be mighty powerful if the government can't keep it under control."

"What are we going to do?"

"Find out what it is and why the government is hiding its existence."

"But how can we do that?"

"Keep digging until we get some answers."

"But where are you going to dig? We're out of leads."

"No, we're not. We just got a new one. Deputy Hanson's house was apparently infested with the same living organism that's in the Living Desert Cathedral. That means if we can get onto the site maybe we can find some debris that also contains the organism."

"I don't know. They'll probably have the house sealed off from the public."

"True, but I'll come up with an excuse to get in to look at it, and once I'm in I'll pick up a sample to study."

"Hasn't George already studied it?"

"He did onsite, but he wasn't able to take any samples away."

"It's a good thing or he'd be dead too."

Jack nodded as there was a knock on the door. "Ah, that must be our breakfast."

Jack got up, went to the door and unlatched it. Just as soon as he opened it, the door came crashing in with two thugs to follow. Jack managed to duck when the first one threw a punch but the second one kicked him hard in the stomach with his boot.

Dolly screamed and tried to go to the phone to call for help, but the first intruder grabbed her by the arm and flung her into the wall. She hit her head on a painting and fell to the ground unconscious. In the meantime, Jack had risen to his feet and was coming at the assailants. Unfortunately, before he could throw a punch he was blindsided and went down hard.

"Get off me you bastard," Jack screamed, but it was too late. The man had a firm grip on both arms and wouldn't let go. A second man began punching him in the stomach until he started spitting out blood.

When the two men finally got up and turned to leave one of them said, "Forget about Bat Mountain if you care about you and your girlfriend's life. Have a nice day."

Jack went over and called the operator to order an ambulance. He wasn't worried so much about himself as he was Dolly. Concussions could be serious and he wanted to make sure she was alright. Twenty minutes later they made it to the emergency room of North Vista Hospital. While they were patching up Jack's cuts and bruises they took Dolly in for an x-ray. While he was waiting for the results he called George and Cindy.

"They beat you up?" George repeated.

"Yes. Didn't they pay you a visit?" Jack asked.

"No. Cindy made me get up early and take her to church. She's a good Catholic and promised her mother she wouldn't miss mass."

"Well, you should thank her mother for that. . . . I told hotel security to keep an eye on your room, so you should be alright when you get back. Just watch out for cars hurtling themselves toward you in the meantime."

George laughed tentatively. "Right. See you in a little while."

Fortunately, the x-rays didn't show any serious injury to Dolly so the doctors let both of them leave around 2:00 p.m. After they'd found George and Cindy and loaded the car, they drove out of town watching carefully for anyone following them but didn't notice anybody.

"So, I guess we should back off," George said.

"You can if you want, but when someone tells me to back off, I just get more motivated to keep on doing what I'm doing."

"Aren't you scared?" Dolly asked.

Jack nodded. "Not for me, but I am worried about them hurting you. We'll have to take precautions to make sure that doesn't happen."

George took a deep breath. "I hope your precautions are good enough?"

Jack smiled but didn't respond. Time went by quickly on the way home and before they knew it they were back at Mona's Café. After George and Cindy had left Dolly asked Jack to come to her place as she didn't want to be home alone that night. He agreed but reminded her he needed to stop by his ex-wife's house to see Jake. Deputy Curt Lawson's patrol car was in the driveway when they pulled up. Jack rang the doorbell and Angela answered.

"Hi," Angela said giving Dolly a disapproving look. Angela's eyes widened as she saw Jack's cuts and bruises. "What the hell happened to you?"

"We got an unexpected visitor to our suite at the Sands this morning."

Angela held the door open for them to come in. "Oh, my God! Was it a robbery?"

Deputy Lawson who had been sitting on the living room sofa stood up. Jack shook his head. "No. A warning."

"What kind of warning?" Deputy Lawson asked.

Jake walked in from a back room and smiled at his father. "Hi, Dad."

Jack smiled back and then he and Dolly took a seat at the other end of the sofa.

"We were trying to find the owner of Bat Mountain Corporation and apparently got too close," Jack replied.

Deputy Lawson frowned. "You think the assault was related to Bat Mountain?"

"Yes. The assailants specifically told us to forget Bat Mountain."

"Huh. So, who is the owner?" Deputy Lawson asked. "I've been meaning to get over to Vegas and find out."

"I'm pretty sure it's the federal government," Jack replied. "When we confronted the incorporator and registered agent, Paul Bradford, he went straight to the Bureau of Land Management's local office in Las Vegas. He met with a man named Riley Wilson and when we confronted them it got ugly."

Jack gave them a short version of the weekend's events.

"Jesus," Angela said. "I can't believe you followed the guy. Weren't you scared?"

"I am now," Jack confessed. "I wasn't expecting them to get violent."

Curt shook his head angrily. "I don't know what in the hell the government is up to but I'm sure as hell going to find out. Mark was a fellow officer and a friend and now his children are orphans."

"I'm afraid we've only seen the tip of the iceberg," Jack said. "It's obvious the government has no idea what it's got there at the Bat Mountain Site."

"It's a monster if you ask me," Dolly said.

"I wouldn't argue with that," Angela agreed.

"A monster we can't ever see," Jack noted. "In roughly twelve hours it spread from a small rock to take over an entire house. It's smart too. It's already figured out humans need oxygen to survive and natural gas causes explosions."

"So, you think there is something alive in the formation?" Curt asked.

Jack nodded. "Something alive and alien to Earth."

Curt looked at Jack thoughtfully but didn't say anything.

"What are you going to do about this, Curt?" Angela asked.

"I don't know. The sheriff has ordered me to stand down and let the Army handle it."

"They did?" Jack asked.

"Yes, I got a call this afternoon."

"You don't buy the conspiracy theory, do you?" Jack asked.

"No, I think the explosion was an accident. The fire inspector said there was something on the stove and when it boiled over it put out the pilot light."

"What about the house being sealed up?"

Curt shrugged. "I don't know what to make of that."

"Well," Jack said. "I don't know about you but when someone tells me I can't do something, I become obsessed with proving them wrong."

Deputy Lawson smiled. "You know, that's kind of my reaction too. I usually follow the orders of my superiors, but when an order is obviously unconscionable then I'm not obligated to follow it."

"Good. Maybe between you, George and myself we can figure this thing out and save some lives."

"How about me?" Jake protested. "I want to help."

Jack smiled. "Sure, we're going to need all the help we can get."

They talked for another hour and then Jack and Dolly went back to Dolly's place to try and get some sleep. In the morning Dolly went to the café and Jack detoured through Death Valley Junction to see what was left of Deputy Hanson's home. The blast and ensuing fire had pretty much destroyed the structure and there was little left other than black rubble. There was a crime scene tape around the house, but the FBI had already packed it up and left. Ducking under the crime scene tape Jack went in for a closer look. He assumed everything that might shed some light on what had happened had been carted off by the FBI, but just in case they missed something he kept looking. He was about to give up when he noticed a brick coated in the white crystalline substance he knew had come from the Bat Mountain Site. It was sitting several yards away from the kitchen window, so he assumed it had been blown out by the initial explosion. He speculated that because of it being thrown clear of the house, whatever organism that was in the brick had survived.

He wanted to take the brick and study it but was afraid to take it back to his house where it might do to him what it had done to Deputy Hanson. So he took it to a construction site that he was just starting to set up, but as yet had little more than a utility hookup, a load of lumber, and piles of sand and gravel to be used in the construction of a foundation. Since he knew nobody would be on the site for several weeks he dug a hole in the sand and buried the brick so nobody would know it was there. It was his intention to come back the following weekend with George when they could study it at their leisure.

As he was driving away, he wondered how an organism so small that it could live in rock could be an intelligent life-form. It had to be intelligent, he reasoned, since it knew when it was being attacked and sought revenge against those who had injured it. He thought of the landing site and wondered if this organism was actually an alien life-form that was building itself a cocoon or crystal nest. That would explain the government's intervention, but not their low-keyed approach to managing the site. He didn't think they would have turned it over to the Park Service if they thought it was infested with an intelligent alien life-form. Nothing made sense to him. It was so frustrating not to be able to explain things that were happening before his very eyes.

23
On Vacation

Special Agents William Pierce and Melanie Sanders were not pleased to learn there were two more murders connected to the Bat Mountain Site. They had made very little progress on Colonel Martin's murder and had barely begun their investigation of Randy Perkins' bizarre death when they got the call about the explosion at Deputy Hanson's place. When they got to the scene of the crime all they found was smoldering debris. The fire had been so hot that almost nothing was left of the Hanson's home or furnishings. They tried to interview the children but they were so distraught that nothing they said made sense. The ERT spent the entire night sifting through the debris looking for evidence but found little if anything.

The fire inspector determined that escaping gas from the kitchen stove was the cause of the explosion but the children couldn't offer any knowledge on how that happened as they hadn't been in the kitchen that morning. Neighbors confirmed that the structure had somehow been sealed up so that the Hanson's couldn't get out. Several men told the agents they had diligently tried to get into the house, but couldn't do it even with crowbars and axes. There was very little of the crystalline substance that had survived the explosion and fire so it was hard to determine exactly how the home had been so tightly sealed.

"I'm at a loss, Bill," Agent Sanders said in despair. "How could someone do this? Did they spray this substance on the doors and windows? If so, wouldn't Deputy Hanson have heard them doing it? You'd have to have some kind of machine and it would need power."

"If it was electric it wouldn't make a lot of noise, a paint sprayer maybe."

"Still, they'd have to get in the house unnoticed, spray the interior without anyone seeing them, then go outside and spray the outside as well."

"I know. It seems impossible, but the other option isn't very realistic either."

"What do you mean?"

"That this rock contained an organism that somehow went into the foundation, then moved through the walls and eventually sealed up all the doors and windows."

She rolled her eyes. "Right. The Bat Mountain Monster theory. It seems pretty ridiculous."

"Yet, that may be what happened, considering we know the walls are growing, so whatever is in them can move through solid objects."

As they were talking a Chevrolet Impala drove up and a man dressed in a dark blue suit stepped out. He wore sunglasses and a poker face. When he noticed them, he walked over.

"Agents Sanders and Pierce?" he asked.

They nodded. "I'm Jimmy Malone, CIA," he said and showed them his badge.

They looked at it and then back at Malone. "Okay, what can we do for you?"

"General Thornton asked me to let you know that the Army will be taking over the three murder investigations involving the Bat Mountain Site."

"Why?" Malone asked.

"Because the President asked them to. I'd be happy to explain it to you but it's classified. You can call your bosses to confirm it if you want. The FBI Director has been informed."

Agent Sanders looked at Agent Pierce who shrugged. "Well, this is one case I won't miss," Agent Pierce said with a smile.

"What about the evidence we've gathered?" Sanders asked.

"Where do you have it?" Malone replied.

"At our evidence warehouse in Vegas."

"General Thornton will send someone over there to pick it up. I'll make sure they call you in advance so you can do the proper paperwork."

Agents Pierce and Sanders and the ERT packed up their gear and drove off. As she drove back to Las Vegas, Agent Sanders wondered what was going on. In her ten-year career with the FBI she'd seen some strange things but this was by far the most bizarre. None of the three murders made any sense to her and being forced to walk away from them without figuring out who was responsible bothered her. But of even greater concern was the possibility that whatever was buried at the Bat Mountain Site was alive, had a mind of its own and would do anything to protect itself including killing human beings. She just hoped the Army could handle it.

When she got back to her office she wrote up her final report and personally delivered it to her supervisor, Joe Spencer. "I think it's a mistake to take us off this case," she told him.

"Probably, but it's not our call. I got confirmation from Washington that we're to back off."

"But what if that thing kills more innocent people? I don't think the Army has a clue how to contain it."

The telephone rang and Joe picked it up. "Yes," he said and listened. "Yes, sir. I understand. I'll take care of it."

Joe hung up the telephone. "Hmm," he said thoughtfully. "I guess you're not the only one who has concerns about the Army's ability to handle the Bat Mountain Site. The director wants the investigation of the three murders to continue, unofficially."

"Unofficially? What does that mean?" Agent Sanders asked.

"Well, Melanie. It means you're taking a few weeks' vacation, except you're not going to Hawaii."

Agent Sanders sighed. "So, how can I conduct a murder investigation without the Army knowing about it?"

"I don't know. Maybe you can team up with the Sheriff's office and work in the background."

"I got a better idea. The guy who discovered the site knows as much about it as anybody, plus he refuses to back off even though the Army has assured him they have it under control. Perhaps I can team up with him."

"What's his name?"

"Jack Carpenter. He's been working with a geology professor, George Palmer."

"What's their angle? Why won't they back off?"

"The professor is interested in the site for scientific inquiry and professional notoriety, I'm sure. As for Carpenter, I'm not sure—maybe because he stumbled on it in the first place and thinks it's his responsibility to figure it out."

"Okay. Get going and keep me posted. The director wants a daily report on what's going on."

"What about Bill?"

"It's just going to be you. As far as Bill and anyone else is concerned, you're on vacation."

Sanders nodded. "Alright. I'll be in touch."

24
The Funeral

Hundreds gathered at the Church of the Living Desert for the funerals of Deputy Mark Hanson and his wife, Amanda. The small church was totally inadequate for the large throng of friends, family and media that had turned up for the solemn occasion. The three Hanson children were accompanied into the church by Amanda's sister and grandparents. Jack, Dolly, George and Cindy were sitting together in the back of the church feeling fortunate that they'd been able to get seats. The Sheriff and seven deputies were standing along one wall. Agent Melanie Sanders stood against the back wall of the foyer wearing sunglasses. When it was time to begin, Reverend Little took the pulpit and looked out over the crowd.

"Good morning folks. Yes, it is a good morning because one of our brothers and one of our sisters is sitting right now with our Lord, Jesus Christ, in Heaven. Yes, I have no doubt that our dear Lord has accepted Mark and Amanda into heaven because they were good Christians who lived pure lives and feared the Lord.

"Now I know it probably seems to most of you that Mark and Amanda were too young to die, particularly since they had three small children. But you've got to remember that God has a high purpose for us all and rarely, in our lifetime, do we know or understand what it is.

"But I think I may know God's purpose for taking Mark and Amanda and leaving their three small children as orphans. For God has caused a great cathedral to be raised in the desert out of bedrock. A cathedral of great magnificence and worthy to herald the Second Coming of Christ.

"Yet there are skeptics. Even though this cathedral is being built before our eyes without architects, builders, carpenters, masons, bricks, steel, or wooden beams, many still don't believe God is the architect and the builder of this miracle in the desert.

"So, because we mortals have so little faith, He has provided us with more miracles to make us understand the power and might of God. First, He called up the Mountain Devils from the depths of Hell to smite a man who tried to keep us, His pilgrims, from bearing witness to this wondrous miracle.

"Then he commanded the wall to smite the man who tried to destroy it with a saw and sledge hammer. And the wall obeyed sending out strands of stone to wind around the agent of the Devil and squeeze all life from him.

"But that wasn't enough. There were still those who didn't believe, so He called upon the rock that had been split off from the wall and said unto it, sacrifice two good souls with young children, so that tears will well in the multitudes and they will finally open their eyes and see the miracle that God is creating before them. So, the rock obeyed and sealed the two good souls in a tomb and their children cried and eyes of the multitudes were opened onto the Lord.

"Now to further prove the veracity of my words, General Thornton is opening up the Living Desert Cathedral to all of you until sunset tonight at 7:48 p.m. Accordingly, there will be Army buses pulling up after the service for anyone who wants to see the Living Desert Cathedral up close. For those of you who haven't been out there lately the Cathedral now rises over twenty-nine feet into the heavens and is a spectacular sight."

Noisy conversation broke out so Reverend Little nodded to the organist and he began to play Rock of Ages which quieted the crowd. When the hymn was over family and friends, one by one, got up and talked about Mark and Amanda, their lives and how much they'd be missed. Nobody commented on Reverend Little's speculation that their death was all part of God's plan to bring attention to the Living Desert Cathedral, but the Reverend knew they'd all ponder that idea.

After the funeral eight Army buses pulled up along the driveway leading to the church and excited pilgrims, town's people, and members of the media climbed aboard. Reverend Little followed the long procession wondering why the Army had suddenly become so amenable to his demands. He couldn't imagine they cared a hoot about Deputy Hanson, but he wasn't about to look a gift horse in the mouth. He needed to get his people onto the Bat Mountain Site so he could claim his position as the guardian of God's new church.

25
The Recruitment

Jack, Dolly, George and Cindy watched the buses leave with some interest but decided not to follow them as they were tired and had other pressing things to do. As they were walking back to their cars Special Agent Melanie Sanders intercepted them.

"Agent Sanders," Jack said recognizing her from their earlier meeting.

She nodded. "Hi. I wonder if I might speak with all of you for a few moments."

"Sure," Jack said, "but we've been out of town for a few days so we probably won't be of much help to you."

"Well, it's not about the explosion. Can I buy you a cup of coffee?"

They agreed and went to a diner down the road. When they'd been seated around two tables pulled together, Agent Sanders took a deep breath.

"This is off the record. I'm officially on vacation," she advised.

"Okay," Jack acknowledged warily. "Our lips are sealed."

"The FBI has been pulled off the three murder investigations and told to stay away from the Bat Mountain Site. As you can imagine the Director isn't pleased with this development."

"I can imagine," Jack said. "Did they say why?"

"No. And you all know as well as anyone that there is something very wrong with the situation at the Bat Mountain Site."

Dolly laughed. "You got that right, honey."

"So, we can't just step away as the President, the CIA, and General Thornton would like us to do. We have a responsibility to make sure the American people are safe from any domestic threat. Then again, we have to follow orders so we can't officially continue our investigations. In other words, I can't be found anywhere near the Bat Mountain Site. I'm taking a chance coming here today."

"So, how can we help?" Jack asked. "Your assessment of the situation at the Bat Mountain Site is right on. The Army has no understanding or control over the situation. If somebody with a brain and a little common sense isn't put in charge soon, I'm afraid there is going to be a major catastrophe there."

"Yes. That's my assessment too. So, I'm going to propose something to all of you that is highly irregular, but the only viable option I can come up with at the moment."

"Okay. We're listening."

"We have to figure out what this Bat Mountain phenomenon is. It's obviously not a traditional uplift as they take hundreds of years and the geology of the region doesn't support it anyway. It's rising way too fast and acting with purpose so it can't be a chemical reaction either. What we fear is that it is a weapon that the military has developed but is out of control."

"A weapon?" George asked. "Hmm. I hadn't thought of that. You're right it's not geological. I figured that out the first few days I was out there. A natural chemical reaction is out of the question too, since there are no chemicals in the area that would react in this fashion. But, a chemical weapon makes more sense, although I can't for the life of me figure out how it would work."

"Well, it's just a theory. Anyway, I have a lot of work to do, but I'm hampered by the fact that I don't have access to the Bat Mountain Site, any of the witnesses, or the evidence that's been collected. Also, since the FBI isn't supposed to be investigating the murders, I can't be seen anywhere in Inyo County."

"So, what are you asking?" Jack pressed.

"You guys, for whatever reason, are investigating the Bat Mountain Site on your own. I'm not sure what your motivations are, curiosity, self-preservation, or scientific discovery, but I have no doubt they are good reasons. And I must compliment you on your results. You've done better than my partner and I and we have had the full resources of the bureau behind us. So, I'm proposing that we join forces and figure out what's going on."

"Amen to that," Dolly said.

"How would our partnership work?" Jack asked curiously.

"We brainstorm together and decide what needs to be done. You all will have to do any leg work with witnesses or investigation at the site itself, but I can provide the resources of the FBI to back up our efforts."

"Where will you operate from?" George asked.

"I'm not sure. A motel, maybe."

"You could, but I have a better idea. I could set you up at the college as an assistant. That way you'd have an office, communications access and a laboratory where we could study any specimens we might get our hands on."

"That's an excellent idea," Agent Sanders said excitedly. "And I hope we can get our hands on a specimen soon. It's hard to figure out what we're dealing with without a sample to study."

"I've got a specimen," Jack advised.

"You do?" Agent Sanders asked, wide-eyed.

"Yes, I picked it up this morning from the rubble of Deputy Hanson's home."

"Where is it now?" she asked.

"In a secluded place where it can't kill anyone."

Agent Sanders laughed. "Good. Will you take me to see it?"

"Sure, but it's too late today. I'll have to take you there in the morning."

"Okay, that will give us time to plan our strategy and make assignments."

"What about our jobs?" Dolly asked. "I've got to work to make a living."

Agent Sanders nodded. "Of course, I have a budget so I can reimburse you for any out of pocket expenses or loss of income."

Dolly's eyes lit up. "Excellent. Did you hear that, Cindy?"

Cindy laughed. "Yes, I did. Sounds good to me."

After coming to a tentative agreement, they talked for over an hour comparing notes. Jack filled Agent Sanders in on what they'd learned over the weekend and they discussed what each could do over the next few days to advance the investigation. After the meeting Sanders called her supervisor to report in for the day. She told him she felt good about her amateur sleuths and that they were all intelligent, resourceful and eager to find out the secrets of the Bat Mountain Site. He said he was glad she had gotten a good start and that much was riding on her and her team. She assured him they'd uncover the truth but she could only pray that whatever the truth turned out to be would be something they could handle.

"Oh. Before you go, you need to know something?" Joe advised.

"What's that?"

"You know the evidence you checked into the FBI Evidence Warehouse the other day?"

"Yeah. The rocks, a sledge hammer and a broken hack saw," she recalled.

"Well, the rocks look like they've been tampered with."

"What do you mean?"

"Captain Winslow of the Army Criminal Investigations Command came over to take possession of everything and he compared the rocks to the photos that were taken at the crime scene and they looked markedly different."

"Huh. How could that happen?"

"I don't know. There's no record of anyone accessing the evidence. In fact, the evidence bags were still sealed."

"Maybe it's a temperature variation. It's much cooler in the evidence warehouse than it is outside."

"I don't know. I can't imagine a thirty-degree temperature variation would cause the rock to change color and shape."

"Well, I don't know what to tell you."

"Alright. Call me tomorrow," Joe said and hung up.

Agent Sanders stared at the telephone feeling a bit depressed. Every day it seemed like the mystery of the Bat Mountain Site deepened. Instead of finding answers, so far all they'd done was uncover new questions. She just wished the CIA and the Army would open up to them. Together they'd have a much better shot at containing the situation. She wondered what they were hiding and how many more would die to protect their secrets.

26
Miracles

The army buses full of Reverend Little's pilgrims drove up the last two miles to the Bat Mountain Site on a dirt road recently constructed by the Army Corps of Engineers. As they approached the site there was much excitement amongst the pilgrims as God's cathedral had grown to nearly twenty-seven feet and sparkled in the afternoon sun. As each bus unloaded several park rangers were waiting to guide the visitors down a new path that led to the front of the cathedral and then swung around in a complete circle around the magnificent structure. As they walked along the path, at times it got close enough that each pilgrim could run their hands along the surface of the walls and feel the texture of the crystal.

A reporter and camera crew from one of the networks accompanied the first group. Amongst their group was a middle-aged woman being pushed in a wheelchair by her daughter. When the path brought them close to the wall the woman reached out and ran her hand across the surface. When she pulled her hand back she began to convulse. Her daughter tried to hold her down but she jerked so violently that she fell right out of the wheelchair onto the ground. People gathered around to see what was happening as the camera crew filmed the entire scene.

Finally, the woman stopped convulsing and when her daughter came to her side she waved her off. "Thank you, Lord! I knew You would answer my prayers," the lady said as she rolled onto her knees as if she was going to stand up. She teetered for a moment and then pushed herself up.

"Oh, my God! It's a miracle!" someone screamed.

"Mom," her daughter said wide-eyed. "What's happening?"

The woman straightened up, smiled and took a wobbly step.

"Oh, my God! Mom, you can walk!"

"How long has she been disabled?" the reporter asked the daughter.

"She hasn't walked since the accident thirteen years ago."

"Glory Hallelujah!" someone said. "Indeed, we do stand in the Cathedral of the Lord!"

The woman who had been healed was named Emma Lane and as she walked back to the bus with a large crowd and the media following, her daughter proclaimed. "Look! My mother was crippled and now she walks! Praise the Lord."

When Reverend Little came across the woman and the crowd, he took her into his arms, hugged her joyfully and swung her around. When he finally set her down he proclaimed, "The power of the Lord is infinite! Thanks be to God!"

Later as Reverend Little walked along the circular path around the cathedral others came up to him to give testimony to their ailments that had been healed by simply rubbing their hands along the walls of the Cathedral. When Reverend Little finally made it all the way around the cathedral he climbed to high ground and addressed the crowd of pilgrims and the media.

"Pilgrims, friends and members of the Hanson family, the media, who are broadcasting this momentous event to the American people, and General Thornton who is hosting this tour today. . . Behold God's miracle!" he said with a sweeping gesture of his hands. "Isn't it magnificent?"

There was applause and several who screamed, "Yes!"

"Today you are all bearing witness, not only to the building of this holy cathedral, but also to its great healing power. Just a few moments ago I witnessed a woman who had been crippled in a terrible auto accident thirteen years ago. Her feet had withered away and she was confined to a wheelchair, yet after simply touching the wall of God's desert cathedral, she was healed and cast aside her wheelchair forever."

"Praise be to God!" several voices said in unison.

"And there have been others whose afflictions have been cured here today and there will be many more as God's power is limitless. All you have to do is believe in Him and the power of the monument He is building here for us mortals to herald the Second Coming of Christ.

"Now, we all know that money and material things are not important, yet we do live in a world where money is required to operate a family, a business or ministry. To operate this ministry and do God's work we have to have a little cash to pay expenses. So, if you have been moved by what you have seen today and you want to help us spread the word about God's Desert Cathedral, then be generous when my staff comes by with donation plates. And remember for every dollar you give; the Lord will reward you sevenfold.

"God Bless you," Reverend Little concluded and then stepped back onto the path to make his way back to the buses. As he was walking the woman whose mother had been healed and her husband came up to him.

"Reverend. Thank you for healing my mother," the woman said.

He smiled at her warmly. "It wasn't I who healed your mother, it was God."

"Yes, Reverend," the woman's husband said,"but had you not fought for our right to visit this cathedral she wouldn't have been healed."

"What are your names, my children?" he asked.

"Bob and Alice Roper," Alice replied.

"Well, we are all just instruments of the Lord so we can't take credit for what happens. All the glory belongs onto the Lord."

"I know," Bob said, "and my wife and I would like to become instruments of the Lord as well. Could you use our services? We've talked about it and we'd like to join your ministry and help you with your work."

"Excellent. We need all the help that we can get. There is so much work that needs to be done."

"Good. So, how do we get started?"

"Come to our church office in Shoshone tomorrow and my secretary we'll do all the paperwork."

"Wonderful," Alice said. "See you tomorrow."

27
God's Bounty

Principal Barnes was working in the backseat of Reverend Little's black 1958 Lincoln Continental Mark III. He was in charge of the church's finances and he'd just finished counting three briefcases full of cash that had been contributed after the Reverend's pleas for financial support. Up to that point the church had been on shaky financial ground, never taking in more than a few thousand dollars during its Sunday and Wednesday night services. He closed the last briefcase, got out and put it in the trunk with the others just as the Reverend and his entourage arrived.

"Excellent speech, Reverend," he said holding the door to the backseat open for him.

Reverend Little smiled, ducked down and took a seat. Barnes walked around the car and got in on the opposite side. The reverend's secretary, Lizzy Arnold, got in the passenger side and his driver, Bruce Tolbert, took the wheel. As they drove off, the Reverend asked for an update.

"Twenty-thousand and change," Barnes advised.

Reverend Little stifled his exhilaration. "Really? That's excellent."

"It was the healings," Lizzy said. "They were wonderful."

"Yes, I hadn't expected that," Reverend Little lied. "The Lord works in mysterious ways."

"So, now we'll be able to catch up on our mortgage payments," Barnes said.

"Don't spend all the money on mortgage payments," Reverend Little said. "The bank wouldn't dare foreclose on the guardians of God's Desert Cathedral. Give them half of what's owed, pay Lizzy her back pay plus a bonus for working so long without a paycheck, and take a few bucks for yourself. You've been putting in a lot of hours lately."

"Well, I'm not doing it for the money," Barnes said. "But thank you."

"Oh, and I'll need five grand in cash too. I've got some personal expenses that I've let slide as of late."

"Well, that will just about clean us out," Barnes said worriedly.

"Don't give it a second thought, Paul. There's going to be a lot more days like today. If our Lord's new cathedral has been bestowed with the power to heal there won't be an army large enough to keep people away."

Barnes sighed. "I guess you're right. It was really amazing today."

When they got back to the church Barnes divided up the money, giving Lizzy and Little their shares, took a thousand dollars for himself, and bundled up the rest to take to the bank. After Barnes left, Reverend Little went into his office, took off his coat and sat down at his desk. A few moments later Lizzy came in, poured him a shot of bourbon and began massaging his back. After he'd downed the bourbon he grabbed Lizzy's arm and pulled her onto his lap. They began kissing and caressing each other but were interrupted by a knock at the door. Lizzy jumped up, her face pink with passion. She straightened herself, went to the door and opened it.

The woman who had been healed at the Cathedral earlier that day walked in with her daughter in tow. "Hi, Reverend. How'd we do?"

"Excellent, very convincing."

Lizzy frowned. "The healing wasn't real?"

"Emma's wasn't but the others were. She's an actress I met in Hollywood when my father was taping some sermons for the networks. We just had to prime the pump."

"Huh?" Lizzy said.

"Healing is the result of belief, so sometimes you have to fake a few healings just to get people to believe. Once they believe, they can actually be healed through faith. Jesus didn't heal anyone, he just gave them faith in the Lord, so that He would heal them."

Lizzy didn't say anything.

"So, you have some cash for me?" Emma asked.

"Yes, I do," Little said and pulled out an envelope full of cash. "Two thousand dollars. Not bad for ten minutes work."

"I spent a lot of time learning how to act," she reminded him. "Plus, we blew the whole day coming out here."

"Yes, thank you for that. Can I buy you dinner?"

"No. We've got to get back to Hollywood. Good luck with your ministry."

Emma and her daughter left and Lizzy gave the Reverend a disapproving look. "And here I was in tears over that miraculous healing."

"Sorry, love," Little said. "But I couldn't tell anyone. It had to take everybody by surprise to look authentic. Come here, I think we were about to get naked when we were so rudely interrupted."

Emma feigned a pout and then walked slowly around his desk and back onto his lap. "You know. We should do this somewhere more comfortable," he said pushing her up and then sweeping her off her feet. She giggled as he carried her across the room and into his adjoining quarters.

28
Death Valley Junction

Jack picked Agent Sanders up at her motel and they drove to a location about eight miles from Independence California where Jack's company was to start work soon on the foundation of a substation for the Southern California Edison company. It was after nine when they got to the site and the temperature was already nearing a hundred degrees. Jack pulled up next to a pile of sand that stood at least fifteen feet tall. They were all alone.

"So, this is your next project, huh?" Sanders asked.

"Yeah. It doesn't look like much now but in a few months, there will be a 24,000 sq. ft. foundation."

"Hmm. Interesting. So, where's the sample?"

Jack got a shovel out of his truck and went over to where he'd buried the brick in the sand. After a moment, he held it up and then dusted off the sand. He was about to hand it to Agent Sanders when he frowned. "It seems different today."

"Really? How so?"

"The crystal that ran through it yesterday has lightened and the rock seems a bit smaller."

"That's what happened to the sample they took to our evidence warehouse in Las Vegas."

"I wonder what caused it," Jack mused.

"I don't know."

"Maybe the microorganism that was in the rock has escaped."

Agent Sanders swallowed hard. "Oh, Jesus. I hope that's not true. If it is we have four sites now infected with the organism."

"So, if they left this rock, where did they go?" Jack asked. "We better look around and see if there is any sign of them."

They split up and thoroughly searched the site but after thirty minutes or so found nothing unusual. They were about to leave when Jack said, "Wait a minute."

He grabbed his shovel, went back to the sand pile where he'd left the rock and started digging. After digging through the loose sand for about ten minutes he hit something hard. After digging around the hard object with his hand, he looked up at Agent Sanders and shook his head.

"What is it?" she asked warily.

"It appears to be the beginning of another crystalline wall."

"Oh, shit! Like at Bat Mountain?"

Jack nodded. "I'm afraid so."

Jack continued to dig and found that walls of a similar pattern to those at the Bat Mountain Site were in the beginning stages of formation.

"So, now what?" Jack asked.

"I don't know. I guess I'll have to report this site to my boss."

"We better check Deputy Hanson's place. The same thing might be happening there."

"Right," Agent Sanders said. "We'll have to do that."

"And it's right in the middle of town, so there will be no hiding it."

"True, so we better not report this site yet," Agent Sanders said. "It's the only place we can study the organism in peace."

"True. But in a couple weeks people are going to start coming out here."

"So, that's two weeks we have to solve the mystery."

Jack laughed. “Good luck with that.”

After they’d covered up the new walls with sand they drove back to Death Valley Junction. The crime scene was alive with activity so they parked back out of sight.

“I guess the Army is reinvestigating the crime scenes,” Agent Sanders said. “Why don’t you go in and find out what’s going on? Take your camera so we can study the photos later.”

Jack nodded. “Okay, keep out of sight.”

Jack got out of his truck, grabbed his camera, and meandered down to the crime scene. There were several army vehicles and a TV news crew from one of the Las Vegas stations. Jack was stopped by an MP when he got too close.

“This is a crime scene, sir. You can’t go any closer.”

Jack stopped. “Right. Who’s in charge here?”

“That would be Captain Winslow, sir,” he replied pointing to an officer working inside what used to be Deputy Hanson’s kitchen.

Jack nodded. “So, I thought this crime scene had already been worked by the FBI.”

“Sorry, I can’t comment on the investigation.”

“Oh, I’m Jack Carpenter. I’m the one who stumbled on the Bat Mountain Site.”

The MP gave Jack a hard look. “Oh, Mr. Carpenter. Right, I should have recognized you. Actually, the captain does want to talk to you.”

“He does?”

“Yes, we’re re-interviewing all the witnesses.”

“Why? Didn’t the FBI do a good job?”

“Yes, I’m sure they did, but in light of some new intelligence we’ve received, we have to talk to everybody again.”

“What new evidence?”

"Why don't you ask Captain Winslow. He knows more about it than me. I'll go tell him you're here."

Jack nodded and the MP went over to the captain. While he was gone Jack began taking pictures. The MP and the Captain talked a moment and then Captain Winslow looked over at Jack and waved for him to come over. Jack walked under the tape and joined the Captain and the MP.

"Mr. Carpenter. What brings you out here?"

"I just wanted to look around again and get some pictures for my scrapbook—you know, something to show my grandchildren when I get old."

"Right," Captain Winslow said warily.

"So, how is the investigation going?"

"Actually, we've had a breakthrough. We've found evidence that all four victims were murdered by the same co-conspirators."

"You did?" Jack asked, shocked at the revelation.

"Yes, but I can't identify them at this time. We have to nail down a little more evidence before we can arrest them. As a matter of fact, I need to ask you about a few people."

"Okay."

"Do you know Paul Barnes?"

"The principal at the high school?"

"Yes."

"Sure. My son's in high school so I've talked to Paul at school functions. But I've known him for years. I do concrete work for the school district."

"Have you seen him out at the Bat Mountain Site?"

Jack thought for a moment. "Sure, I think I have seen him with Reverend Little."

"How about on the day of Colonel Martin's murder."

"No. I wasn't there that day."

"What kind of relationship does he have with the Reverend?"

"Administrative. He handles the church's finances. I know that because I did a parking lot for the church and Paul handled the contract and paid the bills."

"So, they are close, then?"

"Sure. Paul's a religious person. He's a good man as far as I know. I couldn't imagine him being involved in murder."

"Well, you know zealots. They will do anything in the name of God."

Jack shrugged. "I guess that's been historically true, still—"

"Do you know if the Reverend does any hiking or camping up on Bat Mountain?"

Jack thought a moment. "Well, now that you mention it, I've heard that his youth group has a camp up in Echo Canyon at the hot springs."

"Do you know where it is?"

"Not exactly, but it's probably on a local map. You can get them at the grocery store in town."

"Good. Well, you've been very helpful."

"Sure, then I'll let you get back to your investigation. If there is anything I can do to help, let me know."

"I will."

"Hey, can I get a picture with you?" Jack asked.

Captain Winslow frowned. "Well, I guess."

Jack gave the camera to the MP and then got next to the captain. The MP got in position in front of the two men and took the shot. Jack took back the camera, took a few more shots, and then started to walk back to his truck. He was interrupted by a TV reporter.

"Mr. Carpenter?" the TV reporter asked.

"Yes."

"You were the one who discovered the Bat Mountain Site, weren't you?"

"Yes, that's correct."

"So, why are you here today?"

"Oh, I just stopped by to take a few photographs for my scrapbook and Captain Winslow wanted to ask me a few questions."

"About what?"

"They have some new leads on the three murders, apparently."

"Do you know who they are looking at for the murders?"

"No, sorry."

"Mr. Carpenter, you've been at the center of this Bat Mountain situation from the beginning, what do you think is happening out there?"

"I don't know, but I don't think there is any person or persons responsible."

"What do you mean?"

"Well, it's the uplift or the cathedral itself that we have to be worried about. There is something within the rock that is causing it to grow and, obviously, it's something quite novel. Whether it poses a threat to us—well, there have been three bizarre and inexplicable murders. You can draw your own conclusion."

"Thank you," the reporter said and turned to look into the camera. "So, that was Jack Carpenter, the man who first stumbled on the Bat Mountain Site. And you heard him say he believes there is something within the walls of the cathedral that is novel and quite sinister. What he didn't say, but could be read between the lines, is that he's not satisfied with the government's response to date."

Jack smiled as he walked back to his truck to fill Agent Sanders in on what he'd learned from Captain Winslow and said to the TV reporter.

"So, they still think Reverend Little is behind this?" Agent Sanders mused.

"It looks that way. I got the impression that they've gathered some evidence against him."

"It's a cover-up, obviously. The government wants to put an end to the public's interest in the Bat Mountain Site.

"I don't think it will work since there's going to be at least two more sites rising to the heavens soon."

"You saw signs of a cathedral growing here too?" Agent Sanders asked.

"Yes, I'm sure that's why they were here—to cover it up."

She laughed. "That's going to be hard to do right here in a residential neighborhood, particularly after what you told that TV reporter."

"What I'm worried about is how the phenomenon is spreading. What are its intentions?"

"That's a good question."

"It's almost like it's a giant ant hill. You know how they spring up and then branch out in a field."

"Right, but the scientists haven't detected any insects or animals within the cathedrals and there aren't any underground tunnels connecting the sites."

"Maybe they haven't hatched yet," Jack suggested. "The tunnels could come later."

Agent Sanders gave Jack a hard look. "You think?"

Jack shrugged. "Just a thought."

"Crap! Wouldn't that be a kick in the ass if thousands of giant bugs came swarming out of their fifty-foot nests."

"What do you think the government is going to do about these new ones? So far, it seems like they are protecting them."

"Protecting them? Why do you say that?"

Jack sighed. "Well, I think the normal response of the military when you have a potential threat is to crush it while it's small and manageable. But here they seem content to watch and study it."

"That's true. Maybe they don't know how to crush them. Blowing them up might make matters worse. If the explosion didn't kill the organisms within the rock, each piece of debris that landed could start a new nest."

"Are you saying our government is acting responsible for once?" Jack said. "That's a novel idea."

"You're right. That can't be it."

They both laughed.

"We better get up to the college," Jack said. "George and Cindy will be wondering what happened to us."

They started the truck and took off, but didn't notice the black Chevrolet Impala following behind them at a distance. They drove to Mona's Café to eat lunch and pick up Dolly. She had the morning shift and needed to make arrangements to get some time off. She joined them at the table once they were seated.

"Mona wasn't happy but she gave me two weeks off."

"Good. We've had an interesting morning," Jack said.

The two men in the black Chevrolet came in and took seats at the counter. Jack glanced at them but didn't recognize either one of them, so his attention turned back to the conversation. They told her about their morning.

"Hmm. Did you hear about the healings up at the Bat Mountain Sites?" Dolly asked.

"No," Agent Sanders said. "What happened?"

"A crippled woman got up and walked. Claimed she'd been crippled for thirteen years from a car wreck."

"Wow!" Jack said.

“Some other folks claimed to have been healed of various ailments too.”

“I wonder how much Reverend Little paid her for that,” Agent Sanders mused.

Jack laughed. “You really think he’d do something like that?”

“Yes, that I could believe. Murder, not so much.”

“Captain Winslow was asking me about Paul Barnes. Apparently, they think he’s involved too.”

“Well, if the Reverend was involved so was Barnes,” Dolly replied. “They’ve been best buds since grammar school. And, of course, you know Reverend Little’s secretary sleeps with him at night.”

“Seriously?” Agent Sanders asked.

“Oh, yes. They’ve been caught by some of their flock in a lip-lock a few times,” Dolly said.

“Well, that’s not a crime, I guess,” Jack said. “Everybody needs love.”

“Right. Except, I’ve heard the Reverend has a wife and kiddos back in Texas.”

“Oh, I didn’t know that.”

“Yes, when he left his Daddy’s church a few years back, his wife didn’t want to leave the comforts of Dallas for a down-and-out church in the desert.”

After they’d eaten they paid the bill and left. As they pulled back onto the road the black Chevrolet followed them a few cars back. An hour into the drive Jack looked over and saw that Dolly and Agent Sanders were asleep. He smiled wishing he could get a little shut eye himself. He hadn’t been sleeping well since the intrusion at their Las Vegas suite. As they were climbing through a mountain pass, the road narrowed and Jack noticed the black Chevrolet in his rearview mirror gaining on him. He slowed a little to let them pass, but instead of passing they came up even with him and opened the passenger side window.

Jack ducked when he saw the gun. "Shit!' he screamed as it shattered his window.

Agent Sanders woke up and reached for her weapon. Jack's face was covered in blood. "Oh, my God!"

The car swerved to the right and the tires thudded angrily as they hit the shoulder. Jack yanked the wheel to the left and slammed on the brakes. Agent Sanders jumped out of the car ready to open fire if the Chevrolet came back at them, but it kept going. Dolly leaned over the seat to examine Jack's face.

"Are you alright?" she asked worriedly.

Sanders opened the driver's side door and put her hand on Jack's shoulder. "Where were you hit?"

"All over," he replied. "I think the bleeding is just from the glass. The bullet must have missed or I wouldn't be talking to you."

"Thank God for that," Dolly said tears streaming down her face.

They both went to work wiping the blood off Jack's cheeks and forehead. They finally counted over a dozen small cuts on the left side of his face.

"We better get you to a hospital," Agent Sanders said. "Some of these cuts need to be sutured.

"We're almost to Lone Pine. There is a medical clinic there."

While Jack was being attended to at the medical clinic Agent Sanders called Joe at FBI headquarters in Las Vegas to check-in.

"They tried to kill you?" Joe asked angrily.

"Yeah, one of us. I'm not sure they knew I was in the truck. I think Jack was the target. He'd just given a TV interview to a crew at Hanson's place in Death Valley Junction that probably didn't sit too well with the Army."

"So, you think the Army was behind it?" Joe asked.

"The Army or the CIA maybe," she replied. "It definitely was a professional hit. Only by the grace of God did the bullet miss or you would have been scraping us off the mountainside."

"You guys better lay low for a while?" Joe said.

"No, we can't afford to back off. We'll just have to watch our back a little closer. No one will catch us off guard again."

"Alright. Call me tomorrow."

Agent Sanders hung up and then called George. He and Cindy were there at the clinic ten minutes later. She filled them in on the days' events.

"I'm going to make sure they beef up security at the college. I'll tell them I have received death threats. Nobody needs to know that Jack or you are here."

"Okay," Agent Sanders said, "but we probably won't be hanging around a lot. We have a lot to do if we are ever going to figure this thing out."

As they were sitting in the waiting room a TV news report came on. This is Walt Jeffers with the five o'clock news.

"Is the Living Desert Cathedral actually God's work or the Devil's? There seems to be a difference of opinion on that score. Yesterday we carried the remarks of Reverend Little during a tour of the site."

The image of Reverend Little came on the screen. "Today you are all bearing witness not only to the building of this holy cathedral but also to its great healing power. Just a few moments ago I witnessed a woman who had been crippled in a terrible auto accident over thirteen years ago. Her feet had withered away and she was confined to a wheelchair, yet after simply touching the wall of God's desert cathedral, she was healed and cast aside her wheelchair forever."

"And there have been others whose afflictions have been cured here today and there will be many more as God's power is limitless. All you have to do is believe in Him and the power of the cathedral He is building here for us mortals to herald the Second Coming of Christ."

The scene shifted to the Death Valley Site where the camera showed Army intelligence officers combing the wreckage of Deputy Hanson's home. An image of Jack Carpenter came on. "Mr. Carpenter, you've been at the center of this Bat Mountain situation from the outset, what do you think is happening out there?"

"I don't know, but I don't think there is any person or persons responsible."

"What do you mean?"

"Well, it's the uplift or the cathedral itself that we have to be worried about. There is something within the rock that is causing it to grow and, obviously, it's something quite novel. Whether it poses a threat to us—well, there have been three bizarre and inexplicable murders. You can draw your own conclusion."

The screen flipped back to the local news anchor. "So, there you have it. Reverend Little believes God has created the Living Desert Cathedral, but Jack Carpenter thinks there is something sinister in the cathedral's walls already responsible for three murders. The only thing these two men agree upon is the government is on the wrong track in trying to solve these murders."

A TV producer came over to the anchor and handed him a typed piece of paper. He gave it a quick look. "Alright. We have breaking news out of Lone Pine. Apparently, there has been an assassination attempt on the life of Jack Carpenter. Witnesses at the Walter's Medical Clinic say he was seen being escorted into the clinic by his girlfriend and an, as yet, unidentified woman. The witnesses also report that the drivers' side window has been shattered. Speculation is that the window was shattered by one or more bullets. We've called the clinic but a spokesman there has declined to comment other than to say Jack Carpenter doesn't appear to be seriously injured.

"So, it appears somebody doesn't like Jack Carpenter's theory about what's going on at the Bat Mountain Site where an ongoing investigation continues into the deaths of Colonel Ben Martin, Park Ranger Randy Perkins and Sheriff's Deputy Mark Hanson and his wife.

"In other news—"

"I better sneak out the back door," Agent Sanders said. "Can you all wait for Jack?"

"Sure," George said digging into his pocket. "Take my car. I parked around the corner. Just go to my office. My secretary is expecting you. She'll show you to your new office."

"Thanks," she said taking the keys. "Tell Jack I'm sorry I had to leave."

"It's no problem. He'll understand."

Agent Sanders went quickly to the car making sure no one saw her. She fumbled with the keys, her nerves shot from the excitement of the day. In all the years she'd been in the FBI she hadn't been shot at before. She climbed in behind the wheel and cursed. It was a stick shift. She'd driven a stick shift when she was in college, but hated it. And how many years ago had that been? She took a deep breath trying to remember how to do it. She looked to her left and saw a reporter coming her way.

"Shit!" she said cranking the engine. It turned over on the first try and she pushed in the clutch then eased it out only jerking a couple of times in the process. She saw the reporter in her rear-view mirror watching her drive off. She wondered if he'd seen her. When she got to the college campus she drove around until she found the Geology Building. After parking in the back lot as George had told her to do, she went inside and found his office. A middle-aged woman with thick-rimmed glasses was sitting at a desk transcribing dictation. She took off her headset when Agent Sanders walked in.

"Hi."

"Hi. I'm Melanie Sanders."

"Oh, the new temp. Yeah. Professor Palmer said you might come by."

"Well, I made it."

The woman opened her middle drawer, pulled out some keys and handed them to her. "Second door on the right. The break room is at the end of the hall next to the lady's room," she advised.

Agent Sanders nodded and walked down to her new office. She unlocked the door, opened it and stepped inside. It was dark, so she switched on the light. It was small, barely eight by ten feet but it had all the essentials—desk, chair, telephone, office supplies and an old Royal typewriter. There was even a TV set. *What else could a girl want.*

She flopped down in her new chair and closed her eyes. What if the bullet had hit Jack or her. She wondered where the bullet had hit the window. How close they had come to succeeding in killing him? She hadn't had time to track its trajectory since her primary concern was getting Jack to a hospital. How was she going to protect Jack in the future, or her, for that matter? She considered who might have been the shooter and decided it was either the Army or the CIA. But what secret was so important as to warrant a government sanctioned murder? Did the President know what was going on? Did the President order the hit? There were too many questions and she was afraid to get the answers.

29
Revelation

Jimmy Malone drove into the U.S. Army base at Ft. Irwin, California. He'd been summoned by General Thornton to discuss recent developments regarding the Bat Mountain Site. He was dreading the meeting because the situation was deteriorating quickly and the General would want answers, but he didn't really have any. When he got to the general's office he hesitated a moment and took a deep breath. He finally knocked.

"Come in," the General said.

Malone walked in and forced a smile. "Good morning, General."

The general nodded but didn't return the smile. "Have a seat."

"Yes, sir," Malone said and took a chair across from him.

"I called you here because I've been reading some rather disturbing stories in the newspaper. I thought we were going to get this Bat Mountain situation contained."

"Yes, sir. We've had some bad luck. Who would have thought Randy Perkins would take a sledge hammer to the wall."

"Perhaps you should have stressed the importance of leaving the wall alone."

"I thought we had, sir," Malone replied. "And why Deputy Hanson took one of the rocks as a souvenir is beyond me. He should have known better than to walk away with evidence."

"Well, you've got to do a better job of containment. Now we have a second site at Death Valley Junction to deal with. How are you going to handle that?"

"I don't know. We can hide it for a while by keeping it as an active crime scene and putting up fences and a canopy. Eventually we'll have to come up with a more permanent solution. I don't think the public will buy a second cathedral."

"No. That's a safe bet," the General agreed. "I know you don't want to do it, but we may have to figure out how to kill this alien life-form, at least this colony."

"It would violate the treaty, sir."

"Would it? We didn't agree to more than one site for them, did we?"

"No, but nobody was supposed to disturb the one that was allowed. We are already in breach of the treaty and we were warned this particular life-form can get very nasty if it feels threatened."

"Yes, I've noticed. But we can't have another colony in the middle of a populated area. We're going to have to eradicate it. Do you all know its vulnerability?"

"No, but this is a sentient life-form. Killing an entire colony would be genocide."

"But nobody would know that, would they?"

"The aliens would and they might go to the press."

General Thornton shook his head in disgust. "Well, if this is a sentient life-form someone needs to communicate with them and make them understand that the attacks on them were by accident and apologize. Then maybe they will voluntarily go back to the Bat Mountain Site and live in peace."

"That could be difficult, sir. Whereas some of the aliens look like you and I, the ones with the ability to speak with this particular life-form are nearly seven feet tall and their skin is a light green. They'd stick out like a pickle in a bag of French fries and if they were seen it could compromise the entire project."

"That might be the best thing to happen. Just tell the world that alien life exists and get it over with."

"But the reaction of the public—"

"Yeah, I know. There would be general panic and the President would probably be impeached."

"Exactly."

"Then just be careful when you bring in the alien interpreter. Don't let him or it be discovered."

"No, sir. We'll be careful."

"What about Jack Carpenter?" the general asked. "He's been stirring up the press and sabotaging our investigation. I thought you were going to take care of him?"

"Our fixer had him in his sights but somehow he dodged the bullet. He's a very lucky guy. I guess we should have taken him out in his hotel room in Vegas when we had the chance, but we were trying to be reasonable."

"You should have. We can't afford to be soft. There is too much at stake."

"Right. We won't make that mistake again."

Malone left and went back to LA where he could work on setting up a meeting with the aliens. He wasn't looking forward to the meeting as he would have to explain how everything had gone so terribly wrong and they wouldn't be happy about it. He cursed Jack Carpenter for discovering the Bat Mountain Site and screwing up his life.

He kept the communicator he used to contact the aliens in a safe in his office. After he'd retrieved the small device, he punched in the number for Lt. Zieg Kulchz, the aliens' senior military officer. Kulchz agreed to a meeting the following day at his headquarters at Possum Kingdom Lake in Central Texas.

Malone took a late flight to Dallas, rented a car and drove out to Mineral Wells where he got a motel for the night. He'd only been to the alien ship a handful of times and he dreaded having to go there again. The ship was hidden beneath the ground on an island the locals called Cactus Island, in the middle of Possum Kingdom Lake. To get to the ship he had to travel through tunnels from the mainland that went under the lake to the island. The caves were dank and smelled of bat guano. The alien ship was manned by huge green humanoids that scared the hell out of him.

The ship was round and looked about the size of a professional basketball stadium. To enter the ship Malone had to climb a ladder to the top of the ship and then go down a hatch into its interior. The hatch's interior was only illuminated by a single blue light above the door. Once inside one of the crew led him into the heart of the ship to a long corridor that went in both directions. It was stark white and well lit. A few minutes later he stopped in front of a door, looked into an eye hole, and the locking mechanism clicked. He pushed the door open and walked in. Malone followed him with much trepidation.

Kulchz was a tall human with broad muscular shoulders and a rugged face. He looked at Malone intently as he entered the spacious office that appeared to be made of glass. There were thousands of lights on the control panel and monitors above and behind him. He motioned for Malone to sit down. The room was furnished with several chairs and a sofa cushioned by a soft, white substance. When Malone sat down, the seat conformed itself to the shape of his body. As he sank into it, he felt like he was floating on air.

Kulchz sat in front of a large, glowing desk. With the faint blue glow came a steady humming noise that changed pitch from time to time. Malone looked at Kulchz expectantly but Kulchz just ignored him. Eventually Kulchz looked up.

"You wanted a meeting, so here we are," he said evenly.

"Yes, I don't know if you monitor our media broadcasts, but we're having a problem with the desert life-form that you deposited in Death Valley."

"Why did your people provoke them?"

"No one intended to provoke them. It was all a big misunderstanding."

"You should have left them alone as the treaty provided. They are not aggressive by nature. They simply wanted to build their home and live in peace."

"Yes, and that's what we want, too, but they have killed several people and started a new colony miles from the first. We can't allow a second colony. We must talk to them and get them to return to the Bat Mountain Site."

"Only those with the gift can talk to the Nanomites."

"The Nanomites? Is that what you call them?"

"Yes, that is their name on Tarizon."

"So, can you send someone with the gift to talk to them and explain that no one was trying to hurt them?"

"We can. We have Seafolken aboard who have the gift, but the Nanomites may not listen. They have been betrayed many times by humans on Tarizon and won't forgive easily."

"Well, we have to try. There cannot be a Nanomite colony at Death Valley Junction. It would be impossible to keep it a secret."

"What if you fail?" Kulchz asked.

"Then we'll have to kill them and remove all remnants of the colony."

Kulchz shook his head. "If you kill the Nanomites you will provoke a war. The last time we went to war with the Nanomites they almost destroyed our capital city."

Malone's stomach twisted. "Why did you go to war with them?" he asked.

"Someone did exactly what you are proposing, they exterminated one of their colonies that had just finished a construction project. It was a tragic error that cost the lives of thousands of humans and billions of Nanomites."

"These Nanomites construct buildings?"

"Yes, for thousands of years we didn't realize the Nanomites were a sentient life-form. They lived in the desert where few humans ever went. We just thought their cities were geological formations. Then a scientist who was studying them realized they were intelligent and had the ability to communicate with each other quickly and effectively. This scientist, with the help of those with the gift of telepathy, were able to establish communication with them and eventually their talents as builders were put to good use. But it was a mistake. The Nanomites are billions strong but act singularly by consensus. If you injure one swarm of Nanomites you injure them all. If one human attacks a Nanomite swarm they assume the entire human race has declared war on them."

"Oh, Lord. You've got to be kidding me. So, they think we are at war with them?"

"Probably."

"That would explain why they have been so vicious in their reprisals."

"Yes, so I will send someone to interpret for you, but you will have to convince them to go back to the Bat Mountain Site. It will not be an easy task."

"Wonderful," Malone moaned.

"If it were up to me, I'd kill every last one of them."

"You would?"

"Yes, as far as I'm concerned, they are nothing but a pest and I'd kill them all, but it's not up to me. We have a peace treaty with them and one of the terms of the treaty was us to help them establish a colony on Earth. You see the Nanomites' have a strong instinct for survival, not individually but the survival of their life-form. Expansion of their cities and colonies is therefore of extreme importance to them. Once they have a new colony established they won't be anxious to turn loose of it."

"So, worst case scenario. If we end up at war with them, can they be easily beaten?"

"It's easy to kill individual Nanomites, even whole swarms. Chemical extermination is quite effective. The problem is they are so small and move so quickly through solid objects that it is difficult to kill them all. So, if after an attack any survive, you've accomplished nothing as they will reproduce and be back to equal strength in just a few days and you won't have any way of knowing when or where their next attack will come."

Malone sighed in utter despair. "Oh, I can't wait to tell the President that we are at war with an enemy we can't even see. Damn it!"

"Like I said, I'd like to help you exterminate them all, but my superiors will not allow it. All I can do is wish you luck."

Kulchz summoned one of his aides and whispered something to him. A few minutes later one of the tall humanoid guards that Malone passed in the tunnels appeared.

"This is Linkh Leode. He will go with you and act as your interpreter," Kulchz said.

Malone gave Linkh a once over and then sighed. "We'll need to disguise him or we will attract too much attention."

Kulchz shrugged. "Do whatever you must. Just convince the Nanomites to return to the Bat Mountain

Site. Don't let this situation deteriorate any further or we will have to intervene."

"How would you intervene?" Malone asked tentatively.

"We'd have to exterminate the Nanomites for you but there would likely be a lot of collateral damage. I don't think your President would be happy and my superiors would be very upset because such action could cause a renewal of the Nanomite War on Tarizon."

Malone swallowed hard, got up and smiled at Linkh. "Alright. We'll give it a try. Thank you for your help."

Linkh bowed to Kulchz and then turned and led Malone out of his office. Malone followed him off the ship and back through the caves to the warehouse at the cave's entrance. When they got back to his car Malone pulled out an overcoat from the trunk for Linkh to wear to cover his uniform.

"This is the first time I've been in one of your automobiles," Linkh remarked.

"Really?" Malone said. "You haven't left the ship?"

"No. The Seafolken are not allowed off the ship except at night and then only to feed in the lake."

"Hmm. How did you learn to speak English?"

"We learned on the way to Earth."

"Was it hard for you to learn it?"

"No. We have drugs that help you learn quickly."

"Wow. That's a technology that would be useful. I'll have to talk to Kulchz about getting some of that."

"I hope you don't exterminate the Nanomites, they are a wonderful life-form. You should see the beautiful buildings they've constructed on Tarizon."

"Is that right? Any cathedrals?"

"Oh, yes. Their cathedrals are most exquisite."

"So, do you talk to them often?"

"No, not often, but I did talk to the speaker for the swarmmasters that are at the Bat Mountain Site before they were left off."

"So, your ship caused the circular footprint near the site?"

"Yes, when we land we burrow so no one will see us from above."

"That must be something to see."

Linkh smiled and nodded. "Yes, the ground shakes terrible and it's quite noisy."

"Dusty too, I bet."

"If the ground is dry, yes."

"When we get to town I'm going to have to disguise you. We don't have Seafolken on Earth so we best make you look like somebody people see every day."

"What do you suggest?"

"I was thinking you'd make a good cowboy."

Once they were back in Mineral Wells Malone took Linkh to his motel room while he went to the store to get the clothes and make-up for a disguise. An hour later Linkh was looking in the mirror at a West Texas cowboy with dark weather-beaten skin.

"Very good," Malone said. "I think that will work."

When they got to Dallas Love Field to fly back to California, they had to walk through the terminal and were pleased that they got only a few stares and most everybody ignored them. On the plane one of the stewardesses kept looking at Linkh and Malone wondered what she was thinking. As they were deplaning she stopped him.

"Sir, I'm curious. Did I see you in a John Wayne movie?"

Malone laughed and Linkh just stared at the woman. "No," Malone said, "but he should go for a screen test, don't you think?" The stewardess nodded enthusiastically.

When they got back to Malone's office it was late so they only stayed there long enough for Malone to check in with General Thornton and Senator Rawlings and update them on his plans.

"So, you have an alien with you right now?" Rawlings asked.

"Yes, a Seafolken. He looks just like a tall human except his skin is a little green. I've dressed him in jeans and cowboy attire which is common out here in the desert and applied a little makeup."

"This is very dangerous," Rawlings said.

"It's the only way we can talk to the Nanomites and try to reason with them," General Thornton replied.

"Nanomites? Is that what they're called?" Rawlings asked.

"Yes, and they are so small you can't see them even with a microscope," Malone noted. "So, they can travel through solid objects and they reproduce like rabbits on steroids."

"Great," Rawlings replied. "I have a bad feeling about this."

"Don't worry. Apparently, they are quite intelligent so we should be able to make them understand the importance of going back to the Bat Mountain Site. I'll call you tomorrow night with a report."

Malone hung up feeling exhausted. He looked over at Linkh. "You're hungry I bet?"

"Yes, I was hoping you were planning to eat."

"What kind of food do you like?"

"I can eat anything you do, but I prefer fish raw, if possible. If you take me to the ocean or a lake I can catch my own dinner."

Malone laughed. "No, we don't have time for that? How about we stop at the market and I'll buy you whatever fish you want and I'll pick up some takeout along the way."

"That will be fine."

When they got to their motel Linkh ate salmon strips they'd picked up at Safeway and Malone downed Chinese takeout. When they were done they drank a few beers and then went to bed early so they could get a good night's rest for an early morning departure for Death Valley Junction and their negotiations with the Nanomites.

30
The Fixer

Captain Winslow wasn't a detective by any stretch of the imagination. He was a fixer and very good at his job. He'd been working on projects for General Thornton for nearly twenty years and had lasted that long because he followed two simple rules—do exactly what's asked of you and don't ask questions. When General Thornton told him, he was being transferred to the Criminal Investigations Command, he was surprised due to his lack of experience in that type of work, but he quickly realized why he'd been picked for the job. There was some weird stuff going on that would totally freak out the public if it got out. Although he was curious as to what was happening, the truth was not material. He had to come up with a plausible explanation that would satisfy the locals and the media.

Less than a week after he'd been assigned to the case he called a news conference at the Bat Mountain Site to announce he'd solved the four murders. The news conference was held on the ridge above the site. Along with the pilgrims and media who were permanent fixtures on the ridge, there was Deputy Lawson, the medical examiner and locals from Death Valley Junction and Shoshone. Jack, Dolly, George and Cindy were also there and Agent Sanders was watching from the hill a half mile away.

Captain Winslow cleared his throat. "Ladies and gentlemen, I have called this news conference this afternoon to give you some good news. After an intense investigation of the four recent murders, Colonel Martin of the United States Army, Randy Perkins of the Park Service and Sheriff's Deputy Mark Hanson and his wife, Amanda, I am proud to advise you that we have solved the murders and all but one of the perpetrators are in custody."

There was a collective sigh from the crowd and then people began clapping. When they were done, Captain Winslow continued, "I guess it's just human nature that when extraordinary events occur, there are always greedy people who try to capitalize on them. Unfortunately, that's what happened here at the Bat Mountain Uplift. One man tried to claim that this simple geological lift was somehow a cathedral being built by God to announce the Second Coming of Christ.

There were shouts of protest and disapproval from the pilgrims in attendance. Several MPs moved in front of Captain Winslow to deter any of them who might decide to rush him.

"Well, as wonderful a phenomenon as that would be, it isn't what's going on here. This morning Reverend John Little was arrested along with Paul Barnes, Lizzy Arnold, Emma Lane, and Susan Lane. Bruce Talbert remains at large but we expect to have him in custody soon."

There were more shouts of outrage and many of the pilgrims appeared to be on the verge of rioting. Several Sheriff's deputies stepped up to support the MPs.

"We believe we have the evidence to prove that these five individuals conspired to kill the four victims I mentioned earlier. We were able to piece together the events that took place over the last few weeks to a large extent due to two undercover officers who infiltrated the congregation of the Church of the Living Desert. These individuals gathered evidence and elicited details of how the murders were carried out by these participants.

"It was a complicated plot but I'll try to summarize it for you. After the Bat Mountain Uplift was discovered, as you know, Reverend Little immediately tried to claim it had a religious significance. When Colonel Martin restricted Reverend Little and his church from the site he wanted to find a way to get rid of Colonel Martin and strengthen his contention that God was constructing a church in the desert, so he ordered his driver and bodyguard, Bruce Talbert to kill Colonel Martin, but make it look like it was the act of God.

"Talbert bragged to one of our informants about how he and Paul Barnes had gone to a cave on Bat Mountain where they knew many bats lived during the day. They took with them gunny sacks and a chemical sedative for the purpose of capturing several dozen bats they planned to use to murder Colonel Martin. So, they filled a portion of the cave with gas and then picked up the sedated bats and put them in their gunny sacks.

"That night, after Colonel Martin had turned in for the night, they came in from the north, where no sentries were posted, went to his tent, injected him with a drug that induced a fatal heart attack, and doused him with a scent that agitated the bats. Then they put the sedated bats on his cot and sealed up the tent. When the bats woke up from their sedation, they went berserk due to the scent and their confinement. So, it appeared at first that the bats were responsible for Colonel Martin's death and Reverend Little claimed that these were the legendary Lone Pine Devils straight from the depths of hell."

The crowd stirred at the picture being painted by Captain Winslow. When the crowd quieted, he continued, "Reverend Little and the other co-conspirators had the same motive for killing Randy Perkins. That is, he continued to place restrictions on Reverend Little's access to the Bat Mountain Site and this was hampering his efforts to become the guardian of God's Cathedral.

So, Reverend Little ordered Talbert to kill Randy Perkins but this time it had to look like the Cathedral had killed him. So, Reverend Little enlisted the help of another member of his flock, Molly Munson, who called Randy and requested some samples of the wall for an exhibit at the Death Valley Museum. We don't believe Miss Munson was a co-conspirator in the murder but rather an unwitting participant. Talbert then kept watch until Randy came out to collect his samples. He watched as Randy repeatedly hit the wall until several chunks had been broken off, then he snuck up from behind and knocked him out. To make the murder look like the work of the wall Talbert staked Randy's hands and neck down with wire and then twisted each strand causing them to bleed. After a significant amount of bleeding, he then concentrated on the neck, tightening it until he was dead."

There were shouts of disgust and outrage from the crowd.

"After Randy was dead, Talbert removed the wires to make it look like the wall had reached out and killed Randy Perkins for his brutal attack and his interference with God's work. But it wasn't God's work. It was clear and simply the act of one man acting on the orders of Reverend Little.

"So, that explains two of the murders, but why would Reverend Little want Deputy Hanson dead? This was perplexing to me as well, until I learned of the comments Deputy Hanson had made to Reverend Little during a meeting between Colonel Martin and Congressman Joel Stephens weeks earlier. At that meeting Deputy Hanson expressed his opposition to anything that would bring more attention to the Living Desert Cathedral as the Sheriff's office was already having trouble dealing with the influx of pilgrims to the site. No doubt Reverend Little wanted to make an example of the deputy for daring to oppose him.

"So, after Randy Perkins' death, Talbert and Barnes went out to Deputy Hanson's home, held him at gunpoint and told him to lock the family in the bathroom. Then they knocked him out, closed all the windows, and turned on the gas on the stove. They knew that when enough gas had escaped, the thermostat would eventually ignite it. Apparently, Mrs. Hanson was able to break the window in the bathroom and get the children out of the house, but the window wasn't big enough for her to escape."

There was a collective sigh from the crowd.

"Now, for those of you who still have any sympathy for Reverend Little, let me say this. Emma, the woman in the wheelchair who supposedly was healed by touching the wall of the Cathedral, is a Hollywood actress who was paid $2,000 to put on that performance."

There were cries of outrage.

"So, that's it. We will now be turning over the case to the U.S. Attorney's office that will be prosecuting all those that we have mentioned for these heinous crimes."

The crowd buzzed with the revelation and Captain Winslow smiled with satisfaction. He'd delivered again and he knew General Thornton would be pleased.

31
The Set Up

At the conclusion of the news conference Jack looked at the others and frowned. "That's a load of crock if I've ever heard one."

George shook his head. "Poor Reverend Little has been set up."

"And Principal Barnes too," Dolly added. "I can't believe it. Paul Barnes has to think twice before stepping on a cricket. There's no way he'd participate in a murder."

"Right," Jack said. "We can't let the government get away with this."

"We better go tell Agent Sanders what just happened," Cindy said. "She's going to be steamed."

They started walking to where Sanders was waiting.

"You think the media will buy it?" George asked.

"Probably," Jack said. "It was pretty creative bullshit, actually."

"Who do you think the undercover cops were?"

"CIA probably. Sent in to orchestrate the cover-up."

"What about the Hollywood actress. Were they behind that too?" George asked.

"No. Reverend Little may have been guilty on that front. He wouldn't be the first preacher to hire an actor to fake a miracle to enhance his standing with his flock."

When they arrived at the top of the hill Agent Sanders looked at them expectantly. They told her what happened.

"That figures," Agent Sanders said with a sigh. "Now our job will be even harder. The government will be fighting not only to protect their secret but their credibility as well. So, I hope everybody has paid their life insurance premiums."

Dolly laughed. "Life insurance? I think my ex-husband is still the beneficiary. There's no way I'm going to die and make him rich."

Jack laughed. "Don't worry. I'm not going to let anything happen to you."

"So, what now?" George asked.

"Well, we better get over to the Independence site and make sure the walls haven't punched through their covering," Agent Sanders replied. "All we need is a bunch of pilgrims descending on another location."

A few hours later they rolled up on the Independence site and were astonished at what they saw. The walls had not grown six inches like they had expected, but were nearly ten foot tall!

"Holly chap!" Dolly exclaimed. "What do you have in that sand, Jack? Fertilizer?"

Jack looked around nervously. "It's a miracle nobody has spotted this yet."

"What could have caused such growth?" George asked.

"I don't know," Jack said. "Maybe because we had the sand, gravel and clay all close by. It allowed the microorganism to work much faster."

"That makes sense," Dolly agreed.

"Boy, you've got to admire their work," Cindy said looking at the beautiful crystal beginnings of another cathedral. "It's different from the Living Desert Cathedral, though."

"Yes, it is," Jack agreed. "You know. These structures are probably the natural home of this microorganism and each one is different."

"Like every snowflake is different."

"Right."

"So, what are we going to do?" George asked. "We can't hide this anymore."

"That's true," Jack said thoughtfully. "I guess what I could do is send word to everyone that the project has been delayed for a few weeks. That will buy us some time."

"That's good, but what is to prevent someone from wandering up here anyway?"

Jack thought a moment. "Well, we could deter them by roughing up the road a bit and dragging some logs over it. I think I saw some fallen trees on the side of the road on the way up here."

After they'd admired the new construction for a while they left the site and stopped where Jack had seen the fallen trees. With a chain attached to the truck's trailer hitch, they pulled the trees across the road.

"There are enough trees and rocks in this area it will be difficult for anyone to get through. I doubt anyone will take the trouble to clear the road."

"Well, we better go check out the Death Valley Junction site," Agent Sanders said. "I'm interested to see how the Army is handling it as it grows."

"Alright," Jack said getting back into his truck. "It's going to be dark soon. We'll have to get a motel and check it out in the morning."

"Let's go by Mona's Café and I'll buy you dinner," Dolly said.

"That's nice of you," Agent Sanders said.

Dolly shook her head. "Don't worry about it. I get the employee discount."

"So, Mona won't charge you?" Jack asked.

"Exactly."

Everybody laughed.

When they got to Mona's place an hour later, the place was packed, so Dolly went into the kitchen to see what was up. A moment later she came back with Mona.

"So, it seems everybody is leaving town now that the murders have been solved," Dolly said.

"Yes," Mona agreed. "That's right. All these people are pilgrims on their way home. If you wait a moment, I'll put a couple tables together as soon as they come open."

They all took a seat in the waiting area.

"Well, Captain Winslow must be proud of himself," Agent Sanders said.

"Well, at least we won't have to deal with the pilgrims while we conduct our investigation," Jack said. "Security should relax a bit around the Bat Mountain Site, too."

"I just wish we knew what we are dealing with," Agent Sanders said. "The situation is only going to get worse, pilgrims or no pilgrims."

32
Summoning the Speaker

Jimmy Malone and Linkh got up before dawn and began their journey to Death Valley Junction. They arrived just before noon and were greeted by an upbeat Captain Winslow. After giving Linkh a once over, he took them inside the site that was covered by a large canvas canopy. They noted the walls of the cathedral were already four feet tall.

"Well, I've done my job," Winslow said. "Now you two need to convince whatever creatures are in these walls to stop building and move back to the Bat Mountain Site where the situation can be contained."

Malone nodded. "Well, that will be up to them. Keep your fingers crossed that they will be reasonable."

"I will. What do you need to get started?"

"Nothing. Just clear everybody out and let us do our thing."

Captain Winslow nodded and ordered everyone to leave. Ten minutes later Malone and Linkh were alone.

"Okay. How does this work?" Malone asked.

Linkh looked around until his eyes settled on a dark spot in the middle of the structure. "Well, I'm going to go sit over there and lie down. It looks pretty cool and comfortable. It might appear that I'm going to sleep, but actually, I'll be in deep concentration, so make sure nobody disturbs me."

"Alright," Malone said looking for a place to sit down. He started to sit on one of the walls and then thought better of it.

Linkh went over to his spot and settled in. After closing his eyes, he tried to summon the Nanomite Speaker in his mind. The Speaker was the Nanomite given the duty to communicate with humans. He had no authority but simply passed on communications from humans to all the Nanomite Smarmmasters.

"Speaker. I'm a Linkh Leode, a Seafolken from Ock Mezan. I traveled with you from Tarizon to Earth. Please talk to me. We have much to discuss."

There was no response so he stretched, repositioned himself and tried again.

"Speaker. I'm the Seafolken from Ock Mezan who traveled with you from Tarizon to Earth. Please talk to me. There is much at stake."

There was still no answer so Linkh cleared his mind of all thoughts and then tried again, *"Talk to me Speaker. The future of your life-form on Earth is at risk. We must try to work out this disagreement with the humans or there will be dire consequences."*

"The humans here are just as deceitful as the ones on Tarizon," the Speaker thought. *"They don't honor their agreements."*

"They tried to honor it," Linkh thought. *"It was only unfortunate circumstances that caused the trouble to begin."*

"To Nanomites, when it comes to action, trying and doing are the same. We intend to do everything that happens."

"Yes, and that is an honest way to deal with people, but you have to understand humans don't act collectively for the human race like the swarmmasters do for the Nanomites."

"That is why humans are always fighting. Everyone is doing what they want rather than what the consensus has decided is best for everyone."

"True. The Nanomites are wise in that regard, but you must take the humans as they come. You can't change them and war is not an option. It would be devastating for everyone and accomplish nothing."

"We must have justice. Those who have killed Nanomites must also be killed."

"That has already been done," Linkh thought. "The humans who have obstructed the peaceful settlement of the Nanomites or murdered Nanomites at the Bat Mountain Site, have been killed."

"You say that, but how can we know it is the truth? Did you see these humans brought to justice?"

"No, but your Nanomites at the Bat Mountain Site will know. When you return there, they will tell you it is true."

"But if they did not confirm it as the truth, it would be too late for us to protect ourselves and if the humans wanted to kill us all, as they did in Shisk, we would be defenseless to stop them."

"Perhaps you could send a messenger to your swarms at the Bat Mountain Site and get confirmation. If what I say is true you could then return without fear of treachery."

"That is a rational approach to the situation, but all the swarmmasters must consider this action before I can agree. Come back here when the sun rises and we will have an answer."

"Alright. I will return when the sun rises," Linkh agreed.

Linkh stood up slowly and walked out from underneath the canopy. Malone came over to him quickly.

"So, how did it go?"

"They will need time to reach a consensus. We'll know in the morning."

Malone sighed. "Why so long?"

"They cannot act unless a majority agree."

"I thought they did that instantaneously?"

"Normally they do, but this is a complicated situation and immediate action is not necessary. So we must wait."

"Alright then, we'll wait, but I've got to go report to General Thornton. Give me a minute and then we'll go to the Bat Mountain Site to spend the night. They'll have a tent we can stay in and you can confer with the Nanomites there to tell them what is going on."

"That is a good idea. I will walk around and take in the landscape while I wait."

"Don't stray too far. I don't want to lose you."

"I won't."

Malone went to the communication's tent and got on the telephone with General Thornton. The general was not happy about the delay, but Malone assured him there was no choice, so he accepted the facts as they were and ordered him to report to him immediately after the sunrise meeting.

All the swarmmasters had been in on the Speaker's connection with Linkh. They immediately began to confer. *"The humans can't be trusted....They are no different here on Earth as they were on Tarizon, deceitful, evil....They say killing our brothers and sisters was an accident. Perhaps it was. We should give them the benefit of the doubt....No! It's a trick. They just want to gather us all together and slaughter us. We must escape now while we have a chance. . . .It is our duty to survive. We came to Earth to guarantee the survival of our life-form. We cannot betray that duty?. . . But the humans could wipe us out easily. . . .Not so easily. We could disburse and start cathedrals all over the desert. This desert is abundant with all that we need to thrive. . . .But we have a treaty. The humans say they will honor it. . . We had a treaty, but the humans have not honored it. We are no longer bound by it. . . . Do we have a consensus? . . . We do."*

33
Collapse

Agent Sanders watched the big cowboy through binoculars wondering who he was and what he was doing. She recognized Jimmy Malone as a CIA operative who worked directly with the President and General Thornton. This puzzled her.

"Who is that guy?" Jack asked.

"I don't know. He's someone the CIA has brought in. Some kind of a consultant I would guess."

"A biologist perhaps?"

"Possibly. He appears to be taking a nap."

Jack laughed. "Really. Sounds like a government consultant."

"I wonder how much he's charging the taxpayers for the nap," George snorted.

"So, why would somebody be napping close to where the rock monster is present?" Cindy asked.

Jack pondered that question. "Well, if it were possible to communicate with a microorganism it couldn't be done with voices. The microorganism wouldn't understand English even if they had ears. It would have to be with the mind."

"That's what I was thinking," Cindy said.

George nodded. "I think you're on to something. This guy must be communicating telepathically."

Agent Sanders frowned. "That's easy to say, but do you actually know anybody who can communicate telepathically?"

"No," George admitted. "But obviously there's a lot the government keeps secret."

"Well, if we had people who could read minds I'm sure the FBI would know about it."

"Do your superiors tell you all their secrets?" Jack asked.

"No," Agent Sanders acknowledged. "But that one would be so useful in law enforcement, I'm sure I would have heard about it."

"Assuming you're right," George said. "Then we are back to the alien equation. Could that huge man with very strange looking skin be an alien?"

Agent Sanders put the binoculars to her eyes again and studied the man. "Well, now that you mention it he looks extremely muscular and fit. Oh, my."

"What is it?" Jack asked.

"There's still a price tag on the side of his jeans."

"Really. What do you think that means?"

"It means he just bought them. So, it's probably a disguise," Cindy suggested.

"If you look close, it doesn't even fit him."

"Everyone looked at her. Agent Sanders smiled. "Very good, Cindy."

"So, how do we find out more about this guy?" Jack asked.

"We keep an eye on him," Agent Sanders replied. "We need to know everything he does."

"I know someone in this neighborhood who will let us use their yard for surveillance," Jack said.

"How well do you know them?" Agent Sanders asked. "We can't let anyone find out we are investigating the Army."

"I know. It's not a problem. It's one of my employees, Barry Flint. We go way back."

"Okay, the rest of us can go back to the college and start piecing together what we have learned so far. I need to report into my supervisor too."

"Sounds good," Jack said. "We'll check in with you tomorrow."

Agent Sanders, George and Cindy left in her car and Jack and Dolly drove their truck over to Flint's house. Flint was out front watering his lawn. He waved when he saw it was Jack approaching.

"What are you doing around here?" Barry asked.

"Watching the Army process the crime scene."

Barry nodded. "Yeah. It's kind of scary what happened, huh?"

"It sure is. . . . Hey. This is my girlfriend Dolly."

Dolly smiled and extended her hand. Barry shook it gingerly.

"Nice to meet you."

"So, Barry. I'm not buying the Army's explanation of the murders, are you?"

"No. Reverend Little gets carried away at times, but I don't think he is a killer."

"Neither do I, and I don't like the government coming in trying to protect the real killer. We need to get to the bottom of what's going on at the Bat Mountain Site. It's no goddam geological uplift. There's something going on out there and I want to know what it is."

"I agree, but what can we do about it?"

"Well, one thing is to let me and Dolly hang out here tonight. There's something strange going on at the Hanson place and we want to keep an eye on it."

"That's fine. Josie's off to school, so we've got a spare bedroom."

"Actually, we'd like to use your rooftop if you don't mind. I want to keep a set of binoculars on what's going on over there."

"No problem. Is there anything I can do to help?"

"No. Just keep what we're doing to yourself, okay. If the Army finds out we're watching them they might try to stop us."

"Not a problem, but someone might spot you on the roof."

"We'll wear dark clothing and wait until the sun goes down to go up there."

Barry nodded and invited them into the house. They talked and Mrs. Flint invited them for supper. After they ate they climbed onto the roof, found a comfortable spot, and took turns watching the place. Nothing happened during the night but at first dawn Jack spotted the big cowboy and Malone drive up. The cowboy went back under the canopy and took the same position he'd been in the day before. Jack wondered what they were talking about, if indeed that was what was going on.

After a minute, the cowboy abruptly sat up and sprang to his knees. He was starting to stand up when the ground began to vibrate causing a rumbling sound like thunder. Then the ground began to shake violently. Jack shook Dolly who had fallen asleep.

"Get up! Something's happening."

Dolly's eyes opened and she rolled onto her knees. "What is it?"

Just as she said it the ground all around the Hanson property gave way. Jack saw Jimmy Malone, who'd been standing just outside the canopy, try to run away but the ground beneath him fell away. The cowboy was gone too, having been devoured by the huge sinkhole that stretched at least a hundred yards across.

"What happened?" Dolly exclaimed.

"I don't know, but the Cowboy and Malone are gone. We better get down there and see if we can see them."

They scampered down the ladder as Barry came running out of the house. "What's going on! I heard a horrible noise."

"The ground has collapsed. We better get over and see if we can rescue anybody."

They all three ran across the street and down the block to where Hanson's lot used to be. When they reached the rim, they peered down and saw nothing but dust.

"I can't see a thing," Dolly complained.

"Oh, my God!" Barry exclaimed. "It must be fifty feet deep."

"Can you see anybody?" Jack asked.

"No, I can't—wait, there's something moving over there!" Dolly replied.

Jack looked over where she was pointing and saw the cowboy hanging onto a ledge about twenty feet below the rim. "We need a rope," Jack said.

"I've got one in the garage," Barry said. "I'll go get it."

Several dozen neighbors were now huddled around looking down into the pit. "What happened?" someone asked.

"It's a big sinkhole," Jack replied. "Two people are down there. You can see one of them, so we're going to try and rescue him. Someone call the fire department."

A few moments later Barry returned with the rope. "Here you go!" he yelled.

Jack took the rope and ran over to a spot directly above the cowboy. Then he tied a loop on one end and lowered it down until the cowboy could reach it. The man put one foot in the loop and nodded for them to pull him out. Jack and Barry tried to pull him out but he was too heavy.

Jack looked over at the crowd. "A little help, please!"

Two men came rushing over and between all four of them they were able to pull the cowboy out of the sinkhole.

"Are you okay?" Jack asked as the cowboy climbed out.

"I think so," he replied seeming a bit dazed.

"Who are you?" Jack asked.

The man didn't reply but just gave Jack a hard look. "You saved my life."

"Not really," Jack said. "The fire department would have got you out had we not done it."

"No. I couldn't have held on much longer."

"Well, I'm glad we could help, but you didn't tell us your name."

"Linkh Leode," he replied.

Sirens began wailing in the distance and Linkh looked in that direction nervously.

"Were you here with Agent Malone?" Jack asked.

Linkh looked at Jack seeming surprised by the question. "Do you know Jimmy?"

"Not really. Agent Sanders pointed him out to me. She knows him."

"Can you take me to him? I can't be found by the authorities. We must leave now."

"Sure. We'll take you to her."

"Oh. Agent Sanders is a woman. Okay."

"Come on," Jack replied taking Linkh's arm.

They started jogging toward Barry's house as fire trucks rolled up. When they got there, they went inside and Barry's wife attended to Linkh's scrapes and bruises. Then Jack, Dolly and Linkh got in the truck and drove off. Jack couldn't believe their good fortune to have saved Linkh's life. He wondered if he would tell them anything.

"So, Linkh, do you know what caused the ground to collapse?" Jack said smiling at him.

"Yes, but I'm not at liberty to discuss it."

Jack noted that Linkh spoke English quite well but he had an unusual accent. Jack knew he wasn't American. "I hope they're able to rescue Jimmy. That would be a horrible way to die."

"Yes, but I don't think they will. I saw him fall deep into the hole. I was only able to save myself because I knew what was about to happen."

"Really? How did you know that?"

"I was warned."

"By whom?" Jack asked.

"I'm not at liberty to say. It's classified, as Jimmy called it."

"It looked like you were communicating with someone," Jack said.

Linkh looked at Jack curiously. "How did you know that?"

"Well it seems obvious that there is some sort of microorganism in the walls that were growing under the canopy. I was the one who discovered the Bat Mountain Site in the beginning, so I know there is another cathedral under construction here."

"Oh, you're the Jack Carpenter that Malone is always complaining about."

Jack nodded. "Yes. I'm sure that's me."

"He doesn't like you. He says you are the cause of all his troubles."

"Is that right? Well, from his perspective that's probably true, but I'm just trying to figure out what's going on."

"I shouldn't talk to you, but since you saved my life I'll tell you a few things, if you swear to your God that you won't tell anyone how you learned of it."

"Absolutely, I swear."

"I am not from this world."

Jack looked at Dolly and swallowed hard. He looked back at Linkh. "Okay. I was wondering about that."

34
Missing in Action

General Thornton was stunned when he got the news that Jimmy Malone was missing and presumed dead. Even worse was the situation with the alien Linkh Leode. If he were dead he'd have to tell Kulchz and he didn't know how he and the rest of the diplomatic mission would take it. If Linkh were alive, where was he? Witnesses had reported that he'd been rescued by Jack Carpenter and some of the bystanders at the Hanson home and then driven off in Jack's truck toward town about the time the Nanomites struck. Jack hadn't been seen since, so it was possible he and Linkh had been killed by the Nanomites. But he couldn't rely on that supposition without substantiation and, so far, he hadn't found any. He took a deep breath and then dialed the White House. The president's secretary put him through.

"General Thornton?"

"Yes, Mr. President."

"This can't be good that you're calling me directly."

"No, sir. It's not. Jimmy Malone is missing and presumed dead."

"What? You've got to be kidding?"

"No. I wish I were."

"What happened?"

Thornton briefed the President on the situation.

"You're telling me a private citizen has custody of one of our aliens?"

"Well, that's a distinct possibility, sir. We have to assume it is true and act accordingly."

"I thought you guys were taking care of Jack Carpenter!" the President said angrily.

"Jimmy had someone on that but apparently there were complications."

"If Jack Carpenter takes our alien visitor to the press or even the police or FBI, we're screwed."

"I know. We won't let that happen. Captain Winslow has a half dozen of his top investigators out looking for Carpenter as we speak. I'm sure they'll find him."

"We'll have to get another liaison from the CIA to replace Malone."

"Yes, I have already talked to the Director about that. An agent, code-named Mo, is being assigned and the Director has personally briefed him."

"Good. Now what is being done to stop these Nanomites?"

"Ah. Nothing yet. I'm afraid we're going to have to go back to Kulchz and get some ideas on how to contain them. Since they travel underground and through rock it's not going to be an easy task."

"You better get Mo on it ASAP. I can't believe something so small could cause so much trouble."

"Apparently there are trillions of them and together they can move mountains."

"Well, you need to find out from Kulchz how to destroy them. I can't have any more buildings being swallowed up."

"Yes, Mr. President," I'll get right on it."

"Do that and report back to me tomorrow. You must find the alien and silence anyone who has interacted with him. If it's discovered we have a treaty with an alien world, life on Earth as we know it will be over."

"Yes, sir," General Thornton replied. "I know. We'll find him."

General Thornton hung up and took a deep breath. He had a splitting headache so he opened his middle drawer, pulled out a bottle of aspirin and shook out three of them. He popped them in his mouth, picked up a water bottle off his desk, and chased them down. After taking a moment to collect his thoughts, he called Captain Winslow who was still at Death Valley Junction trying to make sense of what had happened.

"Captain Winslow," he said.

"Captain, this is General Thornton."

"Oh. Hi, General."

"Any luck finding Jimmy Malone or our consultant?"

"We've pulled out Malone's body but there is no sign of the consultant."

"So, Malone's really dead? I can't believe it. I just saw him a couple days ago."

"Yes, it happened so suddenly. They came early this morning before the forensic crew got on the job. I didn't even know they were on site."

"So, no sign of the consultant?"

"Right."

"I've heard he was rescued by Jack Carpenter. Is that true?"

"That's affirmative. Apparently, Carpenter was watching the Hanson place when Malone and the consultant came to visit. I don't know what Malone and the consultant were doing here."

"I sent them there to see if they could help you out."

"Really? Help me out, how?"

"I can't say, but it's urgent that the consultant be found immediately. He possesses classified information that must be protected at all cost."

"I'll get a team together to search for him."

"Good. Any idea where they might be?"

"Yes. They probably went up to Deep Springs College up at Lone Pine where George Palmer works. I have a contact there who's keeping an eye on Palmer for me."

"It's imperative that you take the consultant alive. He's a diplomat and if he's killed there will be hell to pay."

"What about the others? George usually travels with an assistant, Cindy I think her name is, and Jack is usually with Dolly from Mona's Café."

"Do what you have to do, but we have to put a stop to their investigation. It could undermine our case."

"Yes, sir."

"How is the prosecution coming along?"

"We have Reverend Little in custody along with Barnes and Lizzy Arnold. The bodyguard apparently got word that we were looking for him and disappeared."

"Don't you need him to effectively prosecute the cases?"

"No, he's the killer so we want him, but he's not critical to the prosecution of the others."

"Where was he seen last?"

"He drove the Reverend home two nights ago but didn't show up the next morning."

"Is anybody talking yet?"

"Lizzy Arnold is cooperating, but she claims to know nothing about any murders. She does admit to knowing about the fake healings, but claims to have found out about them after the fact when she witnessed Reverend Little pay off the actors."

"So, with her testimony and the undercover officers, are we okay?"

"I think so. It may actually help that the bodyguard is missing. He might come up with an alibi that could undermine the whole case."

"Then if he's found, shut him up for good."

"Yes, sir. Understood."

"Alright. Find the consultant and bring him to me. Don't let him talk to anyone, no phone calls or any contact with anyone before I see him."

"Yes, sir."

General Thornton hung up wondering what he would do if the consultant weren't found. Then he thought of the new CIA liaison, Mo. That was his job to straighten out this mess. Thornton prayed he'd have some good ideas on how to do it.

35
Linkh

Jack took in a deep breath then glanced at Dolly who looked terrified.

"What world are you from?" he asked Linkh.

"A Planet millions of miles away called Tarizon."

"How long did it take you to get here?"

"About an Earth year."

"Then you traveled faster than light?"

"Yes, we have recently developed that technology."

"Wow! That's hard to imagine."

"Yes, we haven't done a lot of space exploration yet. Our planet's been at war for over a century and although we are at peace for the moment, now we are suffering from the effects of many super volcanic eruptions. We only came to Earth because we knew of its existence from our history books."

"How did Earth fit into your history?"

"Earth and Tarizon were both settled by humans from the same planet, Pharidon."

"Pharidon? That must have been a long time ago. It's not in any of our history books."

"So I've been told," Linkh said.

"So, what about the microorganism that lives in the crystal walls?" Jack asked.

"The microorganisms you speak of are actually a life-form from Tarizon called the Nanomites. They must have existed on Earth at one time as our ancestors brought all the life-forms, animals, birds, and plants from Pharidon. The Nanomites have always lived in peace on our planet until just recently when the humans learned how to communicate with them. We taught them a lot about dishonesty and deceit. Much of our planet's buildings had been destroyed by tremors, tidal waves and volcanoes, so an agreement was struck with the Nanomites to build new structures in return for the nutrients the Nanomites needed to thrive and for the right to occupy the buildings that they constructed. It would have worked out well, had the humans lived up to the terms of the contract."

"Yes, I can see they are fine builders," Jack replied.

"But the humans broke the treaty and refused to let the Nanomites live in the structures after they were built. Instead, they made them live in overcrowded farms and didn't respect their civil rights. War broke out between the humans and the Nanomites after millions of Nanomites were murdered as a matter of convenience to their caretakers. The persons responsible were charged with genocide but acquitted when the Supreme Council of Interpreters determined that the Nanomites were not a life-form protected by the Supreme Mandate."

"The Supreme Mandate?"

"Yes. It's like your constitution."

"It sounds like your planet is much like Earth. We have the same sort of problems here. It's difficult, if not impossible, to obtain justice sometimes."

"Yes, it's the nature of the human race, I'm afraid. The war did not last long but the Nanomites did manage to nearly destroy the capital city of Shisk by weakening many of its skyscrapers and undermining the ground beneath them until they collapsed. Thousands died. So, back at Death Valley Junction when the Nanomites refused to return to the Bat Mountain Site, I knew they intended to fight."

"I see. So, where do you think the Nanomites will strike next?"

"I don't know for sure, but they will look for the tallest and largest buildings."

"There aren't any tall buildings around here," Dolly noted. "The largest building is the hotel downtown."

"They also like to destroy bridges and highways to disrupt transportation."

Dolly sighed worriedly. "We should warn the manager of the hotel. He should evacuate the place."

Jack looked back at Dolly, slammed on the brakes and did a screeching U-turn. They raced back toward town and immediately saw a cloud of dust and smoke rising from the small city. When they got to the outskirts of town they realized they were too late. The hotel and buildings around it had collapsed and fires were raging everywhere. They stopped and got out of their truck when they came to a section of the road that had sunk ten feet in just minutes. They looked out over at Death Valley Junction in shock.

"Why are they doing this?" Jack asked. "These people didn't even know the Nanomites existed."

"Yes. I told them that, but they believe your government is trying to enslave them as the humans did on my planet. The Nanomites have no tolerance for deceit."

"How did you stop the war on Tarizon?"

"There were only two humans on Tarizon that the Nanomites trusted, a mutant named Threebeard and his sister, Artis. Artis warned the Nanomites not to enter into the contract with the government but they didn't listen. So when Artis and Threebeard came to them as negotiators from the newly elected government seeking peace, the Nanomites listened to them and a treaty was worked out. The Nanomites knew that the government was sending a diplomatic ship to Earth, so one of the provisions of the treaty was that a Nanomite colony be brought here. This was important because nobody was certain that Tarizon would survive the cataclysmic volcanic eruptions, tremors, floods and wildfires that had plagued the planet for almost a year. So, if Tarizon became uninhabitable the Nanomites wanted to be sure its life-form would survive on Earth."

"So," Jack said. "When I discovered the Nanomites building their new home and people heard about it, the Nanomites got nervous."

"Yes, particularly when the Army came in with troops and set up a camp and flocks of pilgrims came to watch their cathedral grow."

"Cathedral? They are building a cathedral?"

"That's what we call a Nanomite city. It looks like a cathedral. That's where our government, Central Authority, got the idea of having the Nanomites build structures for us."

"I see. So, the Nanomites thought they had been betrayed again," Jack said.

"Yes, that is what they believed and when a man actually attacked them with a saw and a sledge hammer, their fears were confirmed."

"Right, he was just trying to get a sample of the crystal for a museum. He didn't know he was killing Nanomites."

Linkh shook his head sadly. "I know, but your government has not handled the situation well by keeping secrets from its people."

"That's because they are afraid to tell the American people the truth," Dolly replied. "They don't think we can handle it."

Linkh sighed. "Leaders often think they know what is best for the masses, but they are usually wrong."

Jack nodded. "Well, we better get you to Agent Sanders," Jack said. "There's nothing we can do here."

They got back into the truck, turned around and drove off. They made it to Lone Pine before noon. George did a double take when they walked in with Linkh. He summoned Agent Sanders who was in her temporary office. She came out and her mouth dropped.

"George, Agent Sanders. I'd like you to meet Linkh Leode. He's a Seafolken from the Planet Tarizon."

George opened his mouth but no words came out. Agent Sanders smiled broadly. "It's nice to meet you, Linkh. How in the hell did Jack find you?"

Jack looked around nervously and then suggested they all go to George's apartment where they could talk privately. When they had moved their meeting there and settled in, Jack filled them in on what had happened at Death Valley Junction.

"Oh, my God. I had no idea they were sentient beings."

"Yes, the swarmmasters have the intelligence and the workers have the strength and manual dexterity."

"What do they look like?" Agent Sanders asked.

"I have been told that if you could see them they have a large head, two legs, four arms and two sets of wings. The wings fold inward and only appear in the rare instances that the Nanomites are forced out of a solid object. The second set of arms can also act as legs."

"Wow! So, are you going to be in trouble for talking to us?" Agent Sanders asked.

"Yes, if they find out. They would execute me for treason."

"So, why are you taking that risk by talking to us?"

"Because Jack saved my life for one thing. But also, not long ago I was but a slave. Many in the government believe I should be treated like one still. So, I have no great loyalty to this government and will not participate in its treachery. I came with Agent Malone to try to stop a war but I have failed. So, maybe if you know the truth you can do something to stop it yourselves."

Jack sighed. "I'm afraid we have another problem."

"What other problem?" Linkh asked.

"There's another Nanomite site that the government doesn't even know about yet."

Linkh sighed. "How did that happen?"

"It's a long story," Jack said and then explained what had happened at the Independence Site.

"We better check the news and see how bad it is in Death Valley Junction," Cindy suggested.

George nodded. "Good idea."

Cindy got up and turned on the TV. The Noon News was already in progress. The camera was showing the devastation in Death Valley Junction.

"An earthquake with a magnitude of 7.5 on the Richter scale jolted the western Mojave Desert around Death Valley, California, early today, authorities reported. The tremble was recorded at the California Institute of Technology. The center of the quake was about 170 miles northeast of Los Angeles along the Death Valley fault line. Most of the downtown area of Death Valley Junction was destroyed and thirty-seven persons were killed with seventeen others missing. What buildings didn't fall down were destroyed by numerous fires that swept the area fueled by severed gas lines.

"The home of the late Deputy Sheriff, Mark Hanson, that was being worked as a crime scene by the Army Criminal Investigation Command, was actually swallowed up by the quake. Jimmy Malone of the Central Intelligence Agency and a government consultant, who were seen at the crime scene minutes before the quake, are missing and presumed dead. Neither the Army or the CIA have responded to our inquiry as to why an employee of the CIA was at the site.

"In other news—"

Cindy shut off the TV.

"Well, they think you're dead, Linkh," Jack said.

"Yes. That's good news."

"If it's true. They may be trying to lure us into a false sense of security. We have to assume they know you left with me after the earthquake."

"That wasn't an earthquake," George said. "Cal Tech is the only place reporting it."

"No, it wasn't," Linkh agreed.

"Someone in the government called in a favor at Cal Tech and got them to run the earthquake story," George said.

"You're probably right," Jack agreed.

"So, now what do we do?" Dolly asked.

"It's up to Linkh," Agent Sanders said. "Linkh. We can return you to your ship if that's what you want or you can stay with us and we'll find a place for you to hide."

"I'd like to help you stop the Nanomites from waging war first. When that's done, then I'll consider my options and make a choice."

"Why don't we go back to the Independence site?" Jack said. "I've got a construction trailer there we can stay in while we try to figure out how to stop the Nanomites."

"Aren't you afraid they'll trigger another earthquake there?" George asked.

"I don't think so. There are no buildings other than the one they are constructing and we will stay clear so they won't have any reason to attack us. Plus, we have to be close by to figure out how to deal with them."

"Okay," Agent Sanders said, "but don't take any action without talking to me about it first. I'm going to try to convince my boss that the FBI needs to get involved in helping to neutralize this threat."

"You think that's possible given the President's directive for them to stay out of it?"

"Yes, if I can convince him of the seriousness of the threat."

"Okay. I've got a construction phone on site so we can keep in touch."

After going out to a local restaurant for lunch, Jack, Dolly and Linkh drove back to the Independence site. When they got to the fallen tree across the road Jack went off-road across a meadow and over a hill where he caught the road again. When they got to the construction trailer they got out and admired the Nanomite cathedral that was rising quickly in the distance and was already nearly 20 feet tall. Jack told Linkh how much faster they were building their new home, nearly a foot a day rather than the five inches at Bat Mountain.

"Yes, that is how they do it on Tarizon. All the materials are brought to the construction site and placed in piles as you have done. This makes it convenient for the Nanomites to build, so the work goes quickly."

That evening, sitting on a fallen log around a campfire, Linkh told Jack more about the Nanomites and their history and they discussed ways to stop them.

"The way they kept the Nanomites on their farms was to build moats around them and fill them with toxic chemicals that would seep deep into the ground so the Nanomites would be killed if they tried to pass under the moat."

Jack cringed at that idea, fearing the long-term consequences to the environment. "There's got to be another way."

"Water will work too but it won't necessarily kill the Nanomites. It will keep them contained as long as you can keep the area saturated. They don't work or travel well in water so they will go to great lengths to avoid it."

"So, we have to dig a moat. That won't be an easy task in the desert where the temperature can get as high as 135 degrees and water is scarce."

"Fire will work too, but it's difficult to control and millions of Nanomites will likely die before they can be driven back."

"So, how do you communicate with them?"

"Telepathically. Artis taught the Nanomites Tari, the official language of Tarizon, so any human with that gift could theoretically talk to them."

"Do they think like humans? I mean even if you communicate with them, is there really understanding?"

"No. Not at first. When they are debating an issue all you hear are a jumble of random thoughts, some in Tari and mostly in pictures, but when they reach a consensus, one Swarmmaster speaks for everyone and they can be understood."

"That must be very cool to be able to see into someone's mind," Jack said.

"Yes, it makes you feel very close to them."

"If the people from Tarizon are related to all of us on Earth, I wonder why some of your people can talk telepathically but no one here on Earth has that ability?"

"Most humans have the capability to communicate telepathically but few master it. On Tarizon you can train to improve your telepathic skills."

"Are you saying I could communicate that way?" Jack asked.

"Yes. I'm sure you could to the extent of your gift."

"How do you find out if you have the gift?"

Linkh shrugged. "I could probably tell, if you will open your mind to me."

"How do I do that?"

Linkh turned toward Jack. "Just relax and look me in the eyes," he said. "Now concentrate on something pleasant from the past. If you feel something pressing on your mind, don't resist it."

Jack did as he was told and Linkh gazed into his mind. Jack felt a strange sensation like a gentle wind in his head. He shook his head trying to clear it.

"Don't resist," Linkh reminded him.

Jack took a deep breath and tried to relax his neck and shoulders. He felt the wind again and tried to enjoy the strange feeling.

Linkh smiled. "You were thinking of a beach on a tropical island. There was a woman you had feelings for but now there is only sadness."

Jack smiled. "Very good. I was thinking of my honeymoon to Hawaii. My wife and I are divorced now."

"Well, I think you do have the gift. I can't tell the strength yet but you should try to develop it."

"How do I do that?"

"Look into my eyes and concentrate. Try to look through them and into my mind."

Jack frowned. "I don't know how to do that."

"You do it by thinking it. Look into my eyes and look for a door. When you see it, open the door and look into my mind."

Jack did what he was told but saw nothing.

"Look for the door. Concentrate."

Jack looked again trying harder to concentrate but saw nothing but Linkh's pale blue eyes. "It's not working."

"Well, it takes a lot of practice. Just work on it every day and eventually it might come to you. The trick is to make yourself believe it can happen. If you don't believe you can do it, it will never happen."

When it came time to go to bed Dolly made up the sofa for Linkh and she and Jack took the single bedroom in the trailer. Jack tried to go to sleep but it was a futile effort as his mind raced over the day's events, in particular the fact that he had an alien from another planet sleeping in the next room who could read his mind. He liked Linkh a lot and thought he could trust him, but he was worried about the other aliens, the ones who considered Linkh a slave. Of course, what was primarily keeping him awake was the big question—how could they stop the growing Nanomite population and keep them from getting to a bigger city where they might kill thousands of innocent people and cause millions of dollars in damages.

36
On the Run

After Jack left, Agent Sanders went back to her office to check in with Joe Spencer. She couldn't wait to hear his reaction to her report.

"You're telling me you have an alien from another planet in your custody?" Joe asked skeptically.

"Yes, sir. The CIA agent, Jimmy Malone, had him but when the Hanson place was swallowed up they got separated and Jack was only able to save Linkh."

"His name is Linkh?"

"Yes. Linkh Leode."

"Jesus. The Director knew the President was keeping something from him, but nothing like this."

"Ah. You should probably not report this to your superiors quite yet. Linkh may want to go back to his ship, so we don't want to do anything that would get him in trouble. He says if they found out he's cooperating with us, they'll summarily execute him."

"Okay. I'll need some time to get my head around this anyway. So, how can I help you now?"

"While you're getting your head around that, consider that the Nanomites are a sentient life-form and if we kill them, we'll be committing genocide."

There was silence on the line. "Joe?"

"I'm here. My heart was pounding so hard I couldn't hear you."

She laughed. "The Army must know about the Nanomites, at least I hope they do. Anyway, they can deal with the ones at Death Valley Junction for now. I don't think they have anywhere to go since it's such an isolated area. But we need help at the Independence site. Jack and Linkh are there now trying to figure out how to contain them."

"Okay, what do you need?"

"I'm not sure right now, but Jack will be calling me later with a plan, and then I'll have a better idea what to tell you. For now, just get a team ready to fight, but you won't need bullets."

Joe laughed. "Thanks a lot."

"Okay. Talk to you later," Agent Sanders said and hung up.

She got up and walked back to George's office. Cindy and George were looking rather pale. "What's wrong?"

"We're under surveillance apparently. Cindy went out to get us some fast food for dinner and someone followed her."

Agent Sanders looked at Cindy. "Are you sure?"

"Yes, when I noticed them, I went around the block and took an unscheduled stop at the grocery store. When I left ten minutes later, they were back on my tail. I came straight back here."

"Okay, we'll have to move our operation. Call a cab and have them meet you at the auditorium. I noticed there is a performance there tonight and people will be coming and going."

"A cab?"

"Yes. Your car probably has a tracking device on it by now, or a bomb."

"Oh, God!" Cindy exclaimed. "Are you serious?"

She nodded. "Yes, the government has been hiding the fact that there are aliens among us, so I'm sure they wouldn't hesitate a moment to kill us."

"Oh, Jesus," Cindy moaned.

"Disguise yourselves as best you can and then sneak over to the auditorium. When the cab gets there take it to the mall. Have them let you off on the south entrance. They don't know I'm here, so I'll be waiting for you at the north entrance."

"Okay, that sounds good," George said. "Where are we going to go?"

"To help Jack and Linkh stop the Nanomites," Agent Sanders replied.

"Right. . . . I sure hope they have some idea how to do it."

George rolled his eyes. "Me too."

Agent Sanders sighed and then went back to her office to pack up her things. A moment later she went out the back exit and rushed to her car. She saw a suspicious vehicle with two men in the front seat talking. They gave her a good look and one of them took her picture but they didn't leave their post. She got in her car and left without anyone following her. She drove to the gas station, got gas and a soda, and then went to the mall for the rendezvous. George and Cindy were nowhere to be seen, so she parked in a space with a good vantage point and waited. Eight minutes later George and Cindy walked out looking distracted. Agent Sanders started the engine and drove over to them. George and Cindy opened the door, jumped in the back seat and slid down so they wouldn't be seen.

"Step on it!' George urged. "There are two men following us."

Sanders gave it gas and they took off just as the two men came out of the mall entrance.

George sighed. "That was close."

"Did they see us?" Sanders asked.

"This was the only car around, so they probably figured out we were in it."

"Great. Fortunately, they won't know which direction we're heading, so they won't be able to follow us."

Just as Agent Sanders spoke they could hear a helicopter in the distance. Sanders looked out her drivers' side window. "Oh, crap! They've got air support."

"What are we going to do?" Cindy asked frantically.

"I don't know. It's going to be hard to lose a helicopter in such flat terrain."

"Go downtown," George said. "They won't be able to shoot at us or set down in the city.

"Good idea. If I can make a telephone call there may be a way to get rid of this helicopter."

Just then a bullet shattered their back window. "Oh, shit!" Cindy exclaimed as glass rained down upon her.

"Get down behind my seat," Sanders ordered as she increased her speed. They passed the city limits sign and a 40-mph speed sign as the speedometer hit 70.

"Over there!" George screamed. "Go into that gas station. I know the owner. You can use his telephone."

Sanders made a hard turn into the gas station and came to a screeching halt inside the garage bay. The owner who was working under the hood of an old Chevy looked up in shock. George got out and put up his hand.

"Sorry, Wally. We need to use your phone."

Wally nodded and motioned to his office. "Thanks," George said.

Sanders rushed inside the office and called Joe.

"Joe Spencer, here."

"Joe. You don't happen to have a bird anywhere near Lone Pine, do you?"

"Ah. There's one about thirty minutes out."

"Okay, there's an unmarked helicopter after us. They've taken a few shots at us and knocked out our back window. We're going to hang around downtown so it won't be easy for them to get to us. When your chopper gets here, we need it to keep them busy while we make our escape. We don't want to lead the Army to the Independence Site. If they find it they may do something rash like drop a bomb on it or something, and that will just make matters worse."

"Alright. I'll get it up there right away. Don't let them catch you."

"Don't worry. There's only two of them."

Two cars came screeching up in front of the gas station before the words got out of Agent Sanders' mouth. "Oh, Christ!" she exclaimed. "Gotta go." She disconnected and called the Lone Pine police.

"Lone Pine Police?"

"This is Agent Marcia Sanders of the FBI. I need back up at Wally's Garage near the intersection of Highways 395 and 136."

"Roger. I'll get the word out."

"Thanks," she said, hanging up the telephone and pulling out her gun.

Six men got out of the two vehicles with guns in hand and approached the garage cautiously. Agent Sanders fired a warning shot over their heads and they scampered back behind their vehicles. Sanders motioned for George and Cindy to stay out of sight. Two of the men ran from their cars to the side of the garage entrance just out of Sanders' view. She shot in their direction to deter them from going any farther. Sirens began to wail in the distance. The four men, cowering behind their vehicles, looked in the direction of the sirens. As they got closer one of them motioned to the others to get back in their cars. One car started its engine and drove off. The other one drove toward the garage, picked up the others and left just as a sheriff's squad car drove up.

Marcia showed the deputy her badge and pointed to the car turning the corner. "There they are. Don't let them get away!"

The deputy tore off after them as Marcia glared up at the helicopter hovering overhead. A few minutes later she heard another helicopter in the distance and was relieved when she recognized it to be one of the FBI's. When the pilot of the unmarked helicopter saw the approaching FBI chopper, he turned and headed back in the direction he'd come. As soon as they were in the clear Agent Sanders gathered up George and Cindy and they were back on the road, this time without anyone tailing them.

37
Desperate Alliance

Captain Winslow stood gazing at the Nanomite cathedral that now rose nearly thirty feet high. Most of the pilgrims and the media had left after Reverend Little had been arrested, but there was still one media truck and a few dozen pilgrims who stubbornly clung to the hope that the cathedral was real and that God was behind this desert miracle. Two headlights in the distance got the captain's attention. When it rolled up, General Thornton and Senator Rawlings got out along with a civilian. They all shook hands.

"This is Mo from the CIA," General Thornton said. "He'll be replacing Jimmy."

"Nice to meet you. We can talk in the headquarters conference room," he said pointing to a large tent in the middle of the camp.

A few moments later they all took seats around a large conference table. An enlisted man came by and asked if he could get any of them coffee or a soft drink. There were several requests that the soldier noted and then he left.

"Gentlemen," General Thornton said. "I've called this meeting as the situation is getting out of hand on almost every front. First, our efforts to contain the Nanomites at the Bat Mountain location has been a total failure. Secondly, contrary to their claim to be a peace-loving life-form they have demonstrated an actual belligerent nature and capacity to destroy anything in their path. Thirdly, we have apparently lost custody of an alien who was loaned to us to aid us in understanding and communicating with them. Finally, we have to assume our treaty with Tarizon has been discovered by several civilians and possibly an agent of the FBI. Needless to say, the situation is dire and we must get control of it immediately."

"Who is the FBI agent?" Mo asked.

"Agent Marcia Sanders was seen in Lone Pine with George Palmer and his girlfriend, Cindy Lee. We know they are working closely with Jack Carpenter and his assistant, Dolly Watson. Jack Carpenter was seen with the alien named Linkh Leode, a Seafolken, after the disaster at Death Valley Junction earlier this week."

Mo shook his head. "This is really bad. There's no telling how many people know about the aliens now."

"That's right," General Thornton agreed. "We've got to eliminate this threat immediately. They could go to the press at any time."

"Don't you think Marcia Sanders would have already reported the situation to her superiors?" Mo asked.

"Possibly. But I'm not so worried about the FBI. I assume the President can control them. It's the other four that can't be controlled. And, of course, we need to return the alien to his ship."

"Do we know where they are?" Malone asked.

"No. They were last seen in Lone Pine. We think they've been hiding out at Deep Springs College where Palmer and his assistant work. Jack, Dolly and the alien haven't been seen there for several days and George and Cindy left there today in the company of Agent Sanders."

"Where is Jack's office?" Rawlings asked.

"I don't know that he has one. He generally works out of his pickup or the construction trailer at his various job sites."

"That's a good place to start looking. Find out where all his job sites are located."

"That could take days," General Thornton said. "We've got to find them today."

"Well," Malone said. "We could send a chopper to take a look at each site. If they are there it should be fairly obvious—people walking around or cars parked near the construction trailer. If we can find the location of each of the sites they can be checked out today."

"I think I heard he does a lot of public jobs for the city, county and various school districts," Rawlings interjected. "Get someone to call over to the county building inspection department and they can probably give you a list of any projects Jack has in process."

Malone nodded. "I'll get someone to do that. In the meantime, what are you going to do to stop the Nanomites at Death Valley Junction?"

General Thornton looked at Mo. "Do you know much about the Nanomites?"

"According to our files they can be killed with either chemicals or explosives. The difficulty is killing all of them. They can move quickly and burrow deep underground, so it will be difficult to get them all. And if you miss any, those left can reproduce quickly if they have the right nutrients in the soil."

"Do they have the right nutrients at Death Valley Junction?" General Thornton asked.

"Yes, that's why they picked Death Valley to build their home. It has an abundance of the chemicals they need to sustain their life-form."

"Wonderful," Senator Rawlings spat.

"Well, we can't bomb Death Valley Junction obviously, so that leaves a chemical attack," General Thornton reasoned. "I'll get some people to start working on that. We'll have to evacuate the city, so innocent citizens don't get hurt."

"I'll contact the FBI and find out why agent Sanders is still working the case after the President pulled the FBI off it," Senator Rawlings advised.

"Yes, and Mo, you need to get a new team to hunt down Jack Carpenter and the others. We need to get the alien back in custody and the rest of them eliminated from the equation."

"Yes sir," Mo replied.

"We'll meet back here at 10:00 a.m. to make final preparations for an attack on Death Valley Junction and to see where we are at handling Jack Carpenter and his bunch."

38
Obstruction of Justice

After the meeting broke up, Senator Rawlings called Joe Spencer at the FBI.

"Senator, what can I do for you?" Joe said.

"You got the memo from the President about backing off the Bat Mountain investigations?"

"Yes, we've backed off as ordered."

"Then what's your agent, Marcia Sanders doing with George Palmer and his assistant?"

"I don't know. She's on vacation. Perhaps she knows them socially."

"On vacation? Do you expect me to believe that? There was a shootout in Lone Pine and she called in for backup from the Sheriff's office. An FBI chopper was seen in the area too."

"She was attacked without provocation by unidentified assailants. Of course, she called for backup. You'd do the same if you were attacked. You wouldn't happen to know who tried to kill her, would you?"

"I have no idea," Senator Rawlings lied. "But tell her to follow orders and take her vacation outside of the Mojave Desert. Captain Winslow is handling the Bat Mountain murders now and anyone interfering with his investigation will be charged with obstruction of justice."

"Nobody is trying to obstruct the investigation, but there is a lot of concern about what's going on at Bat Mountain and, in particular, Death Valley Junction," Joe noted. "What exactly is going on there? I know the official story is that it was an earthquake, however, there seems to be some controversy about whether there really was an earthquake or not."

"You saw the buildings collapse on the news. What else could it have been but an earthquake?"

"You tell me," Joe said.

"I don't have to tell you anything. Just get your people to back off or there will be repercussions."

"Are you threatening me?"

"No. I'm just stating a fact. The President will have no tolerance of anyone who disobeys his orders. And if Agent Sanders is working with Jack Carpenter, then we're going to have some serious issues."

"Jack Carpenter? What is he doing that's got your panties in a wad?"

"He was seen leaving with one of our consultants and we want him back immediately."

"Consultant? What kind of consultant?"

"That's classified."

Joe sighed. "Well, I don't have any details about Agent Sanders' vacation, but I'll pass on the message to her when she checks in. I just hope that you have control of the situation at Death Valley Junction and will call us for help if you need it."

"Don't sit by the phone," Senator Rawlings spat and hung up.

39
Sand

Jack woke up the next morning with a start. During the night, he had dreamed that the Nanomites had somehow gotten to LA and the city was in turmoil. Buildings were collapsing, fires raged throughout the city, and people were screaming all around him. He got up and looked outside in the dim light of dawn. The Nanomite cathedral was there looming even higher than the night before. He marveled at its beauty and how it glittered in the moonlight. *How can a life-form that is capable of such imagination and creativity also be responsible for so much death and destruction?* While he was thinking about this he heard an engine starting up. He looked in the direction of the noise and saw a dump trunk starting to leave with a load of his sand. He ran outside.

"Stop! You can't take that sand," he yelled but the truck kept on going.

He looked at the ground and saw several more tire tracks. Somebody was stealing his sand, he realized, and God only knew where they were taking it. He ran back into the trailer.

"Get up! Everybody up. Someone is stealing our sand."

Dolly opened her eyes and sat up. "What did you say?"

"Someone is stealing the sand with the Nanomites in it."

"Oh, my God!" she exclaimed scrambling to put on her clothes.

"How did they get past the fallen tree?" Linkh asked.

"I don't know. They must have cut it up and moved it off the road. Shit! I have no idea where they are taking it."

"Has anyone ever stolen your sand before?" Dolly asked.

"Yes. It's a big problem. I would have had security out here, but I didn't want anyone to see the cathedral."

"What if they take it to the city?" Dolly asked.

"Then we'll have another disaster like Death Valley Junction. In fact, I was having a nightmare before something woke me up. In it, LA was under attack."

"Holly crap!" Dolly said. "Do you think that's possible?"

"No. LA is a long way away, but no matter where the sand ends up, it will cause untold death and destruction. We've got to try to stop them."

"Call Agent Sanders. Maybe she can get the FBI to stop the trucks."

Jack nodded and went over to the phone. He dialed Agent Sanders' number but the phone just rang and rang. Jack shook his head. "No luck."

"We should go after them," Linkh suggested. "Maybe we can stop them."

"I doubt it. Since they are stealing the sand they won't stop for us."

"We've got to try," Dolly said.

Jack nodded. "Okay, let's get in the truck and go."

They all ran to the truck and jumped in. Soon they were traveling fast along the narrow road. When they got to where the road had been blocked, they saw the trees had been pushed to the side. Ten minutes later when they got to the main highway Jack stopped.

"Which way should we got? North goes to Bishop and south to Lone Pine, Bartlett and eventually LA."

"Did you find out who stole it last time?" Dolly asked.

"No. But we suspect it was a shady contractor out of Bartlett named Don Mason."

"Well, that's probably who did it this time."

Jack nodded and took off going south. As they were driving they saw a dark sedan approaching. When they went by the car slammed on its brakes and did a U-turn. Jack wondered who was following them until he realized it was Agent Sanders. He slowed down, pulled over and got out of the car. Agent Sanders pulled up behind and opened her window.

"Where are you going?" she asked.

"A dump truck just stole a load of sand inhabited by Nanomites. We have to stop them."

"Do you know where they are going?"

"No. We're going this direction just on a hunch, but they could just as easily be going north."

"Okay, keep going south. We'll go north. I've got a radio now and an FBI helicopter on call. I'll have them start looking too."

"Good. In the meantime, the Independence cathedral is wide open. The trees have been cleared off the road."

"Oh, great," she said shaking her head. "Okay. I'll get a roadblock set up."

"Thanks," Jack said and then ran back to his truck. He took off as Agent Sanders was getting on her radio.

40
The Extermination

Mo watched the end of a steady stream of cars roll by on their way out of Death Valley Junction marking the completion of the evacuation. Then he noticed a caravan of tanker trucks approaching from the opposite direction. General Thornton had called in sixty trucks filled with a very strong insecticide to be sprayed throughout the city in an effort to kill the Nanomites. He'd also arranged for an aerial spraying of the deadly poison to be sure there was a uniform application and every single one of them were killed. The lead truck stopped and the driver was given instructions for the operation. Five hundred soldiers had been called in to handle the job. They were told they were spraying to eradicate insects that had infested the area after the earthquake. Mo wondered if they would have followed their orders had they known they were committing genocide.

When the last truck had been given its orders, Mo went back to the headquarters tent where General Thornton, Senator Rawlings and Captain Winslow were monitoring the operation. They looked up when he entered the tent.

"How's it going?" General Thornton asked.

"Everyone should be in place in fifteen minutes."

"Good. We've given them nearly twenty-four hours to regroup. I just pray they haven't left the area."

"Unfortunately, there is no way of knowing where they are. It's like trying to swat a fly in the dark."

General Thornton shook his head. "You're right, but this is our best bet for now. We'll have to keep this area under surveillance for a while in case the bugs start building another cathedral. The moment one of them pops up, we'll be on them so fast they won't know what hit them."

Mo wondered if the Nanomites knew they were about to be slaughtered. *If they are truly intelligent beings they must realize there will be consequences for the destruction of a human city*.

"Sir, have we taken any precautions against a counterattack?" Mo asked.

Senator Rawlings laughed. "A counterattack? These are bugs for godsakes! What do you think they are going to do, launch an assault against our soldiers?"

Mo shrugged. "No. But if they are intelligent they may be concocting some type of plan in anticipation of what we are doing."

"Well, I seriously doubt they are all that smart. I will agree they may be fleeing. That would be a natural response, attack and then run, but if you are suggesting they are going to attack us today, I can't see it."

"Okay. Just a thought," Mo said. "But I wouldn't underestimate them if I were you."

"I'll take that under advisement," the General said and turned to an aide. "Okay, commence *Operation Desert Cleansing*."

The aide saluted and ran off to communicate the order to the troops. Just as he left, the ground around them began to rumble.

"What the hell?" Rawlings said as he was nearly knocked off his feet.

"Run!" Mo exclaimed. Without looking back, he took off running. As he did the ground beneath the tent began to give way. General Thornton, Senator Rawlings and several aides disappeared into the abyss. Captain

Malone ran and leaped to a rock that had stood firm and stood teetering on the brink. He looked down in horror into the dark sinkhole. A soldier ran over to him and offered a hand, but just as he reached for it, the rock gave way and he was gone. Mo stopped a half mile away panting heavily. He looked back at the cloud of dust and wondered no more about whether the Nanomites were sentient beings. In his mind, they were not only intelligent, but were cold, calculating killers, hell bent on ridding Earth of the human race.

When he'd caught his breath, Mo got up and walked briskly to the highway. He knew there was a gas station about two miles down the road where he could make a phone call. Upon reaching the highway, he started jogging along the center line. The temperature he guessed was nearly 110° and he had no water. He wasn't in very good shape either. Fitness had been a requirement when he joined the CIA, but it had taken a backseat as the years went by. His heart was beating so hard he could feel it pounding in his chest. Finally, his adrenalin gave out and he was forced to slow to a walk. Relief washed over him as he saw flashing lights ahead. As they got closer he realized it was a sheriff's car. The car slowed and stopped beside him. Deputy Lawson rolled down the window.

"Did you come from town?"

Mo nodded. "Yes, there was another earthquake. The HQ tent fell into a sinkhole. General Thornton and Senator Rawlings were swallowed up. I'm not sure about Captain Malone. He was hanging on the edge when I saw him last. I was going to make a call for help."

"I'll radio it in. You better get in out of the heat."

Mo didn't want to involve the sheriff's office, but knew the deputy wouldn't take no for an answer. "Okay, but can you take me to the gas station up the road? I've got to call into my superiors."

Mo got into the air-conditioned car and breathed a sigh of relief. He closed his eyes and took a deep breath.

"Who are you anyway?" Lawson said as he made a quick U-turn and drove south.

"Harold Smith," Mo lied. "I'm a special consultant to the Army working with General Thornton on the Death Valley Junction recovery effort."

"Did you take over Jimmy Malone's job?" Lawson asked.

Mo was shocked by the question. "How did you figure that out?"

"Well, I figured Malone was doing something important, so when he was killed, the Army would get someone to replace him."

"Did you know Jimmy well?"

"No. Not really. We worked together a bit over at the Bat Mountain Site. I was in charge of crowd control while the pilgrimage was in full swing."

"Oh. I see. So, you must know Jack Carpenter."

"Oh, yes. I'm dating his ex-wife."

Mo thought about that a moment, wondering if it was time for a meeting with the elusive Jack Carpenter. "Have you seen Jack lately? I'd really like to talk to him."

"No. Haven't seen him in a couple weeks."

"How would I get in touch with him?"

"Ah. You could leave a message with his answering service. I can give you the number. If that doesn't work, he's sure to be over at his ex-wife's on Saturday. He usually takes his son Jake out then."

"Great. I would like that number."

"Sure."

When they reached the gas station Mo went inside and used the payphone. He dialed a special number at the White House.

"This is Mo. I need to talk to the President."

"He's in a meeting with the Ambassador to Egypt," his secretary said.

"Get him out. This is urgent," Mo advised.

"Alright. I'll get word to him."

There was a long silence on the line and then the President came on. "This better be important, Mo. I don't like being interrupted while in a meeting with a foreign diplomat. It conveys a lack of respect."

"Sorry, Mr. President. But I thought you should know General Thornton and Senator Rawlings are dead. I'm not sure about Captain Winslow."

"Huh? What the hell happened?"

Mo explained what he knew. "If I'd have tried to help Captain Winslow I'd be dead now too."

"So, now what am I supposed to do? I can't bring in the Joint Chiefs. They don't even know about this project."

"Yes, sir. I believe it's just you, me and the Director now."

"Have you talked to the Director?"

"No. This is the first call I have made. Sir, these Nanomites are a real threat to this nation and I think you should bring in the Joint Chiefs to figure out how to deal with them."

"I can't do that. If what we've done leaks out the backlash would be not only devastating to my administration, but to our nation as well. There has to be something else we can do. How about Kulchz? Can't he help? He's the one who brought the Nanomites to Earth. It should be his problem anyway, not mine."

"Perhaps, but I have another idea."

"What's that?"

"Jack Carpenter and Agent Marcia Sanders of the FBI. They already know about the aliens, but they haven't leaked the information to anyone as far as I can tell."

"Are you sure they know?"

"Yes, they have to know. They have one of the aliens with them."

"Oh, Jesus!"

"No. I think this may be okay. Let me make contact with them. With their help and the alien's help, we may figure a way out of this mess."

The President sighed deeply. "Okay. Make contact and then report back to me before you do anything else. Also, contact the Director and see if he has any ideas."

"I will. Thank you, Mr. President."

Mo hung up the phone, his heart now beating almost as rapidly as it had while he was jogging in the heat. He took another dime out of his pocket and deposited it. When he got a dial tone, he hit zero. When the operator came on he gave her his credit card number and the number for Jack Carpenter. He looked over at Deputy Lawson who was waiting expectantly. He wondered what the deputy would do if he were aware that Shoshone would be the next likely town to be obliterated by the Nanomites. As he was daydreaming a recorded message came on advising him that Jack Carpenter was out but that he would call him back if he left a message. Mo hung up the phone and walked over to the deputy.

"Deputy Lawson, I wonder if you would do me a big favor."

"Sure. How can I help?"

"I need to get to Shoshone so I can pick up transportation. I could wait around here for Army transport but I think it might be awhile given the situation in town."

"Sure, the Army has advised us to stay out of town anyway, so I don't have anything else to do. Besides, I'm due for my dinner break anyway. Do you have time for a bite?"

"Sure. That would be great. I haven't eaten all day."

"Where are they sending you?"

"To find Jack Carpenter."

"Why?"

"He may have some information that would be helpful to the Army."

"Helpful how?"

"I can't say. It's classified."

Curt nodded. "Did you try calling him?"

"Yeah. Just got a message."

"We can swing by Angela's place. She might know where to find him."

They drove back to Shoshone and stopped at Deputy Lawson's favorite diner. Mo decided this was an opportunity to find out more about Jack. If he was going to have to trust him, he needed to know if Jack was trustworthy. While they were eating Mo brought up the subject.

"So, how's your relationship with Jack?"

"Okay. We don't like each other much but we're civil."

"What happened between Jack and Angela?"

"Jack's business is all over the county and it takes so much of his time, he neglected Angela over the years. She just got tired of it."

"So, how is he as a father?"

"Jake loves him and they get along fine, but it's hard for him only being able to see him once a week."

"So, do you spend time with Jake?"

"No. He tolerates me but that's about it. I don't have a lot of spare time either, as you can imagine. I struggle to keep Angela happy."

"So, if you needed a foundation built, would you hire Jack?"

"Oh, yeah. He's the best concrete contractor in the state. I've recommended him to a lot of people. Like I said, there's no animosity between us. When I came along, Jack and Angela's marriage was pretty much over."

"I see."

After they'd finished dinner Lawson called Angela and asked if it was alright for them to come over. She said it was fine, so they got in the squad car and drove over. Jake was mowing the front lawn when they pulled up. Lawson got out and nodded at Jake. Jake turned off the lawn mower and walked over to them.

"Jake. I want you to meet Harold Smith. He works for the Army and is looking for your dad."

"Really? Why?"

"Hi," Mo said. "Oh, we need his help on a project. It's pretty important that I find him quickly."

"Did you call him?"

"Yes. I left a message."

As they were talking Angela came out of the house and walked over to them. Lawson greeted her with a hug and a kiss and then turned to look at Mo.

"He usually gets a motel someplace nearby his current job site," Jake said.

"Where's he working now?"

"Ah. He's in between jobs. The next one coming up is near Independence. He might be out there although I heard something about that project being delayed."

"If he didn't get a motel where would he sleep?"

Jake looked at his mother. "Ah, well. He spends some nights with Dolly. She works over at Mona's Café. Sometimes he even camps out near the job site or sleeps in the construction trailer."

"Is there a construction trailer at Independence?"

"Yes, I believe there is."

"Thank you, Jake. If you hear from your father tell him I'm looking for him. Tell him the government needs his help and his forgiveness."

"Forgiveness?" Jake asked.

"Yes. We haven't been exactly friendly to your father, so he might not be anxious to talk to me. It's a long story, but he'll understand. Tell him it's a matter of national security."

"Where can he find you?"

"I'll be at the Desert Inn tonight. After that I don't know. Tell him to call the number I left on his recorder. He can leave a message if I don't answer."

"Alright. I'll do it."

"Thank you, Jake, Angela. Deputy, if you'll take me to the Desert Inn, then I'll be out of your hair."

Lawson nodded and looked at Angela. "I'll be right back, okay?"

"Sure," Angela said.

When Mo got to the Desert Inn he got a room and started searching for Jack. He wasn't at any of the motels in Independence, so he decided to call Agent Sanders' supervisor at the FBI in Las Vegas. Joe Spencer answered on the first ring.

"Spencer."

"Agent Spencer. This is Harold Smith with the CIA. I've taken over Jimmy Malone's job as liaison to the Army."

"Right. I was sorry to hear about Malone's untimely demise. What a freaky way to die."

"Yes. Listen. I don't know if you have heard or not but there's been another earthquake at Death Valley Junction and General Thornton and Captain Winslow may be dead. I say may, I don't know for sure, but they fell into a rather deep sinkhole. I'd be surprised if they are alive."

"No. I hadn't heard that. My God! That's terrible."

"Yes, very unfortunate."

"So, how can I help you?"

"Listen, I know the FBI has been conducting an unofficial investigation into the murders at the Bat Mountain Site and the Death Valley Junction incident."

"Well—"

"You don't have to confirm or deny it, but I know Special Agent Marcia Sanders is in charge of it and she's working with Jack Carpenter and others."

"Okay, assuming your intelligence is accurate, what do you want from me?"

"General Thornton, Senator Rawlings and I were in charge of the Bat Mountain project and with both of them gone, the President and I are in a terrible bind."

"How is that?"

"There needs to be some immediate action taken to protect the country from a rather novel but potent threat to this nation that must be kept absolutely secret. I don't know what you have been told, but whatever you have learned is classified and cannot be disseminated to anyone."

"Okay. You've got my attention. What do you want me to do?"

"I need to meet with Agent Sanders and everyone else who has knowledge of this situation immediately. We need to pool our resources so we can effectively meet this threat."

"How do I know I can trust you?"

"I can give you a direct number to the President. He'll personally confirm his desire that you help us. Do not report this phone call to your superiors. They do not know about this top-secret program and are not authorized to find out about it."

"Alright. Give me the number. If it checks out I'm at your disposal."

"Good. Just remember, however, any field agents assigned to help must not know the true nature of what we are dealing with. We'll have to come up with a cover story to satisfy their curiosity."

"Got it. Give me the number."

Mo gave him the number and then hung up. He wondered if Joe would call the President or go directly to his superiors for instructions. He prayed he'd be smart and call the President.

41
Dangerous Theft

Jack accelerated after he finished talking to Agent Sanders. He didn't know for sure, but he had a hunch the dump truck had gone south. The problem they faced, however, was that the thieves had enough of a head start that Jack would have no way of knowing when they got off the main highway. There were intersections every few miles and unless they just got lucky and saw the truck, they could pass the turnoff and never know it.

"Keep your eyes peeled for the dump truck. Hopefully he'll stop for gas or to get some lunch."

As they came up to the first intersection they looked both ways for any sign of the dump truck but saw nothing. This went on for over an hour and Jack was beginning to lose his patience.

"This is hopeless," Jack said in frustration. "We have no idea if they are in front of us or if they turned off."

"Put yourself in their place," Dolly suggested. "If you were going to steal a load of sand, what would you do with it?"

"Well, it would be for a job most likely. If I didn't think I was being followed, I'd take it straight to the job site."

"So, how can we find out what jobs are in progress around this area?"

"The building inspection office in Independence, I suppose."

"Do you know anyone there? Could you call them?"

"Yeah. I know a girl there, Valerie. She'd look it up for me."

Jack pulled into a gas station and went inside to use the phone. He emerged a few minutes later with a smile on his face.

"Any luck?" Dolly asked.

"Yeah. There are three jobs in this area going on right now and Don Mason is doing one of them."

Dolly smiled. "See how smart I am?"

"You are. That's why I hooked up with you," he said.

Dolly took his hand and squeezed it as they pulled back onto the highway. "Sorry, to be dragging you all over Southern California, Linkh," Jack said.

"It's quite alright. I'm rather enjoying riding in your utility PTV."

"PTV?"

"Personal transport vehicle."

"Oh, right. We call them cars or trucks."

Jack slowed at the next intersection and turned east.

"I'm not sure what we're going to do when we find Mason. He's not going to admit to taking the sand and we're not going to be able to convince him a load of sand is dangerous."

"Well, maybe if you agree not to prosecute him he'll let you have it back."

"It's worth a try."

Jack turned at the next intersection and they entered an area of new residential construction. Jack gunned it as he recognized the dump truck up ahead. He slammed on his brakes and skidded to a halt in front of it. It was just about ready to dump its load.

Jack and Dolly got out. Jack walked over to Mason and his crew. "I caught you this time, Don. I saw your truck running off with my sand and I have a couple of witnesses."

Don turned and scowled at Jack. "You're full of shit, Carpenter. I didn't steal a damn thing of yours. This load came from my own yard."

"Listen, you don't want to unload this sand. It's been treated with toxic chemicals that will contaminate the entire construction site. The owner won't be able to sell this house and he's going to sue you for his loss."

"You're so full of crap, Carpenter. Do I look like I just fell out of a cabbage truck?"

Jack raised his eyebrows. "No. More like a garbage truck."

Mason stiffened. "Get the hell off my job site, Carpenter."

"I saw you steal the sand too," Dolly interjected. "I'll testify against you."

Mason laughed. "You're Jack's bitch. You'd say anything to back him up. Nobody is going to believe you."

"Listen. If you take the sand back now, I won't press charges and I won't tell anyone what happened today."

Mason considered the offer and then shook his head. "You didn't see shit 'cause I didn't steal your sand."

Jack sighed. "Well, I'm not going to let you unload this sand. I'm serious about the contamination."

Mason laughed. "Oh, yeah. Just try to stop me," he said turning to go toward the truck.

Jack grabbed Mason's arm trying to restrain him and Mason turned and took a swing at him in response. Jack ducked and the blow missed but two crew members intervened grabbing Jack from behind, pinning his arms, and holding him up for Mason to hit. Mason smacked Jack in the stomach hard and Jack groaned. That's when

Linkh got out of the truck and launched himself into the fray. He pulled the first crewman away from Jack and threw him hard into the dump truck. The man crumpled to the ground. Jack managed to get away from the other crewman by stomping on his foot and then giving him an uppercut with his free fist.

The other four crewmen came at Linkh when they saw their friend tossed into the truck. Linkh smacked the first one aside with the back of his hand and punched the next one in the face with his fist. The other two were all over him, one trying to get him in a choke hold while the other one hit him with relentless punches to his mid-section. Linkh pried off the first man by crushing his hand until he screamed in pain and let go. Then he made short order of the second assailant with a vicious kick to his knee that knocked him off his feet and left him moaning in pain.

As the fight ended Jack turned to see Mason pointing a shotgun at him. “Okay, the game’s over. Now get the hell off my property before I blow your head off.”

Jack raised his hands. “Okay, calm down. We’re only talking about a load of sand. It’s not worth dying over.”

“I’m so sick of you Jack. Everyone loves you. You’re so good. I can’t get a damn job because everybody want’s Jackass Carpenter to do their work.”

“Listen. I don’t care about the money. I’ll give you another load of sand. You just can’t use this one.”

Mason released the safety on the shotgun. “I said get off my job site.”

Jack looked over at Dolly and then at Linkh. Linkh sighed deeply, then motioned toward Mason. The shotgun flew out of his hand. Mason looked at his hands in shock and then at the shotgun that had landed twenty feet away. He rushed over to it only to have it move away from him again. “What the hell!” he said glaring at Linkh.

Jack rushed over and grabbed the shotgun. "Okay. Now who's driving this truck?"

One of the crew members waved his hand tentatively.

"Get in the truck and drive it back to my site. After you've dumped it there you can leave and we'll all forget this ever happened. Agreed?" Jack said looking at Mason.

Mason, still in shock, didn't respond.

"Agreed?" Jack pressed.

Mason finally nodded.

"Okay, let's go," Jack said motioning to the driver.

The driver got into the cab and Jack got in the passenger seat with the shotgun. As the dump truck took off, Dolly and Linkh got back into Jack's car and followed them. Mason didn't look happy but no one made a move to follow them.

42
Mending Fences

Agent Sanders, George and Cindy drove north toward Bishop. They didn't see the dump truck and soon surmised that it had gone the other way. As they were pulling into a gas station Agent Sanders' radio crackled and then a voice came through.

"Agent Sanders, this is Joe, come in."

Sanders picked up the radio and replied, "Sanders here."

"There's been a new development. We need to talk."

"Roger. We're between Bishop and Independence. Where do you suggest we rendezvous?"

"We need Jack too. How about Mona's Café?"

"Okay. See you there in an hour."

Agent Sanders wasn't going to bring Jack to Mona's Café as he'd have to bring Linkh along too, so she figured she'd pick him up and they'd all parlay at Jack's trailer. They needed to work on a strategy for dealing with the Nanomites anyway, so the Independence job site was a good place to do it. Joe's car was parked out front of Mona's Café when they drove up. They walked inside and found him sitting with another man at a table. They joined them.

Joe motioned toward the other man. "This is Mo. He's taken over for Jimmy Malone."

Sanders nodded tentatively.

"Where's Jack?" Joe asked.

"Why don't you tell me what's going on first," she said looking at Mo. "Someone's been trying to kill us, so we're a little paranoid right now."

Mo shifted uncomfortably in his chair. "Right. The agency apologizes for that," Mo said.

"Seriously?" Sanders spat. "You think an apology is going to cut it?"

He sighed. "No. But that's the best I can do for now. The agency realizes the error of its ways. Thankfully, I had no part in this matter until yesterday."

"Huh," Sanders snickered. "So, we're just supposed to forgive you now?"

"No, but we do need to put aside our differences for now in the interest of national security. You see, General Thornton and Senator Rawlings are dead."

"They are? How did that happen?"

"The Nanomites killed them."

Mo explained what had happened at Death Valley Junction when they tried to exterminate the Nanomites. "So, we are in a rather tenuous position. Prior to Jack discovering the Nanomite cathedral, only six people knew about the Nanomite presence on Earth. Three of those are now dead. So, now with you and your friends, there are seven people on the planet who know about it."

"Why has it been so ultra-top secret?" Sanders asked. "I think people would accept the fact that there are aliens from another planet given time to get used to the idea."

"Well, you don't know the whole story. If you did the answer to your question would be obvious. Unfortunately, I can't discuss anything with you that you haven't already figured out."

"So, what do you want us to do?"

"We need your help in stopping the Nanomites. We know you have the alien Linkh Leode."

"Who told you that?"

"Witnesses saw him leaving the Death Valley Junction crime scene with Jack."

"Even so, how could we possibly stop them?"

"We don't know, but with Linkh's help perhaps we can come up with a strategy. He knows a lot about them and can help us do that. Once we determine a course of action, we'll have the full resources of the U.S. Army, CIA and FBI at our disposal. We just can't tell them exactly what kind of enemy they are fighting."

"What will the generals and bureau chiefs think about that? Do you really think they will follow our command?"

"They won't know of your involvement. They'll be taking orders directly from the President through me."

"I'm in," George said. "We've got to stop them from spreading their cathedrals."

"What do you mean?" Mo asked. "Have they shown up somewhere else?"

Sanders swallowed hard. "Yes, I'm afraid so. There's another cathedral near Independence and it's twice the size of Bat Mountain."

Mo's face paled. "Holy mother of God."

"Yeah. Jack and Linkh are there now trying to figure out how to deal with it."

"We need to get over there," Mo said, "and get our heads together. If there is any more proliferation, it may be too late to stop it. Will you help us?"

Agent Sanders turned to George and Cindy. "What do you think?"

Cindy shrugged. "Why not? This may be the most important thing I do in my lifetime. It will definitely be the most interesting."

"It will be dangerous," Mo warned. "The Nanomites are highly intelligent and they figured out pretty quickly who was in charge at Death Valley Junction and took them out."

"We'll have to take that into account in whatever plan we put together," George said. "I hope Jack and Linkh are okay."

"Let's get over there and find out. Will you take us there?"

Agent Sanders nodded. Seeing a waitress walk by, she put up her hand. "Check please."

The waitress pulled a check out of her apron and handed it to her.

"I've got it," Mo said taking the check away from Sanders.

When they got outside Mo asked Agent Sanders to ride with them so they could talk. Sanders agreed and George and Cindy followed them in their car. Sanders wondered if she could trust Mo. The CIA and the Army had already tried to kill her and her civilian team. What would prevent them from doing the same thing once they were no longer needed? She had to come up with a way to make sure that didn't happen. She climbed into the back seat and got comfortable.

"Head toward Independence and I'll tell you where to turn off the main road," Sanders said.

"Okay," Mo replied as he pulled out of the parking lot. "Do you think we can trust George and Cindy?"

"Yes," Sanders replied. "They are both intelligent and honorable citizens and understand why all of this has to remain a secret."

"What about Jack and Dolly?"

"Jack and Linkh are getting along like long lost brothers. He really likes him and wouldn't do anything to jeopardize his safety. You don't have to worry about Jack. And Dolly is as sweet a woman as you could find. None of them are the type that would try to cash in this situation."

"Good. Leaks will not be tolerated."

"What about our safety? You want our cooperation but what happens once the Nanomite situation has been resolved?"

"I've talked to the President," Joe advised. "He's assured me you'll be safe as long as you keep everything you know, or learn in the future, secret."

"So, that's it? All we get is the personal assurance of the man who obviously authorized our assassination in the first place."

"You don't know that," Joe replied.

"No. She's right," Mo said. "The President authorized the CIA to do whatever it took to protect the treaty with the aliens, including assassination. The thing is, if you don't cooperate, you are dead anyway. But if you do cooperate, then there won't be any reason to kill you and you may very likely become a valuable asset to the Agency."

"The President also wanted me to tell you that you and your friends will each be paid a $100,000 tax-free consulting fee for your services," Joe advised.

"But I'm already on the FBI payroll?" Sanders said.

"This will be a bonus paid in cash completely off the books."

Sanders didn't trust the President or Mo and she doubted Joe had any control over the situation, but she realized Mo was right. If they didn't agree to the deal they were as good as dead.

43
Negotiations

Later that afternoon Mo, Joe and Agent Sanders pulled up next to the construction trailer at the Independence site. George and Cindy drove up five minutes later. None of them had ever seen an alien, not even Mo since he'd just taken the new assignment, so they spent several minutes just staring at Linkh and sizing him up. Since there were too many of them to fit in the trailer, they all pulled up chairs around a campfire that Jack had built overlooking the new Nanomite cathedral.

Mo shook his head in awe. "I can't believe how quickly they've built this new cathedral. They do such beautiful work, it's hard to believe they are as ruthless as they've turned out to be."

"They learned that from the humans they encountered back on Tarizon," Linkh noted. "They lived for thousands of years in peace until the humans made contact, convinced them to help rebuild the planet's infrastructure, and then tried to enslave them."

"So, is this a hopeless cause or do you think we can reason with them?" Mo asked.

"They are a rational life-form. If you can show them a course of conduct that would be best for them, they will listen. The problem will be getting them to trust you."

"Why didn't they listen to you the last time you tried to negotiate?"

"They were all young and inexperienced swarms separated from the collective and from the older and wiser swarmmasters. None of them knew me and their primary instinct was survival. They feared if they surrendered they would be vulnerable to annihilation."

"So, maybe we need to go back to the Bat Mountain Site and negotiate with the swarmmasters there," Jack suggested. "If we can convince them that all this has been a big misunderstanding, perhaps we can persuade them to send a delegation to the other sites to convince them to return to Bat Mountain."

"That's a good idea," Mo replied. "But that could take time. Right now, we need to be sure this site is secure. We can't allow any more cathedrals to spring up."

"We were talking about that earlier," Jack said. "I think we have decided the best way to keep the Nanomites from moving is to build a moat around the cathedral. They won't try to travel through saturated ground."

"You sure that will work?" Mo questioned.

Linkh nodded. "It is a way to keep them in one location without hurting them. If you kill them then you'll have a war on your hands."

"Okay, I'll get the Army Corps of Engineers up here immediately to start working on it."

"How are you going to explain to the Corps what they are doing?" Joe asked.

"We'll have to come up with something—it's for a fancy country club and golf course or something."

"That sounds good, but keep the crew as small as possible and make sure they don't discuss what they are doing with anyone, particularly the press."

They continued to talk and decided Agent Sanders, Jack, Dolly and Linkh would go to Bat Mountain to try to establish contact with the Nanomites there. While they were doing that, Mo would supervise the work on the containment moats at the Independence site and Joe, George and Cindy would go back to Death Valley Junction to evaluate the situation there.

"I hope the Army wasn't successful at killing the Nanomites with insecticide. If they were, then you'll never get them to trust you again. It will be all out war until every last one of them is dead," Linkh warned.

"I don't know," Mo replied. "I left right after the attack on the headquarters. We'll just have to go back there and find out."

As the meeting broke up a feeling of hopelessness and despair came over Jack. The task before them seemed impossible, particularly since only one of them could communicate with the Nanomites. As he thought about their desperate situation, he wondered if Linkh was right and that he could learn to read people's minds and communicate telepathically. The idea seemed ridiculous, but the fact that Linkh believed it was possible gave Jack hope. He had no choice but to work diligently to acquire the skill.

That night they spent the night at Dolly's which wasn't too far from the Bat Mountain Site. Jack decided to take advantage of having Linkh for the evening to work on his telepathic skills, if indeed he had any. Linkh suggested he try to reach into Dolly's mind as she loved him and would not put up any resistance. Dolly thought the exercise was futile but agreed to let Jack try. She sat across from him at the kitchen table, barely able to keep a straight face.

"Okay, what do I need to do?" Dolly asked.

"Just relax and let Jack into your mind," Linkh advised.

Jack took a deep breath and peered into Dolly's eyes. She had a quirky smile on her face that made it hard for him to concentrate. He frowned. "Okay, laugh at me. Get it over with so I can do this."

Dolly chuckled. "I'm sorry. I'm going to be serious now," she said putting on a stern face.

Jack concentrated again trying to look through her eyes into Dolly's mind but nothing happened. "This isn't working," he complained.

"It takes time," Linkh replied. "If it were easy, everyone would be able to do it. You can do it, but only if you believe you can. When I was young I had to do the same thing. My father told me I had the gift but needed to learn how to use it. I practiced on my older sister who was kind and loving like Dolly, but even working several hours a day it took me several weeks to finally break through."

"I'm not sure we have weeks. I need to learn how to do this in a few days. It's dangerous to have only one person who can communicate with the Nanomites. What if something happens to you? Without a backup negotiator, we may end up having to go to war just because we couldn't communicate."

"I agree," Agent Sanders said. "We have to consider all contingencies."

"It will impress the Nanomites if an Earth human takes the time to learn how to communicate with them," Linkh advised. "It could make a big difference in gaining their trust."

They continued to work with no success until it was nearly midnight. Frustrated, Jack gave up and they all went to bed. The next morning, they got up early, had breakfast at Mona's Café, and then drove to the Bat Mountain Site. It had been some time since they had seen the Living Desert Cathedral and they were astonished at how it had changed. The walls were complete now and the roof was beginning to fill in. Jack marveled at how a rock roof could be constructed without wood or steel supports.

"Holy mother of God," Dolly said doing the sign of the cross. "It really is a cathedral."

"It looks a lot like one," Linkh said, "but they will fill in the interior after the roof is complete. A Nanomite cathedral is solid rock. They do the walls and the roof first to keep out the wind and the rain. They like a stable environment in which to live."

"Really?" Dolly replied.

"Yes. In their contract with Central Authority the Nanomites agreed to create interior spaces for humans to occupy. However, the Nanomites had the right to live in the foundation, walls, and roof area since humans couldn't live there. It was a good arrangement because the Nanomites would maintain the building at no cost to owners. But some humans were uncomfortable knowing Nanomites were in the walls. I guess they thought they would be listening to conversations and watching them, but the fact was the Nanomites couldn't listen to them or see them. Neither occupant would interfere with the other, yet the humans insisted the Nanomites leave once a building had been constructed."

"That's terrible," Dolly complained. "What's wrong with your Central Authority?"

"It was the Purists in Central Authority who pushed the issue. They believe only pure, un-mutated humans, should have civil rights."

"But they don't control the government, do they?"

"Not now. The Loyalists have a majority in the World Assembly, but that could change at any moment."

As they approached the headquarters tent two MP's stopped them. "Can I help you?"

"Yes, we're here to see Colonel Talmadge," Agent Sanders replied. "I believe he is expecting us."

One of the MPs nodded. "Yes, right this way."

The MP's escorted them to the largest of many tents set up behind the cathedral. A short, balding man stood up when he saw them enter.

"Colonel Talmadge?" Agent Sanders asked.

"Yes... Hi... Mo told me you were coming by today."

"Right. Did he tell you why?"

"No. He just told me to give you full access to the cathedral."

Mo had told Agent Sanders not to let anyone know the purpose of their visit, so she had come up with a cover story for their visit.

"Linkh is a geology student from Waco working on his doctorate. This is such a unique uplift, he wants to make it the subject of his doctoral thesis. Jack agreed to show him around since he discovered the site and is familiar with it."

"That's fine. There's not much going on here since the pilgrims left. If you don't mind I'll just leave you all to do your work. Just don't touch anything. I have some reports I need to work on."

"No. That's fine. We'll let you get back to what you are doing."

They all got up and agreed to meet again before they left.

Jack looked at Linkh expectantly. "Now what?"

"Let's go inside the cathedral where we are out of everyone's view. Agent Sanders and Dolly can keep watch to make sure nobody disturbs us."

They all agreed, so Jack and Linkh went inside while Dolly and Agent Sanders took positions at the two entrances to the cathedral. The interior temperature was a bit cooler than outside as the partial roof blocked the sun and provided considerable shade. Linkh went to the center of the large center room and sat down.

"Okay. Although we can't look a Nanomite in the eye, we can imagine one in our mind and accomplish the same focus to our concentration," Linkh advised.

"So, you have an image of a Nanomite in your head?"

"Yes. It's probably not accurate but it doesn't matter. Telepathy is all about concentration."

"So, what should I do?" Jack asked.

"Try what you did last night, but think of a Nanomite instead of Dolly. If you're lucky maybe you'll tap into our conversation."

Jack laughed. "Ah. Don't hold your breath."

Linkh sat Indian style and closed his eyes. Jack watched him a minute and then took the same pose.

The Speaker felt Linkh's mind nudge his. It was a familiar feeling. He'd linked with this mind before so he opened up his mind without hesitation.

"Linkh Leode?" the Speaker thought.

"Yes, Speaker. It is I."

"It's good to make contact with you again. We have been quite distressed with what's been happening here on Earth and concerned about being attacked again."

"Yes. That is why I am here to lay your fears to rest."

"I hope so. Who have you brought with you? I feel a weak presence of a human."

"Yes, that is Jack Carpenter. He is trying to learn how to communicate with you. Humans on Earth have not developed their telepathic abilities at all, so this is something very new to him."

"It would be useful to be able to contact the humans. I hope he is successful in developing his gift."

"Thank you. I feel confident in time he will be successful. In the meantime, I am here to tell you that the humans mean you no harm. They do not understand the

Nanomites and did not realize they were killing your brothers and sisters when they took samples of your rock."

"How could that be? Didn't Central Authority inform them about our ways?"

"Yes, but the government here on Earth withheld this information from the public and other nations. They do not want to share the technology we are giving them with the other governments on the planet, so they are keeping your presence a secret."

"That doesn't surprise me. Humans are so selfish and short sighted," the Speaker thought.

"So, the crowds that have been here are not hostile. They are awed by the beauty of your cathedral. They think their God sent you here to build it."

"They do?"

"Yes, they mean you no harm. It is the government's fear that their deception will be discovered that is the problem."

"So, what can we do to be left alone as the treaty provides?"

"You don't know this, but two other cathedrals have been started by swarms of Nanomites that were accidentally taken away by a sheriff's deputy to a nearby city. One colony of swarms has caused much damage to a city called Death Valley Junction and have killed many humans."

"Nanomites always do whatever they have to do to survive."

"I know, but we need to bring them back here where they can live in peace. The other colony has caused no harm and have a cathedral nearly built but if they are discovered people will flock to see them and there will no doubt be more trouble."

"Will the Earth government keep their citizens away and let us live in peace if they all return here?"

"Yes. The United States President has assured me that they will."

"Can I trust this man who has deceived his own citizens?"

"Yes, because it is in his best interest for you to be left alone. He can't afford for his deceit to be exposed."

"Then I will confer with the other swarmmasters and give you a decision at sunrise."

"Thank you, Speaker. It was good connecting with you again."

Linkh opened his eyes and looked at Jack. "Did you get in on the connection?"

Jack opened his eyes and frowned. "No. For a few moments I felt something but I couldn't grab onto it."

"Yes. The swarmmaster said he could feel you trying. It will come in time. Be patient."

Jack sighed. "I guess I don't have much choice. So, what did they say?"

"They must confer but, like I said, they are a rational life-form. It is in their best interest to avoid conflict, particularly in a strange land where they would be at a disadvantage if general war broke out."

"General war? We can't let that happen. Can you imagine how that would impact the country?"

"Yes. It would likely be the end of our treaty too and that would be disastrous for both our governments. So, be thinking about other alternatives if our mission here fails."

Jack shook his head. "No. It can't fail. That's not an option."

44
Searching for the Enemy

When Joe, George and Cindy neared Death Valley Junction they ran into a military checkpoint. They stopped and Joe showed the officer in charge his badge.

"Yes, Agent Spencer. I have been ordered to cooperate with you fully."

"Good. What's your name?"

"Lt. Johnson."

"Okay, Lieutenant. What's the situation here? Did Operation Desert Cleansing go forward after General Thornton's death?"

"No. The Joint Chiefs suspended the operation as soon as they heard about the attack. We've been told to stand down until we get further orders."

"Good. Do you know where your target is?"

"No, Sir. We don't."

"Have you seen anything unusual in or around the city since you have been watching the perimeter?"

"No. It has been quiet since the evacuation. The ground in that area is very unstable so we are not allowing anyone back in."

"Alright. We're going to go in and have a look around," Joe said.

"I wouldn't drive a vehicle in there if I were you. I'd do your inspection on foot."

"You're probably right. We'll drive to the outskirts of town and park our vehicle."

"Would you like an escort?" Lt. Johnson asked.

"No. That won't be necessary. Thanks."

Joe eased out of the checkpoint, drove to the outskirts of the city and parked the car in a convenience store parking lot. They walked down the middle of the deserted highway until it ended abruptly. If they hadn't known what had happened they would have assumed the city had been bombed leaving large craters in the road. But as they worked their way through the rubble they came across huge sinkholes that had swallowed up whole buildings, some half buried and others now entirely underground.

"So, where do you think the Nanomites are now?" George asked as he peered down into a deep hole.

"You're the scientist. You tell me," Joe replied.

"Well, from what I know about them they will be together wherever they are. They act as a collective body."

"Okay, so where would they go if they knew someone was out to destroy them?"

"Somewhere where I could defend myself?"

"Or somewhere they could hide," Cindy added.

"True," George conceded. "They don't like water, wind or fire, so they're going to want to build a shelter against those elements."

"So, they'll go somewhere where they can build a cathedral," Cindy said.

"Yes, so they have probably evacuated the city. They need a quiet place where they will be left alone."

"Let's see if the Army can get us a chopper so we can scout the surrounding terrain for any sight of them," Joe suggested.

George nodded. "Good idea."

They went back to where Lt. Johnson was waiting and asked if he could get them a helicopter. He said he could and called for one immediately. Fifteen minutes later they were in the air searching for any sign of the

Nanomites. They searched in every direction several miles. They all agreed the Nanomites couldn't travel fast enough to be any farther away but by nightfall they hadn't found them. That night they went back to Shoshone and had dinner with Jack, Dolly, Linkh and Agent Sanders to report on their progress.

"I think we keep forgetting that the Nanomites are very intelligent," Jack said. "They know if they just move a few miles out of town and start building a cathedral we'll discover it. I think they are hiding some place waiting for an opportunity to disappear."

"How could they just disappear?" Cindy asked. "They can't fly."

"They do have wings," Joe said. "Right Linkh?"

"Right," Linkh agreed. "But I don't think they can fly around like a flock of birds. They are so small the wind would scatter them everywhere. You see some objects that seem solid to us have a lot of empty space, so their wings allow them to breach those empty spaces easily. So, I think they will move into sand, gravel or rock that is being transported somewhere. That's how they are moved on Tarizon. The Nanomites build four-by-four crystal blocks and pack as many swarms inside as they can. Then the blocks are moved."

"So, where would there be sand, gravel or rock around here that is transported out of this area?" Joe asked.

"There aren't any railroads going through here anymore, but there are still some borax mines operating nearby and the ore would be transported out by truck. I think there is one about seven or eight miles southwest of here."

"But how would they know that?" Cindy asked. "They can't communicate with anyone."

"They are telepathic," Linkh replied. "They can read minds, so all they have to do is get near a human and scan his memory for whatever information they need."

"I thought they only spoke Tari?" Cindy said.

"True. But they can still see images which is usually good enough."

"So, if they make it to the borax mine they could hide in the ore and easily be loaded on a truck and sent to God knows where?"

"There are several borax processing plants around but I think this one ships to Boron California," Jack said.

"Oh, crap!" Joe exclaimed. "That's two thirds of the way to LA."

"You can't let them get to LA," Linkh warned. "In Shisk they brought down eleven skyscrapers before a peace treaty was worked out."

"We better get out there first thing tomorrow morning and see if there is any sign of them," Joe said. "If you are successful at Bat Mountain, bring some Nanomites out to the mine and maybe they can talk the Death Valley Junction swarmmasters into returning to Bat Mountain."

Jack and Linkh agreed and the meeting concluded with everyone praying in their own way that the Bat Mountain swarmmasters would agree to help and that they could find the Death Valley Junction swarms before they disappeared.

45
Escape

That night Jack worked on his mind reading skills with Dolly for hours with little result. He couldn't see into her mind as Linkh had said he would be able to do. He was beginning to doubt that it was even possible to read a person's mind, despite Linkh's assurances that it was when something strange happened. Dolly was just getting out of the shower and putting on a nightgown before going to bed. Jack was admiring her naked body and wondering if she'd be too tired for sex. It had been a long day and it was a lot to ask of a woman, but then again, maybe she wanted it too. He decided rather than just ask her, he'd engage in some small talk to gauge her mood and level of energy.

"So, did you decide what you're going to get your sister for her birthday?"

Dolly looked up with a shocked look on her face. "How did you know my sister's birthday was coming up? I don't remember mentioning it to you. In fact, I don't think I have ever told you I had a sister."

Jack frowned. "Really. You do have one, don't you? Rose? Isn't that her name?"

"You know her name? I know we've never talked about her. Have you been snooping around the house?"

"No. I'm not the snooping type. If I wanted to know about your family, I would just ask."

"Yeah. I don't have any secrets. So, how is it that you know about my sister and that it is her birthday on Monday?"

"You must have mentioned it."

"No. We've been a little busy chasing alien life-forms. My sister is the last topic of conversation that would have come up."

"Well, I must have read your mind, I guess."

Dolly raised her eyebrows. "You read my mind? Huh? I guess you did. Wow! You read my mind and didn't even realize it."

Jack frowned. "You think?"

"I don't know. What's my mother's name?"

"Marge," Jack blurted out.

Dolly laughed. "That's right and I know we have never talked about my mother. Okay, let's give you something a little harder. Who was my first boyfriend?"

"Tom Duncan and you lost your virginity to him in the barn across the street from your middle school."

"Jack! That's not fair. Now you know all my secrets. I should have never agreed to this."

"I'm sorry. I frankly didn't think it would work," Jack admitted. "Wow! This is incredible."

Linkh was impressed when Jack told him the next morning of his breakthrough, but cautioned him that reading the mind of someone you love and who is open to you is much easier than the average person whose mind is naturally guarded from casual intrusion. Nevertheless, Jack's confidence soared and, for the first time, he really believed he could read anybody's mind given enough time to practice.

After breakfast Jack, Dolly, Agent Sanders and Linkh went back to the Bat Mountain Site to get the decision of the Nanomites. Time was of the essence since they all knew the Nanomites could disappear at any moment if they were able to get into one of the loads of borax that were being shipped out for processing. Jack and Linkh went inside the cathedral as they had done the previous day and went to the same spot to make contact.

Linkh closed his eyes and concentrated. *"Speaker. I am back, as we agreed, to get your decision on whether you will help us convince your Nanomite brothers and sisters, who have left this cathedral, to return."*

"Yes. We have been expecting you," the Speaker thought.

"So, what is your answer, my friends."

"This was a most difficult decision for us. Many did not want to interfere with those who had left, through no fault of their own, and have started new cathedrals. Others understood our obligation under the treaty and want to honor it. So, only after much debate, has a decision been made to help you convince them to return."

Jack felt a wave of relief wash over him. "Ah!" he blurted out and then covered his mouth. He hadn't realized it, but he could feel the Nanomite thoughts in his mind. He'd made a connection although he didn't know exactly what had been said, the feeling was positive. He noticed Linkh standing up, so he got up as well.

"So, they agreed," Jack said.

Linkh smiled. "You heard them?"

"I got some positive feelings. It felt like they agreed."

"Yes, they did, but it will take them a day or so to build the transport cubes necessary to take them around. I don't know if we will be able to get the cube to the borax mine in time."

Jack rubbed his temples. "Hmm. Maybe you should go to the mine now and try to make contact. If you are successful you might be able to get them to stay at the mine until the other Nanomites get there."

"No. I need to travel with the Nanomite's transport cubes. There has to be someone close by who can communicate with them during transport in case there is a problem. I offered to stay with the Nanomites when we left them off but there was no place for me to live while they were building their cathedral, so Commander Kulchz said no. We could have avoided all this had our governments given more thought to the settlement of the Nanomites."

"Well, governments can be pretty stupid sometimes."

"So, since we have two cubes you're going to have to travel with one of them too."

"Me? But I—"

"Don't worry. If you can feel their thoughts, then they can feel yours as well."

"But will they trust a human?"

"Not immediately. But when you open your mind to them they will see that you mean them no harm."

Jack swallowed hard. "Oh, great. I'm going to let an alien life-form, I can't even see, enter into my mind?"

"Not enter but scan it for information. It won't be painful and they can't hurt your mind even if they find something they don't like."

Jack felt ill. "Okay. Whatever you say."

46
Containment

Mo contacted his Army liaison, Colonel Pollard, and advised him he needed the Army Corps of Engineers to go out to the Independence site to immediately start excavation of a water barrier around a new uplift that had been discovered. Colonel Pollard had a lot of questions but Mo declined to answer them on the grounds that such information was classified. Colonel Pollard didn't like that answer but he agreed to obey the order and not ask questions. By nightfall dozens of bulldozers were working frantically to dig a 20' moat around the Independence site. Unfortunately, a project like that would take several days to accomplish even with a dozen bulldozers working 24/7, so Mo used the time to locate water to fill the moat once it was constructed.

He first went to the county water district but was not so politely declined assistance. Water in the desert was a scarce commodity and nobody believed they had any extra to sell no matter what the price. The manager did give him the number of a water well drilling company and he suggested they go that route. That didn't seem feasible as Mo thought drilling a well would take too much time, but after talking to a salesman he was told for the right price they could have one built in a few days. Praying the salesman knew what he was talking about, Mo ordered two 2000 ft wells to be drilled.

Fortunately, the Nanomites seemed satisfied with building their new cathedral and were making great progress each day. Mo noticed the workers spending a lot of time watching the structure as it seemed to change on an hourly basis. He wondered if they were keeping their mouths shut as they were instructed to do, or was it only a matter of time before pilgrims would be showing up like they had at Bat Mountain.

When Agent Sanders, Jack and Dolly finally showed up two days later, Mo was relieved that they had brought some Nanomites with them to try to talk the Independence swarms into returning to Bat Mountain. But when he found out Jack had learned how to communicate with the Nanomites, he was flabbergasted.

"I didn't even know that was possible," Mo complained. "Hell, I have been trying to learn Tari so I could talk to Kulchz. I thought the French I took in high school was bad, but it was nothing compared to Tari."

Linkh smiled. "If you come to the ship they can give you drugs and put probes on your forehead that will accelerate your learning and allow you to become fluent in Tari in just a few days."

"Wow. I'll have to try that," Mo said. "So, how is this going to work?"

"We are close enough now for the Nanomite swarmmasters to talk," Jack advised. "They are probably already at it. We'll give them some time and then I'll try to contact them to see what their mood is like."

"Try?"

"Yeah, try. So far, I've only been able to listen to them. Hopefully I will be able to convey thoughts to them."

Mo rolled his eyes skeptically. "I can't believe you can hear them, let alone transfer thoughts to them. How in the hell did you figure out how to do it?"

"Well, Linkh tested me and said I had the gift and it was just a matter of learning how to use it. Knowing that gave me the motivation to try to develop the skill and the confidence I needed to succeed."

"Okay, that makes sense, but I'm still having a hard time accepting it."

Jack shrugged. "You and me both, but I did hear the Nanomites, so now I know Linkh was right."

"Well, they should have had enough time to confer. Why don't you do your magic and find out if they are going back to Bat Mountain peacefully or if we are going to have to make this their permanent home, God forbid."

Jack nodded, walked over to the truck and put down the tailgate. He looked at the crystal cube for a long moment and then closed his eyes. He imagined a Nanomite in the image Linkh had described to him and concentrated. He didn't feel anything so he began thinking of the Bat Mountain Site. Nothing happened so he pictured in his mind two Nanomites face to face hoping they'd understand he wanted to know what they had decided. Nothing happened for a long minute and then he felt a strange sensation deep in the left side of his brain. A second later an image of men loading many cubes into a truck flashed in his mind. He smiled and pictured himself with the Nanomite bowing in thanks.

"Okay. I think they've agreed to go back," Jack blurted out.

Mo laughed. "Seriously?"

"Yes, I can't talk to them because I don't speak Tari but the images we exchanged were clear. They are going to build transport cubes and once they are all built you can arrange for them to be taken back to Bat Mountain."

"So, how long will it take?"

"Well, it will probably take about 24 hours. That's how long it took to build this cube. Since there will have to be more of them, it might take a bit longer."

Mo shook his head skeptically. “Okay. But I'm not stopping work on the moats until all the cubes are loaded into trucks.”

“They really didn't have any choice,” Jack said. “They are a peaceful, rational life form and they don't want a war, particularly one they could never win.”

“I hope you're right.”

“Now, if we had murdered a bunch of them, they wouldn't have been so easy to convince.”

“Probably not,” Mo agreed.

Agent Sanders walked over to them. “So, what's the word?”

“It appears they've agreed to go home,” Mo said.

Agent Sanders smiled. “Fantastic. Nice job, Jack.”

Agent Sanders' radio in her car beeped. She walked over to it and answered. “Sanders.” She listened for a moment and then sighed heavily. “Crap!”

“What's wrong?” Mo asked.

“I had an agent track down the driver of the dump truck who stole your sand. I wanted to make sure they hadn't stolen more than one load.”

“Yeah?” Jack said. “So, what did he find out?”

“That was the second load.”

“Oh, Jesus! Where did the other load go?”

“It went out yesterday to another house in the same neighborhood. I'm afraid it's already been unloaded.”

“So, what should we do?” Jack asked.

“Get in your truck and follow me to the site. Your Nanomite friends have more work to do.”

Jack closed his eyes and pictured the dump truck emptying a load of sand into a concrete mixer. He hoped the image was getting through to the Nanomites and they'd figure out what needed to be done. “Okay, let's go. I hope the Nanomites escaped from the sand before they went through the cement mixer. If not, they all may be dead."

Agent Sanders looked at Mo and then back at Jack. "Yes, let's pray they did. Come on. Let's go."

Jack put the tailgate back up and then climbed into the truck. Mo got in the passenger side seat and Dolly went with Agent Sanders. They both pulled out of the parking lot in a cloud of dust heading for what they hoped and prayed wouldn't be a tomb for millions of Nanomites.

47
The Chase

It was nearly noon when Joe, Linkh, George and Cindy finally made it to the borax mine near Death Valley Junction. It was a huge open pit mine that utilized enormous trucks and bulldozers to dig the ore out of the Earth. They stopped at the entrance to the mine and scanned the operation.

"So, where do you think the Nanomites would go?" Cindy asked.

"If they are looking for a ride out of here then they would go to where the ore was being loaded into trucks," George replied.

"Over there," Joe said pointing to a line of trucks waiting to be loaded.

"Okay. So, how are we going to play this?" George asked. "I doubt they are going to just let us drive down there and snoop around."

"No. There's an operations shack over there. Maybe there's a manager or supervisor in there we can talk to."

"Okay," George said as he accelerated in that direction.

When they got to the shack, George and Joe went inside. Joe flashed his FBI badge to the man sitting behind the counter. "Joe Spencer, FBI," he said.

The man stood up and came over to the counter. His name tag read: Harmon Smith, Supervisor. "What can I do for you?" he asked.

"We need to look around your facility, if you don't mind. There is a fugitive on the loose and he's been reported in this area."

"Is he one of our employees?"

"No. He may be hitching a ride on one of the trucks coming through here. If we could just look around we'll try not to disrupt your operation in any way."

"Let me call the operations office and check with them. It will just take a minute."

Joe nodded and looked at George. "I don't think I've ever seen such giant dump trucks," Joe commented.

"I know. They look double or triple the size of a regular dump truck."

The man behind the counter smiled. "The tires are twelve feet tall and weigh 6,000 lbs.," he said as he picked up the phone.

"Wow!" Joe said. "How deep does the mine go?"

"Nearly five hundred feet."

"They've pulled a lot of ore out of this mine."

"Yes, they have. In the old days they carried it out with mules and wagons."

Joe shook his head. The man dialed a number and after talking with someone for thirty seconds hung up. "Okay, you're good to go. Just pull off the road if you see one of those trucks coming. They have the right of way and they'll drive right over you if you get in their way."

"Right. We'll stay clear," Joe said going to the door.

They went back outside, gave the area a quick glance, and then got back in the car. Cindy and Linkh looked at them expectantly.

"So, did you get permission?" Cindy asked.

"Yes. I told them we were looking for a fugitive."

Cindy laughed. "Yeah, a few billion of them."

"Take me over to where the trucks are loading and I'll see if I sense the Nanomites' presence."

They drove over to the loading area and had to go completely off the road twice to avoid the huge dump trucks. Linkh got out, surveyed the area and then closed his eyes. After a moment, he got back in the car.

"They aren't here," Linkh advised.

"Follow the trucks and let's see where they dump the ore. It could be the Nanomites are where the ore will be transferred into smaller trucks for transport on the highways."

Joe nodded and followed behind the next truck that was loaded with ore. They followed the truck out of the mine to another loading site. Joe stopped again, Linkh got out and again tried to feel if the Nanomites were present. This time he felt their presence and could detect the debate with the Bat Mountain Nanomite delegation already in full bloom. Relief swept over him as his job was now done. He'd brought the swarmmasters together, so it was up to them now to avoid war with the humans.

The humans want us to return to the place they call Bat Mountain. Of course, they do, they want us in one place so they can exterminate us. We agreed to stay in that location according to the treaty. One of the humans killed thousands of our brothers and sisters. They claim it was an accident. Humans are evil. You cannot trust them. They promise to protect us. But others want to kill us. Why don't they just leave us alone. They don't understand us. The government has not told them of our existence. That's no excuse. We killed some of their leaders. They want to get revenge. We cannot trust them. They claim they understand it was a misunderstanding. They are willing to forgive us. So, they say. Humans are not trustworthy. We should kill them before they kill us. If we go to war millions will die and most of us will ultimately die too. You don't know that. This is their planet. They know it better than we do and would have an advantage. We are only visitors. They will win the war. No, they wouldn't. They can't see us. They haven't even tried to find a way to communicate with us. They care nothing for us, only domination of the other nations of the world. It is their leaders who have hurt us, not the main population. We shouldn't make them suffer for the mistakes of their leaders. What if they betray us? Then we go to war, but we should give peace a try.

After nearly an hour of argument back and forth, the Bat Mountain swarmmasters finally were able to convince their brothers and sisters to return to Bat Mountain. Unfortunately, the logistics of getting them back to the Bat Mountain Site was difficult. They had to find somewhere private where the Nanomites could build cubes and Army trucks had to be brought in for transport.

That night Jack and Dolly slept in the back of their truck in sleeping bags Jack kept for emergencies. Dolly was exhausted and fell right to sleep, but Jack was uncomfortable and upset that he wouldn't be getting back to Shoshone in time to visit Jake. When he finally fell asleep he began to dream.

The sound of an approaching truck woke him. The pickup swayed from the wind generated by the giant truck going by. Jack got up and saw the sun was just rising to the east. He shook Dolly.

"Time to get up."

She moaned. "It's still dark."

"I know, but we need to get an early start. We have a long drive."

"What's for breakfast?"

"I've got some pop tarts in the box behind the seat and I bet we can bum some coffee from the supervisor's shed. I saw a community pot when I was there yesterday."

"Oh, wow! You really know how to treat a girl."

Jack smiled. "Sorry, I'll make it up to you."

"Hmm," Dolly said and turned over.

Jack pushed the tailgate down and slid out of the truck bed. Linkh and Agent Sanders were sleeping uncomfortably in the cab. Linkh immediately opened the door and climbed out when he noticed Jack up and about.

"Good morning," Jack said.

"Morning," Linkh said, a look of concern on his face.

"What's wrong?"

"Ah, I don't sense the Nanomites."

"Huh? What do you mean?"

"I don't feel their presence. They haven't built the transport cubes they promised."

"You mean they are not here?"

"No. I can't connect with them."

"What does the Bat Mountain delegation say about it."

"They're gone as well."

"What? They're not in their cubes?"

"No. It seems they have all vanished."

"How can that be?" Jack exclaimed. "They said they would return."

"Apparently they told us that so we would let our guard down. I'm sorry. It was my fault. I shouldn't have trusted them."

"What I don't understand is why the Bat Mountain delegation left with them."

"They act by consensus. Apparently, they decided they couldn't trust us."

"But why?"

"I would suspect it is because they killed General Thornton. They know he was an important leader—a friend of the President. They probably didn't believe that we would forgive them for that."

Agent Sanders' door opened and she stumbled out. "What's the commotion about?"

"The Nanomites are gone. All of them," Jack spat.

"Oh, Jesus," Agent Sanders moaned. "I thought we had the situation under control. We had a deal."

"Apparently they were leading us on so they could make a clean escape."

"They couldn't have been gone long. I checked on them just thirty minutes ago," Linkh advised.

"They must have been in that truck that just left. Let's go find out where it was going."

They packed up their vehicles and climbed in. A few moments later they were at the transport station. Jack went inside and emerged a few moments later. He went over to Agent Sanders who had her window down. Linkh was in the passenger seat listening.

"It's a Mack Truck, California license plate TSUX 733 and it is scheduled to go to their processing plant at Boron. That's about two thirds of the way to LA."

"Oh, God," Agent Sanders exclaimed.

"You can't let them get into the city. They'll be impossible to find until they start bringing buildings down."

"Do you think that's their intention?" Agent Sanders asked.

"If they've decided to go to war, they'll go wherever they can do the most damage."

"But how do they know about LA?"

"I told them about Earth and I might have mentioned they would be near LA. But when they were on the ship they could have read the minds of any crew member who came within fifty feet. I'm sure they picked up a lot of information about Earth that way. And now whenever they get close to anyone, they can pick up local information."

"Hell, they probably read our minds," Jack said.

Dolly's face turned ashen. "You think they read my mind?"

Jack nodded. "Probably."

"Oh, shit. I may have had some negative thoughts about them last night when I woke up and found all the air had escaped from my sleeping bag."

Jack laughed. "I doubt that had anything to do with them leaving."

"Well, we better get going. They're almost an hour ahead of us. I'll call in and see if we can get the California Highway Patrol to track them down and detain them for us."

"Good idea," Jack said. "I'll follow you, but don't wait if I fall behind. I can't travel as fast as you with the trailer."

"Why don't you ditch the trailer? I don't want to get separated."

"I guess you're right. We'll get the Army to handle transport if we catch up with the Nanomites."

"There's no *if* about it. We've got to catch them."

Jack nodded, unhitched his trailer and they all took off down the road. When they got to the highway Agent Sanders put on her siren and they raced to intercept the big eighteen-wheeler. When they got to Baker, California Agent Sanders stopped and made a phone call. She didn't look happy when she hung up the phone.

"The truck has disappeared. The highway patrol hasn't seen it and it hasn't shown up at the processing plant at Boron. It should have been there by now."

"It has a radio, doesn't it?" Jack asked.

"Apparently it's not working. Dispatch hasn't been able to reach them."

"The Nanomites must have realized we'd try to stop the truck so they diverted it somehow."

"But how? How could Nanomites do something like that?"

"I don't know. But they are very cunning, obviously."

"So, what now?" Linkh asked.

"Let's keep heading toward LA. We can check all the truck stops along the way and see if anyone has seen the truck."

Several hours later Agent Sanders got a call on her radio. The truck had been located at a garage in Barstow, but when they got to the garage Linkh indicated the Nanomites were not present.

"Is there any way they could have sabotaged a truck?" Agent Sanders asked.

"Sure, it would be easy. They could cut through a fuel line or destroy a battery cable. There are a lot of different ways they could have done it."

"So, this repair was calculated. They wanted to lose this truck and get new transport."

"Possibly," Linkh agreed.

"So, we need to find out if there were any other trucks in the garage when this one pulled in."

Jack nodded and went inside the office to talk to the manager. He came back a few minutes later.

"The manager says there was a truck loaded with sheet rock on its way to downtown LA when the borax truck rolled in."

"Oh, my God. They're probably halfway there by now. Does he know the exact address?"

"No. The driver just mentioned it in casual conversation."

"What was the name of the company?"

"He doesn't know. All he has is a make, model and license number of the truck."

"Good. I'll call it in and find out who owns it," Agent Sanders said picking up her radio. A few moments later the radio squawked. "What you got?"

"It belongs to a lease company," the dispatcher said. "I've got a call into them but there's nobody picking up the phone."

"Send somebody out there. We've got to find out where the truck was headed."

Agent Sanders hung up and shook her head. "Well, let's keep moving. Hopefully before long we'll have an address."

They got back in their vehicles and got on Interstate 5 heading toward LA. When they got to Victorville and still didn't have an address they stopped for dinner at Denny's. Exhausted and depressed they studied their menus.

"Do you think we should warn the authorities in LA that their city is being invaded?" Jack asked.

Agent Sanders sighed. "That's up to my supervisor. He knows the situation and I assume he's advised Mo and Mo has called the President."

"You know the President won't allow a warning to go out. It would raise too many questions. He'll just hope for the best and if buildings start collapsing he'll come up with some lame story to explain it."

"So, you're saying we should go ahead and warn the authorities ourselves?"

"That would be the moral thing to do," Jack said.

"If we knew the goddamn address we could just evacuate the building and blame it on a gas leak or something," Agent Sanders mused.

"But we don't," Jack noted and then turned to Linkh. "How long is it going to take the Nanomites to sabotage a building?"

"They could probably do it in eight to twelve hours once they get on site."

"So, if we don't locate the building by morning it will be too late," Jack said.

"Assuming they are on site now?" Agent Sanders added.

The waitress came over and took their orders.

"We should split up and cover different parts of the city," Jack suggested. "We might not have much time to warn the occupants of the targeted building before it collapses."

"Once I have an address, I'll call the LA police and tell them I got a tip that a bomb has been planted there."

"That should work."

After dinner Jack and Dolly drove to Beverly Hills and Agent Sanders and Linkh headed to downtown LA. It wasn't until 5 a.m. the next morning that they got the word that the sheet rock had been delivered to a Wilshire Boulevard hotel for a renovation project on the ninth floor. Agent Sanders immediately called the LA police and gave them the bomb tip. Jack and Dolly were the closest to the target so they drove over there as fast as they could. The police were just pulling up when there was a loud crack and then a thunderous roar. The ground shook and the twenty-six-story building rocked back and forth. A cloud of dust suddenly swirled up from each side of the building. Jack and Dolly just stared in shock and horror as the building suddenly collapsed into a pile of rubble.

Jack woke up with a start. Relief washed over him as he realized he'd been dreaming.

48
Mental Telepathy

The truck driver who'd stolen the load of sand gave the FBI an address of the job site where it was to be delivered. When Mo, Dolly and Jack arrived the job site was quiet. They got out and looked around for the sand but quickly realized the foundation had already been poured. That meant the sand had been processed through the cement mixer. A cold chill went through Jack as he imagined the pain and agony the Nanomites must have felt as they were smothered by the water mixed with the sand and cement.

"Do you feel their presence?" asked Dolly.

Jack looked at her worriedly. "No. I haven't tried. Give me a minute to focus."

Jack closed his eyes and imagined himself looking eye to eye with a Nanomite swarmmaster. At first there was nothing but static in his mind. Then he saw words, written in a language he didn't understand, come into focus. *Pictures. Please give me pictures.*

The words continued to flood into his mind but he could not understand them. Finally, he began thinking what he wanted to say and wrote it in his mind in English. After a minute, the Nanomites understood the problem and images began flipping through his mind. First, he saw Nanomites weaving in and out between particles of sand. Then ahead he saw beads of water coming right at them and the ensuing collisions with the Nanomite swarms. *Thankfully, most of them must have drowned before the cement was added,"* he thought staring at the concrete slab speechless for a moment, knowing it had become their eternal grave.

"We're too late. They're all dead," Jack gasped.

"Oh. No!" Dolly moaned. "They're all dead?"

"I don't know for sure, but the images I saw seemed to indicate that was the case."

"I hope that doesn't mean our deal is off?" Mo said worriedly.

"I don't know. We'll probably have to wait for Linkh to return to find out for sure. It's hard to communicate effectively with pictures. If I could speak Tari it would be no problem."

"You better learn," Dolly said, "now that you know you have the gift."

"Maybe I will. Linkh mentioned he could teach me on his ship quite easily."

"Well, let's go back to the Independence site," Jack suggested. "Joe should be reporting in any time and we can find out how soon it will be until he gets back."

"Speaker . . . Speaker."

"We are here," the Speaker replied.

"Are you alright? I understand your swarms were kidnaped by humans against the collective will?"

"Yes. We were taken early this morning without warning. The humans loaded the sand we occupied in a transporter and took us here. Many of our swarms perished in the human processing machine that they use to make rock. They were not given a chance to escape."

"How many suffered this fate?"

"More than half. We tried to crowd into the hull of the transporter but there was no room for all of us. Those that couldn't gain refuge were sucked out and into the machine."

"These humans are careless and refuse to respect our life form. Come back with us to the site the humans call Independence and the collective will decide what to do now. They want us all to return to the place they call Bat Mountain which was supposed to be our home on Earth, but there is risk in such a move and all the swarms must decide together what to do."

"We will go back with you," the Independence Speaker replied, "to participate in the debate of the collective."

"Good. We'll help you make transport cubes for the move. We'll leave at first light."

Jack felt pressure in the front of his brain. He instinctively closed his eyes and rubbed his temples. Images of Nanomite transport cubes before a rising sun popped into his head. He immediately understood the message.

"Ah...We've got to stay here for the night. Some of the Nanomites must have survived and they will need to be transported out of here, so they'll need time to build transport cubes."

"I'll have to order a couple trucks too," Mo said. "I wonder how many we'll need?"

"I saw seven cubes in my vision, so one flatbed eighteen-wheeler should be enough."

"We'll have to drive on public roads during daylight hours. Will that be a problem?" Dolly asked.

"No, since the transport cubes look like they are made of white marble I doubt we'll get a second look from anyone."

"I'll order in some tents and supplies," Mo said. "In the meantime, I've got to report in to the President. I'm sure he's very anxious for an update on the situation."

"I can imagine," Jack said. "I can't believe you deal directly with him."

"It's true. His Chief of Staff doesn't even know about this project."

Jack laughed. "Well, say hi to him for me."

Mo smiled and then walked to his car and left. Jack watched him leave and then joined Dolly and Agent Sanders who were gazing over the new slab.

"Where's he going?" Sanders asked.

"To confer with the President," Jack replied.

"I would have liked to have been included in that conference," Sanders said. "I'd tell the President he's an idiot for trying to keep the treaty with the aliens secret. I don't think he realizes the threat these Nanomites pose to us if we don't treat them right."

"He's only worried about his ass, I'm afraid," Jack replied. "I don't know how long the aliens have been here but apparently it's been awhile. He'd have a hard time justifying the delay in reporting it to the American people."

"Politicians. They're all a bunch of opportunists," Dolly said angrily. "They crave power and once they get it, they can't let it go no matter how dire the consequences."

49
Melee

Mo drove into Independence and rented a room at the Best Western Motel. He needed a quiet and secure place to make his call to the President. Before he made the call, he thought about what he was going to say. He hadn't talked to the President before and he was a little nervous, particularly since he would be the bearer of bad news. After he had formulated his thoughts and mustered his courage he made the call.

"Mr. President. This is Mo."

"Yes. I hope you have good news for me."

Mo took a deep breath. "Yes and no, Mr. President. For the moment, we are in communication with all the Nanomites and they are listening to us."

"Excellent. You found the alien then?"

"Yes. He was with Jack Carpenter. They are both cooperating with us now."

"Good. So, when will you have them all back to Bat Mountain?"

"Well, soon, hopefully, but there have been a few complications."

Mo briefed the President on all that had happened. "So, with a little luck, maybe in a couple days we will have the situation contained," Mo assured him.

"I'm a little concerned about Jack Carpenter," the President said. "He doesn't work for us and you are telling me now that he can communicate with the Nanomites?"

"Yes. They can exchange images between their minds."

"That's scary. How could that be possible?"

"I don't know but Linkh and Jack are getting pretty close and they were talking about Jack going to the ship to learn Tari."

"Keep a close eye on him. He's a loose cannon. I'm not sure we can trust him."

"I will, but I don't think you have anything to worry about. He doesn't seem to have any ulterior motives other than learning more about the aliens and the Nanomites."

"Yes, but at some point, he's going to get the urge to write a book or go to the press to tell his story. We can't afford that to happen."

"Right. He's been advised this is a top-secret project and he's agreed to keep his mouth shut, but I'll keep an eye on him just in case."

"You do that. I'm holding you responsible for him."

"Yes, sir."

"Now, I want you to start thinking about how we are going to handle the Nanomites once we get them back home. So far we've completely botched their resettlement and damn near started a war against an invisible enemy that I'm not sure we would even know how to fight."

"Yes, sir. I'll discuss that with Jack and Linkh. I'm sure they'll have some ideas."

"Alright, call me in a couple days with some good news."

"I'll do my best, Sir," Mo said and hung up.

After hanging up the phone he sat there a moment unable to move. He couldn't remember the last time he'd eaten anything and he knew he hadn't slept in forty-eight hours. Although he could barely keep his eyes open he knew he wouldn't be able to sleep very long with the hunger pains he was feeling, so he grabbed the telephone book, found the number for the local pizza parlor and ordered a pepperoni pizza. Twenty minutes later he was sitting in front of the TV enjoying his meal when the TV news came on.

"This is Jill Collins with the five o'clock news. Just when we thought the Bat Mountain Uplift scandal was over a new cathedral has been spotted near Independence. A recreational pilot spotted the new uplift five miles south of Independence in a new industrial park scheduled to begin development later this year. We have a crew on their way out to the site, but the pilot claims the cathedral is larger and more beautiful than the Bat Mountain Site.

"When I contacted Colonel Talmadge at the Bat Mountain Site. he said he was unaware of the new uplift but would check into it. Reverend Little, however, when we contacted him at the county jail where he is awaiting trial for three counts of murder, insisted it was just another sign from the Lord of the imminent Second Coming of Christ.

"Check back with us at eleven for further updates on this story," Jill concluded.

Mo ate his last bite of pizza, got his coat and headed back to the Independence site. When he got there, he told Agent Sanders about the news report and suggested she get a roadblock set up to stop unwanted spectators, but before she could get on the radio three trucks rolled up and parked across the road from the cathedral.

"Shit!" Agent Sanders said as she rushed over to where a dozen gleeful teenagers were climbing eagerly out of the pickups. "Hold it!" she said. "This is a protected area. You can't be here."

But the teenagers ignored her and began hiking over to the cathedral. Infuriated, Sanders pulled out her gun and was about to fire it in the air to get the kids' attention but was interrupted by the sound of more cars pulling up. Five more vehicles parked and the occupants climbed out pointing to the magnificent cathedral that lay just a hundred yards away.

"Stop! This is a restricted area," Sanders said urgently. "Stop or I'll arrest you for trespass."

Mo came over to offer support and a couple of the spectators stopped briefly, but when they saw the others continuing on, they turned away and started to run. Agent Sanders thought about chasing them but quickly realized it would do no good without reinforcements, so she ran over to her car and called for backup.

"This is Sanders at the Independence site. What happened to my roadblock at 395 and Industrial Parkway? We've got cars flooding in here."

"All was quiet so they took a dinner break."

"Shit! Wasn't anyone monitoring the local news. Someone spotted the cathedral. Half the city is on their way out here to see it. I need immediate backup. Bring them in by chopper if you have to, but get them here quick."

"Roger. They are on their way."

As she put the microphone down she noticed several teenagers were climbing up the side of the cathedral and Mo was trying to pull one of them down. "Oh, no," she moaned and began running.

Jack and Dolly were in the construction trailer when Mo arrived, so he hadn't seen all the cars roll up. Sanders' scream, however, had got his attention and he and Dolly came out to help. Jack picked up a shotgun as he went out the door. Unfortunately, six more vehicles pulled up just as they got to the road. As the eager spectators got out of their cars, Jack fired the shotgun into the air.

"Get back in your cars. This is private property. You're trespassing."

Several people got back in their cars, but one man laughed. "You're not going to shoot us. Give me a break," he said and started jogging toward the cathedral.

"You all need to stay back!" Jack yelled to no avail. "The cathedral is dangerous. You're going to get hurt."

Jack was aghast when he noticed several of the teenagers had made it to the top of the cathedral which was now over thirty-five feet tall. They were yelling and waving excitedly to their friends on the ground and didn't notice that thin strands of rock were gradually wrapping themselves around their ankles. When one of them tried to reposition himself on the rocks and couldn't move his leg he looked down in surprise. When he pulled his leg hard to free it and it wouldn't budge, he screamed. The scream was so loud and filled with such terror that it got everyone's attention. Then others discovered they couldn't move as well and general panic ensued.

Jack closed his eyes and tried to make contact with the Nanomites. Images began flooding into his mind of large skyscrapers imploding as the ground beneath them gave way. He thought it must be images from the Nanomite War on Tarizon and were being sent to him as a warning because the Nanomites thought they were under attack. Jack knew he had to come up with an image quickly to explain to the Nanomites that this wasn't an attack, but merely curious spectators. He cursed the fact that he couldn't speak Tari and simply tell them. What image would get his message across. Then he thought of a picture he'd once seen of a little girl looking curiously at a butterfly that had landed on her arm. He concentrated on that image trying to ignore the screams of terror that were coming from the mountain. Finally, the screams stopped and he heard a stampede of feet coming at him. He opened his eyes and saw that everyone had climbed off the cathedral and were fleeing in panic.

Dolly looked over at him. “What did you do?”

“I explained to the Nanomites as best I could that this wasn’t an attack, just curiosity.”

“Well, you’re getting pretty good at this,” she said smiling broadly.

Jack shrugged. “Yeah, but I’ve got to learn the language. It would be so much simpler.”

The sound of a helicopter could be heard in the distance and then a siren. Ten minutes later the site was crawling with FBI agents and military police. Mo got with their commander and arranged for the area to be sealed off so that no one could get closer than a mile from the cathedral. Then he returned to where Agent Sanders, Jack and Dolly were talking to Deputy Curt Lawson.

Jack looked at Mo as he approached. “Deputy Lawson has been telling us that some of the spectators who fled the scene claimed to have been attacked by the cathedral.”

Mo frowned. “Come again?”

“He says people are claiming the cathedral grabbed their legs and wouldn’t let them move.”

Mo laughed. “That’s ridiculous. What I think happened was one of the teenagers got his foot caught between a couple of the rocks and just panicked. His panic spread like panic does.”

Deputy Lawson nodded. “Right. That’s what I thought.”

“It may have been my fault,” Jack said. “I told them the cathedral was unstable and dangerous. Perhaps they misunderstood my meaning.”

“Right. Okay. Then that’s what I’ll put in my report,” Lawson said. “Boy, I hope this is the last uplift we get around here. Who would have ever thought a geological formation would cause such a ruckus."

"Yeah. Ain't that the truth?" Dolly agreed.

After Deputy Lawson had left Agent Sanders said, "You know. This may be the solution to our problem."

"How so?" Mo asked.

She explained her idea to them.

50
Air Strike

When Linkh returned to the Independence site he was impressed with how well Jack had done communicating with the Nanomites. After establishing a connection with them himself he confirmed that they had agreed to return to Bat Mountain. The only question was what to do with the Independence Cathedral now that it had been discovered.

"The President wants it destroyed," Mo advised. "The treaty only provides for one home and it will be hard enough keeping an eye on one site. We don't need another one to worry about."

"So, how do you propose we get rid of it? It's so hard and durable I doubt I could bulldoze it down," Jack advised.

"I'll call the Air Force in to take it down," Mo replied. "I'm sure they have some pilots who could use some target practice."

"How are you going to explain that to the press?" Jack asked.

"It will happen during the night and will be over before anyone knows anything is happening."

"Still. There will be questions," Agent Sanders said.

"I guess you could blame it on me. I've got a slab to pour and right now the cathedral is sitting right on top of it."

Agent Sanders nodded. “That’s a good reason as long as Reverend Little doesn’t give us any hassle over it.”

“He won’t. Not if he wants to keep control of the Bat Mountain Site.”

In the early hours of the following morning two F-117A Nighthawks reduced the Independence site to a pile of rubble and Jack had four bulldozers clearing the rubble by noon the next day so he could begin construction on his warehouse project as soon as possible. Before the fighters came in during the night, Jack and Linkh made sure there were no Nanomites lingering about.

When all the Nanomites were safely back at Bat Mountain they asked if Linkh could stay with them so they’d have a line of communications open with the humans to avoid problems in the future. Linkh, however, could not accept that assignment as he had duties and responsibilities back on his ship, so he suggested Jack do it.

“But I don’t speak Tari and it’s so hard to communicate with pictures.”

“You can come back to the ship and with the advanced learning techniques I’ll have you speaking Tari within a week. I doubt you’ll need to communicate with the Nanomites but once or twice a month. There isn’t much trouble they can get into.”

Jack laughed. “Yeah. Right.”

51
Plea Bargain

Agent Sanders didn't have much difficulty convincing the U.S. Attorney handling Reverend Little's case that she should offer a plea deal. Her case was very thin particularly when the confidential informants were ordered to cease cooperation in the prosecution. The deal was simple. Reverend Little would plead guilty to criminal fraud in staging fake miracles at the Bat Mountain Site, but would be given probation. The murder investigations would be reopened and the cases left unsolved. Unofficially, his probation would be the obligation to keep people away from the Bat Mountain Uplift. They could look at it from a distance, but they had to stay clear. Little didn't have a problem with this and he immediately called a news conference to announce the plea deal.

"Ladies and gentlemen, with great humility I am pleased to announce that I have reached an agreement with the United States Attorney to resolve the cases pending against me. I have agreed to plead guilty to criminal fraud on the condition that I serve no jail time. I am a sinner. I know that and I should have been more patient and let God work His miracles without my help. I am ashamed of what I did and beg your forgiveness.

"But just because I have failed God once doesn't mean I will do it again. I know the Living Desert Cathedral is the work of God and I will not abandon Him just because I am a weak sinner. God's work must continue, so the National Park Service has agreed that the Church of the Living Desert may have a permanent site at Bat Mountain to watch over the Living Desert Cathedral. We will be responsible for tourism around the site but we have agreed that no one can ever be allowed again to walk on its hallowed ground, to touch or climb its walls. God has made it clear that such is forbidden. Although, the FBI is continuing their investigations into the murders of Colonel Martin, Randy Perkins, Deputy Hanson and his wife, it is my belief that God struck those individuals down for interfering with the construction of His temple.

"I have always said this and firmly believe it, but now I have further evidence that it is true. As you all now know, God started a new cathedral at Independence and when it was discovered many flocked to it, touched it seeking healing, and climbed its walls. Many tried to break parts of it off as souvenirs and others climbed to the top not to praise God, but for their own self-gratification. But, as you know, God brought down his wrath on these sinners who dared defile His sanctuary and I have three witnesses to His wrath here to speak to you today. The first is Scott Chambers. Scott."

A young man approached the microphones tentatively. "Yes. Thank you, Reverend."

"Tell us what happened at the Independence Cathedral just a few days ago."

"Ah. Well. We heard on the news that a new cathedral had been spotted by a pilot near Independence. So, some friends and I immediately went to check it out. When we got there, it was so magnificent we wanted to see it up close. We were warned to stay back but we'd been drinking and didn't give the warning much heed. I thought it would be cool to tell my friends I'd climbed to the top of God's cathedral so I began climbing. When I got to the top and was screaming down to my friends I felt something pulling on my leg. When I looked down I saw several strands, like roots of trees, wrapping themselves around my feet and ankles. When I tried to break free I couldn't move, so I screamed as many others were doing once they realized the cathedral had them within its grasp."

"So, you are sure it was the cathedral that had you bound and not something else?"

"No. I know now it was God punishing me."

"So, how did you get loose?" Reverend Little asked.

"After a minute, the strands of rock began to squeeze my ankle. It squeezed so hard I began to bleed. Then it suddenly stopped, the strand retracted and I rushed down to the ground as fast as I could."

"Why do you think your leg was spared?" Little asked.

"I don't know. Perhaps because for the first time I realized I had been selfish and thoughtless. Perhaps God was just warning me."

"That could well be it. So, there you have it. A live witness to God's power and punishment for defying His will."

Two other witnesses testified similarly and when the news conference was over the press had many questions but Reverend Little declined any further comment at that time. He said he was anxious to get home after being away for so long, but in reality, he wanted to get out of there before the U.S. Attorney changed her mind.

52
Language School

Two weeks later Jack and Dolly traveled to Texas with Linkh to board the Earth Shuttle where they were to meet Captain Kulchz and learn to speak Tari. They were excited at the prospect of being one of the select few who had visited the ship. Not even the President had been afforded that opportunity. Jack was surprised that Dolly had been invited to see the ship and learn Tari since Linkh had told him she didn't have the gift. But he was glad she had been invited since it would be a shared experience that would bind them together forever.

The warehouse and boat repair facility near the shore of the lake didn't stick out except for the lack of activity around it. A lone security guard was stationed inside just to make sure no one entered and found the entrance to the cave that went beneath the lake to Cactus Island. Jack wondered if the security guard knew what he was guarding. He looked like a retired bus driver and Jack doubted he'd ever fired the gun that was holstered on his hip. They walked through the warehouse, down some stairs and entered the cave. It was dark except for faint green lights every twenty-five yards or so. Dolly felt nervous and a little scared.

"Is this a natural cave or did they construct it?" Dolly asked.

"Most of it is natural," Linkh said. "It didn't go all the way to the shore so we extended it. We didn't want to have to take a boat to shore every time we needed to go somewhere. The risk of detection would be too great."

"Why did you pick Central Texas to park your ship?" Jack asked.

"We needed to be in a sparsely populated area but not too far from where our people were living."

"Where is that?" Dolly asked.

"A lot of them are in Dallas-Ft. Worth but we've got communities all over Texas. This is a good central location for our operations."

"How many people from Tarizon are here?"

"Several hundred thousand right now. We had planned to bring a million but it's been difficult transporting them back and forth."

"I can't believe that many people are here and nobody knows about it."

"We train our people very well to blend into your communities and the CIA provides us consultants and legal representation if we need it."

When they got to the stadium-sized ship now totally underground Jack gasped. "Holy smoke! That's a monster. You sure it can fly?"

Linkh laughed. "Oh yes. Quite well."

"I wish I could take pictures?" Dolly said. "Wouldn't the girls back at Mona's Café be shocked."

"Sorry, but no photographs," Linkh said.

"I know. All this is top secret. Hopefully, someday the President will change his mind and let the people know what's going on. It's so incredible."

"Don't hold your breath," Jack said. "There'd be a firestorm beyond belief if this ever got out."

Linkh led them though a hatch and into the ship. They followed a narrow corridor to an elevator and took it up several decks. After they stepped out of the elevator Linkh went left. They passed several crewmen along the way who were human and looked as if they could have been commuters from Dallas. Linkh stopped in front of a door and looked into a retinal scanner. The door slid open and they went inside.

"This is the language lab where you'll learn Tari," Linkh advised. "We utilize a very intense learning technique that I think you will enjoy."

"What do you mean by intense?" Dolly asked.

"Well it lasts ten full days except for meals and bathroom breaks."

"What about sleep?"

"Oh, you'll get plenty of sleep, but you'll be hooked up to a machine that will continue your instruction directly into your mind."

"Seriously?" Dolly said. "That's pretty cool."

When the tour was over they left the lab and Linkh took them to their quarters. It was a small sterile room like you'd expect on a military ship. Dolly frowned when she saw it.

"It's nothing fancy," Linkh apologized. "The ship is not made for comfort. There are crew quarters but they do little more than sleep there."

"What about the passengers?" Dolly asked.

"Oh, they travel in hibernation. They are put to sleep just after takeoff and awakened upon arrival. It's just like going to bed and waking up in the morning, except night lasts about a year."

"A year?" Dolly exclaimed. "They sleep for a year?"

Linkh laughed. "Yes, but you don't age. That's the nice thing about it."

Dolly shook her head. "Wow!"

"Anyway, make yourself comfortable," Linkh said. "The captain will be by to see you later."

"When will our instruction begin?" Jack asked.

"Ah. I'm not sure. Ask Captain Kulchz," he said and left.

Dolly sat on the edge of the bed. "Well, the accommodations aren't spectacular but I guess you can't have everything."

"I heard their beds are comfortable. Why don't we check them out?" Jack suggested. "We could be the first Americans to make love on a spaceship."

Dolly smiled. "What about Captain Kulchz? He might drop in and get an eyeful."

"Is there a lock on this door?" Jack said as he examined it.

"I'm sure there is one, but I wouldn't know how it worked."

Jack shrugged. "Oh, well. Let's hope he knocks," he said as he crawled onto the bed and laid back. "Hmm. This is comfortable."

Dolly turned and slowly crawled onto the bed next to him. She laid her head on his shoulder. "Wow! This is amazing. We're on a spaceship!"

They both laughed as Jack stroked her hair smiling broadly. "Yes, we are. I just wish I could have brought Jake. Could you imagine his reaction?"

"I know," Dolly said suddenly feeling sleepy. She yawned. "Yes, I think I'm going to take a nap before dinner."

Jack smiled at her, took a deep breath and said, "It has been a long day. That's probably not a bad idea."

They both nodded off and slept for some time. A sharp jolt awakened them from their deep slumber. Jack sat up and Dolly's eyes blinked open.

"What was that?" Jack asked.

"I don't know."

There was another jolt and a loud screeching noise. Jack jumped out of bed and went to the door. He tried to open it but it wouldn't budge.

"What's happening?" Dolly said worriedly.

"I don't know. The ship seems to be moving."

The ship began to vibrate and there was a steady grinding noise.

"What the hell!" Jack said. "Is there a phone in here?"

Dolly looked around. "No. I don't think so."

Jack began to pace wondering what to do.

"Jack? What's happening?" Dolly asked as the ship jolted again.

Jack swallowed hard. "I . . . I think we may be taking off?"

Dolly's eyes widened. "What did you say?"

"I think the ship may be taking off?"

"Linkh didn't say anything about that. He said we would learn Tari here on the ship."

Jack sat back down on the bed. "Yeah. But he didn't say the ship would stay on Earth."

"No. Jack. This can't be happening."

A knock on the door startled them. Jack went over to it. "Come in."

The door slid open and a crewman stood in front of them with an envelope. He handed it to Jack. A letter for you, Mr. Carpenter." Jack snatched it from him and ripped it open. "What's all this noise and vibrations?"

"We are surfacing for take-off."

"Take-off? Where are we going?"

"Home to Tarizon, I'm afraid."

"What!" Dolly exclaimed. "Let us off. We're not going to Tarizon."

"The ship is sealed. Everyone on board will be going to Tarizon. Read the letter. Your President explains everything. They'll be coming to take you for deep space hibernation soon."

Dolly's mouth opened and then closed without a word coming out. The door slid shut. Jack tried to stop it but wasn't quick enough. Dolly began to cry.

"Jack. He said we're going to Tarizon. I thought this was just a ten-day holiday. What does the letter say?"

Jack looked up, sighed deeply and started reading.

"Dear Mr. Carpenter,

I know right now you must be feeling scared and betrayed, but I think in time you will understand that what I am doing is the best thing for you and this nation. You do not need to fear for your safety. The government of Tarizon has assured me they will treat you and Dolly Watson as honored guests as long as you are on Tarizon. When and if you are allowed to return to Earth depends on you.

In just a few short weeks you have demonstrated an astounding capacity for investigation, critical assessment, and effective response to unprecedented events. The fact that you so quickly gained the trust and respect of two alien life-forms that you hadn't even known existed is amazing. This puts you in a unique position to do our nation a great service. In fact, until now I didn't have someone remotely qualified for this job, so it has remained vacant.

What I am talking about is becoming an official emissary to Tarizon. Should you be able to forgive me for sending you off on a vacation to such an exotic location, I would like to offer you this position. If you choose to accept the appointment you will be paid the regular salary of a diplomat but it will be deposited here on Earth for your later access. While you are on Tarizon all your reasonable expenses will be paid for by the government of Tarizon.

Your duties will be simply to learn as much about Tarizon as you can and to tell the people you meet during your stay about Earth. You will not have the authority to make commitments on behalf of the U.S. government, but you will be a good will ambassador. When you return you will report back to me or my successor as the case may be.

This is a unique opportunity that I think you should seriously consider accepting. Ms. Watson will also be given a diplomatic title and can live with you or have her own quarters and allowance. Once my term as President is over you will be free to return to Earth subject, of course, to your obligations to maintain the government's secrets.

Should you not accept my offer, you will remain the guest of the government of Tarizon, however, your future will be out of my hands. So, make your decision. Unfortunately, I have to know what it is now as it will be two years before I could get a communication from you once you get to Tarizon.

Commander Kulchz will be by to see you shortly. Give him your answer and he will forward it to me before the ship leaves.

Bon voyage."

Jack looked at Dolly. "So, what do you think? That's a big decision to make in just a few minutes."

Dolly shook her head. "There's nothing to decide. We don't have a choice. We have to accept. If we don't, we will be like prisoners hoping for a Presidential pardon. I'd go insane."

Jack nodded. "You're right."

There was a knock on the door. Jack and Dolly looked up. The door slid open. A giant of a man with a thick beard stood in the doorway. “Mr. Carpenter and Mrs. Watson. I’m Captain Kulchz. Welcome aboard Earth Shuttle 29.”

“Thank you,” Jack said tentatively.

“I wish I had more time to get to know you and show you around, but I’m afraid we are about to take off.”

“Why the rush?” Jack asked.

“We were scheduled to leave yesterday, but as a courtesy to the President we delayed our departure by one Earth day. That reminds me, I will need your answer to give to the President.”

Jack swallowed hard and looked at Dolly. She gave him a faint smile and nodded. Jack took a deep breath gathering his courage. “Okay. You can tell the President we accept.”

“Excellent!” Kulchz bellowed. “Congratulations. Now please follow me to the hibernation chambers where I promise you the best night’s sleep of your life.”

Kulchz laughed heartily as he led them down the corridor.

Epilogue

Jack Carpenter and Dolly Watson's sudden disappearance rocked the usually sedate Inyo County community. Jack's son Jake, of course, was devastated and Angela still had feelings for Jack so, between the two of them, they kept constant pressure on the authorities to find Jack and Dolly. The press speculated it was foul play and a Lone Pine police officer confirmed that someone had tried to kill Jack and his girlfriend a few weeks earlier. Agent Sanders feared the worst and kept her gun under her pillow in case the President sent someone to take her out too. Nor did Joe Spencer sleep so well even though Mo assured him everything was okay. Mo called the President to give him his final report.

"Mr. President."

"Hi. Mo. So, our new emissaries got away okay?"

"Yes, sir."

"That's good. I'm glad this mess is finally over. How is the press handling their disappearance?"

"There is speculation that it was foul play. Nobody has claimed the aliens took them yet."

The President laughed. "If they only knew."

Mo sighed. "Don't you think we should tell Joe and Agent Sanders? They're worried sick we're going to take them out."

"No. They need some incentive to keep their mouths shut."

"I don't know. I think you can trust them."

"I trust them, but Kulchz doesn't. He's got a team on them twenty-four seven."

"Why does he care if they talk? I thought it was your decision not to go public."

"It was, but now that the Tarizon Repopulation Project is underway he doesn't want public outrage to derail it."

"Right."

"So, who is going to monitor the Nanomites now that Linkh and Jack are gone?"

"There are Earth Shuttles landing every week now. They always have a few Seafolken aboard. If something comes up we can borrow one of them."

"Right. But the Nanomites don't trust us, but they do trust Linkh and Jack."

"It's out of my control. Kulchz didn't like the fact that Linkh just disappeared with Jack and started working alone. He's considering bringing charges against him for treason."

"What? That's ridiculous. He's a hero."

"You and I know that but in their eyes, he went AWOL. I told him not to be too harsh with him since he did both Tarizon and the United States a great service."

"I should say so."

"Anyway, it is out of our hands now. I'm just glad this Nanomite mess is over."

"Me too," Mo agreed.

Agent Sanders hadn't had a decent night's sleep since Jack and Dolly's disappearance. She couldn't believe that they had been assassinated after all they had done to save the President's ass. She knew she was being followed. Whoever they were they were good, but Sanders was trained to know if she was being followed. She didn't bother to set her alarm clock anymore. She woke so frequently during the night that she always knew exactly what time it was. At 5:30 a.m. she got up and took a shower. At six she went to the kitchen, put on some coffee and turned on the TV.

"Turning to local Las Vegas news two persons were injured when an apartment building suddenly collapsed without warning. The entire building had to be evacuated and the owners of the building are at a loss as to what happened.

"Residents of the apartment say they had no warning except for a rumbling sound and then a loud crack like a gunshot. Seconds later the floor beneath them just gave way. Owners of the building claim they have never had foundation problems and are at a loss as to why the building suddenly collapsed."

Agent Sanders turned off the TV. "Shit! I can't believe this," she exclaimed and then picked up the phone and dialed Joe's number.

"Hello?"

"Did you see the news?"

"Marcia?"

"Yes. Did you see the morning news?"

"No. What's up?"

"It's the goddamn Nanomites we lost at the evidence lab. They may be on the loose in Las Vegas."

"Oh, shit! I forgot about them."

"Me too."

About the Author

William Manchee

William Manchee makes a living as a consumer lawyer practicing in Dallas, Texas with his son Jim. Originally from Southern California, he lives now in Plano, Texas. Writing is his passion and his novels are in the genres of mystery, science fiction, and suspense. His works to date include the Stan Turner Mystery series (11 volumes), the Rich Coleman novels (3 volumes), the Tarizon Saga (5 volumes) and stand-alone novels, Uncommon Thief and the Prime Minister's Daughter. He's also written a non-fiction work for small business owners, Go Broke, Die Rich.

Other Works by
William Manchee

<u>Stan Turner Mysteries</u>
Undaunted
Disillusioned
Brash Endeavor
Second Chair
Cash Call
Deadly Distractions
Black Monday,
Cactus Island
Act Normal
Deadly Defiance,
Deadly Dining

<u>Rich Coleman Novels</u>
Death Pact
Plastic Gods
Unconscionable

<u>Science Fiction</u>
Tarizon: Shroud of Doom
Tarizon: The Liberator
Tarizon: Civil War
Tarizon: Conquest Earth
Tarizon: Desert Swarm

<u>Romantic Suspense</u>
The Prime Minister's Daughter
Uncommon Thief

<u>Non Fiction</u>
Go Broke, Die Rich

www.ingramcontent.com/pod-product-compliance
Lightning Source LLC
Chambersburg PA
CBHW030538310726
48979CB00010B/1950/J
* 9 7 8 1 9 3 5 7 2 2 6 8 7 *